To my DESERT BUDDIES Ron & DOTTIE
MAY YOUR SWINGS ALWAYS BE SWEET

Creative
Authors
Press

THE
SWORD
OF
JUSTICE

RON SHARROW

Creative Authors Press
P.O. Box 1814
Rancho Mirage, CA 92270

www.CreativeAuthorsPress.com
E-mail: CreativeAuthorsPress@gmail.com

Library of Congress Cataloging in Publication Data:
Library of Congress Control Number: **2006925218**

Sharrow, Ron
The Sword Of Justice: A Lawyer's Revenge

Printed in the United States and London

The Sword Of Justice: A Lawyer's Revenge / by Ron Sharrow

FICTION/Humorous - IC016000
FICTION/Legal - FIC034000

ISBN-13: 978-1-929841-40-X   Hard Cover
ISBN-10: 1-929841-00-0   Hard Cover

ISBN-10: 1929841-39-6   Paperback
ISBN-13: 978-1-929841-39-4   Paperback

First Printing 2006
Second Printing April, 2006

For
Jamie and Melissa

PROLOGUE

The sword of justice has no scabbard

—Joseph De Maistre, 1821

1

"*I was startled from a deep sleep by a man standing over me with something sharp pressed against my throat. I was terrified! I screamed as loud as I could.*"

"*And then what happened?*"

"*Well, he told me if I made another sound, he would kill me.*"

My mind drifted away from the victim's testimony, back to the day several months earlier when I first heard the name of the man against whom she was testifying, Jefferson Wilkes.

As I recall, that was a day that began when I stepped from the elevator into my office with no memory of the events leading up to that moment. I had no memory of leaving home, driving to work, arriving at the building, parking the car, or pushing the button on the elevator. I did know where I was, which under the circumstances was a good start.

This state of amnesia wasn't something that

happened to me all of the time. It occurred mostly on the mornings after a night of revelry at the Bear's Den, one of Baltimore's local watering holes. It was a popular hang out among the recently separated, recently divorced and currently running-around-married folks.

The Bear's Den, from all outward appearances, is an ordinary looking neighborhood joint in a somewhat run-down, blue-collar part of town. It occupies the basements of two eighty-year-old row houses. The thick foundation walls had been broken through to combine the two spaces. At some point in time when the old buildings had been restored, the plaster was chipped off the walls to expose the original bricks, which now are a part of the decor. The dropped acoustical tile ceiling which has become yellowed with age and discolored from cigarette smoke gives you the feeling that you have just been swallowed by some giant creature, probably, not too much unlike Noah's experience with the whale.

To enter this fine establishment, patrons must descend four or five steps from the sidewalk to a door several feet below the level of the street. As the door swings open, you are immediately struck by the cacophony of loud voices straining to be heard over the blaring music from the jukebox. Once inside, you must descend yet more steps from the landing inside of the door to the basement floor. The acrid smoke drifting upward in its search for an escape from the windowless edifice and the stench of stale beer, combine to assault your eyes and nose so that your first reaction to the place would be best described as a teary-eyed gasp. This is before you even catch a glimpse of the mélange of humanity stirring in the haze on the floor below. No food is served in the place, so the establishment is able to avoid the smoking prohibitions imposed by law. And even if the place is not exempt from the smoking laws, nobody gives a shit anyway, because none of the customers are in any position to complain.

Actually, the Den doesn't really qualify as a neighborhood bar, because no self-respecting, blue-collar neighbor would set foot in the place. Yet, most week-nights people are four deep at the bar and the place is literally bulging at the seams. As one steps into the throng of young nubile bodies, there is a sense of being swept away on a pulsating tide of human flesh engaged in some kind orgasmic frenzy. There's no entertainment other than a jukebox screaming from a corner of the dance floor, and no apparent reason for the establishment to be so busy every night, every night, that is except the weekends. The mood of the place provokes a feeling of unfettered frivolity. Interestingly, not one person in the joint, including Charlie and Bill, the bartenders, lives anywhere near the Den, and therein lies its attraction. It's safe! It would be highly unlikely that you'd accidentally bump into an acquaintance from your real life.

The place swarms during the week with a smattering of newly separated women and the cheaters and assorted losers from Pikesville, an exclusive, upscale, upper-middle class sprawling neighborhood of businessmen and professionals on the other side of town. The Pikesville men flock to the

Den, as it is affectionately called by the hangers-on, in search of the women who flock to the Den in search of the men who flock . . . Well you get the picture!

The Bear's Den patrons are mostly married, but not to each other. These people are attracted like magnets to each other, forming liaisons reminiscent of *"Captain's Paradise."* It's like having two spouses, one on either side of town. They are all miserable being married, yet they mate with one of the other unhappily married cheaters, travel in cliques, party together and go out to dinner and movies in their little groups just as if they were married to each other. Then on the weekends they switch to their real spouses. Some of them even travel in the same circles, but never to the Den. This of course is the reason you can shoot a cannon in the Den on Saturday or Sunday night with not even a remote chance of hitting anything.

None of this makes sense to me, but the intrigue almost makes me wish I were married again. Actually, I probably wouldn't mind marriage, but not for the same reason. But, that's a whole other story.

Eventually, these folks will get divorced. Some will even marry their paramours. Those pathetic relationships will soon dissolve into hatred and they will resurrect their adulterous behavior. Most lamentable though is the fact that the Bear's Den then becomes off-limits. My remedy for this nonsense, which I share generously with my friends, and which I am pleased to share with you, is relatively simple. Just find a woman you hate from the start; buy her a house and give her half your money! It saves a lot of time, a lot of wear and tear, and virtually eliminates the emotional trauma and financial stress caused by divorce.

It wouldn't be unreasonable to ask why a successful, single, 36 year old, lawyer would want to hang out in an iniquitous sinkhole like the Den. I don't live in Pikesville. I'm not cheating on anybody. I'm not a loser. I mean. I lose sometimes; hell, everybody loses sometimes, but I don't . . . like . . . lose all the time. I mean, I'm not lost in life like the other habitués of the Den. The women? Nah! That's just a secondary benefit. I go there not to hang out with the losers, but to hang around them. Even though I am reluctant to reveal one of my most closely guarded secrets of success, let me tell you why I hang around a bunch of losers. Cheaters and losers always have problems; mostly legal problems. I have created a very busy little law practice helping to extricate the inveterates of places like the Bear's Den from the quagmire of their perpetual legal problems.

Yes, I'm a lawyer. Try to keep in mind, and if for no other reason than just for the sake of this story, that all lawyers are not really bad people. Lawyers don't exactly enthrall me either, but I'm really different. You'll see. I really want you to like me. Maybe you even know a nice girl for me! I hope you will grow to admire my firm and continuous desire to insure that the people I represent are rendered that, which is their due. In the story I am about to relate, you will observe first-hand the application of my keen Justinian sense of fair play.

I enjoy what some would, no doubt, consider a warped sense of humor. I'm often . . . strike that . . . less than often would be more accurate . . . charitable, understanding, compassionate, considerate and sympathetic. I try not to overdo any of these admirable traits, strongly believing in moderation for all things. I have also been known by some, just a few, to be a genuine son-of-a-bitch, but only as may be dictated by time and circumstances.

So, anyway, there I was, standing at the threshold of my office. C. Bruce West, Attorney-at-Law, slightly battered by the night before, but still quite dapper in my navy blue, seven-ounce gabardine, Super 100, twelve hundred dollar, Canali suit. My mere presence, I am sure, lighting the life of Kelly Clark, my secretary for the past eight years. Kelly is captain of the watch, protector of the fortress, confidant, straight man, office manager, receptionist, bookkeeper, paralegal, messenger, chauffeur, confessor and whatever else may be demanded of her from time to time. We have a great relationship. There's a lot of good-natured teasing, good humor and a fair share of bullshit, but the job gets done. No romantic fantasies. Kelly is happily and comfortably married to a super guy and has two adorable little kids.

She's from a large Irish Catholic family. Her parents were strict disciplinarians, who taught their children by example to adhere to an almost extinct work ethic. If the job is from nine to five, get in at eight-thirty and leave at six. If the work isn't done, take it home with you. When you have a good job, work there until you die. If your boss is under fire, stand in front of him to take the bullets. That's Kelly. Dedicated, loyal, honest, committed, protective, and dependable. Whoever said a dog is a man's best friend, couldn't possibly have known anyone like Kelly.

I occupy a comfortable suite of offices in the tower of a twenty-story office building in downtown Baltimore. The suite fills the entire fifteenth floor of the building, which sounds like a big deal, but from the twelfth floor up, the tower is rather narrow, so the suite is only about eighteen hundred square feet, and I share that with three other lawyers and their secretaries. Kelly's desk is within earshot, just outside of the door to my office. We have a little combination file-room/kitchen, an impressive library, and a comfortable conference room. Clients are genuinely impressed when the elevator doors open and they step out right into our waiting room. The ambiance declares our success. We have magnificent views of Baltimore's inner harbor and the world-renowned Harbor Place. In the summer, I walk the three blocks to one of the many outdoor cafes in the Harbor Place Food Pavilion, and have lunch at the water's edge.

"What brings you here so early?" Kelly greeted me. "Up all night?"

"Why? What time is it?"

"Quarter to ten."

"I have a really good excuse. Do we have any coffee?"

"Every morning you ask if we have coffee. Every morning we do have coffee. We always have coffee! Why would you ask if we have coffee?"

"Okay, okay! Can I have some then?"

"No!"

"No! What do you mean, no!"

"Today, we don't have any!" she teased. "You want coffee; help yourself"

"Where is it?" I asked, feigning helplessness.

"It's in the coffee pot, where it always is!"

"Did the check come?" I called out from the coffee pot in the file-room, just to keep up the early morning banter.

"What check?"

"Any check!"

"No checks," she hollered back. "You got here before the mail."

"Did he call?"

"He? Who?"

"The President of IBM, who else?" I hollered.

"Why, does he hang out at the Bear's Den?" she retorted derisively.

"Well, if not him, then, anybody? Did *anybody* call?"

"Matter of fact, Jennifer Dunn called. Said you'd remember her from the Bear's Den."

"Jennifer! I was expecting her call," I lied. "Did she say what it was about?"

"No, but I'll get her for you."

A couple of seconds later, Kelly called out, "Miss Dunn is on line one."

"Tell her to hold for a minute. Where's the sugar?"

"Oh Jesus! Get the phone. I'll get your coffee!" She said it in an exasperated tone of voice to be certain that I understood she knew all along that she would end up getting the coffee. She really didn't mind, though.

"Jennifer!" I gushed into the phone. "Great to hear from you." I attempted to sound as if my life was finally back on track now that she called.

"Do you remember me from the Bear's Den?" she asked, somewhat puzzled, I supposed by my gushing into the phone. She probably could tell that I had no clue who she was.

"Of course; what's up?"

"I didn't think I'd be needing your services quite so soon," she said, somewhat distressed.

"Well, what can I do for you?" I tried to sound very concerned.

"It's not really for me. It's for an employee. You know I'm the resident manager of the Western Creek Apartments. Our maintenance man was arrested this morning. It sounds pretty serious. He called from jail and asked me to help him. He asked me to get him a lawyer. I only met you last night, and you're the only lawyer I've met since I've gotten to Baltimore."

Wanting to get right to the heart of the matter, I asked, "Jennifer, how is he going to pay for a lawyer?"

"Oh," she replied, I assume somewhat taken aback by my direct manner. "Well, he has a check here for two weeks pay. Do you think you might be able to help him?"

"How much is the check for?" I asked, trying not to sound overly eager, or too avaricious.

"A little over five hundred dollars."

"I might be able to help him a little bit," I responded, thinking to myself that a little bit is about all you can expect for five hundred dollars.

"Why was he arrested?"

"I'm not sure. He said something about a rape, but he didn't do it. I just know he didn't. He couldn't have," she added. "You know what I mean?"

Now, why the hell does everybody always ask if you know what they mean? Most of the time you haven't the slightest notion, but to be polite you feel compelled to say you do.

"Sure, I understand," I said sympathetically. "Where is he? I mean which jail? The police station? City Jail? Which one? Do you know?"

"Baltimore City Jail, I think."

I wasn't really sure who Jennifer was. I had met several new people of the female persuasion the night before at the Den. Maybe she was the little blonde who was sitting at the end of the bar talking to Ted Kaufman, the owner of the Den. She wasn't exactly a stand-out, but was kind of cute.

"What's his name?"

"Jefferson," she answered.

"What's his first name?"

"Jefferson," she said again.

"Okay, what's his last name?"

"Wilkes." She spelled it for me, "W-I-L-K-E-S."

"Where does he live?"

"Here at the apartment complex. He's on call most of the time, so they give him an apartment. It's one of the benefits of the job."

"Tell you what, Jennifer. I'll go over to the jail and

pay Jefferson Wilkes a visit. Get more details; see what he's charged with and see if I will be able to help him. "Then," I suggested, "why don't you and I meet somewhere for a drink. Say around seven this evening?"

"I'd like very much to do that," she said, "but my car is in the shop." She sounded as if she might start to cry.

So here's where it gets to be serious. I'm going to go to jail to see Jefferson what's his name, but I don't get to pass Go or collect the five hundred and change.

"Do you have his check?"

"Yes."

"Do you think you can maybe redeposit his check and write one payable to me?"

"He asked me to get him a lawyer, so I guess that would be okay."

"Great! How about this? I'll pick you up at your place around seven this evening and then we can talk about the situation over a drink?"

"Okay," she replied, a bit hastily I thought.

"Where exactly do you live?"

"I live in the apartment complex too," she replied. It's one of the perks of my job also."

"Okay. Hang on a second. I'll put my secretary back on the phone. Give her your address and I'll see you at seven. Will that work for you?"

"That'll be fine. I'm looking forward to it," she said.

"Thanks for thinking of me Jennifer. I really appreciate it."

I put her on hold. "Kelly!" I called through the open door of my office.

"Yeah, yeah; I know. Get the address. Jesus! What the hell do you have that all these women are after? I don't get it," she mumbled in a tone of bewilderment.

"If you weren't married, I'd show you."

She groaned, "Spare me."

If the truth were known, what I really have is an empty life. It might not be readily apparent, because from the outside looking in, it would seem I have everything. *Bon vivant* on the outside, but empty on the inside. The ambiance of wealth; lots of playmates, a lucrative business, a nice home, a nice car, but no one of any significance with whom I wish to share it. It's the old story of money not being able to buy happiness. Sadly the only happiness I have is what I am able to buy. Somehow, true happiness has eluded me. I'm not particularly looking for a shoulder to cry on, or for anyone to feel sorry for me. I just start feeling sorry for myself when people remind me that despite outward appearances, only I know what's really going on inside.

I suspect that my parents are to blame for my lack of success in finding the perfect mate. Not for the usual reasons that people blame their parents for everything that happens to them, but because of the truly wonderful life they share with each other. Here are two people so well suited that they spend every day of their lives together, and never to my knowledge have had an argument in the 40 years of their marriage. They are completely devoted to each other and created a home full of love, happiness, peace and comfort. It is the kind of place you would rush to after work; a haven to escape from the day-to-day pressures of life. For me, as a kid, it was a place to gather with my friends. It was the place I looked forward to going after school. There was always the excitement of going home. I had no way of knowing that marriage could be a living hell on earth; that home could be the place from which you longed to escape. I just naturally assumed that the home I grew up in was the paradigm of what I would have when I married. *Au contraire, bon ami*; I was totally unprepared for the realities of matrimony.

It's possible that my marriage failed simply because of the unrealistic expectations resulting from my observation of the extraordinary relationship of my parents. In any event, for me, marriage was a Promethean nightmare. Thus, I have brought to each new potential relationship a frivolity that would impede the development of a serious romance. Unconsciously, I guess I have avoided women of any real quality, or at the very least, have searched for love in all the wrong places. Deep within, I know that God created a younger version of my mother and that she's drifting around out there someplace waiting for fate to thrust us into each other's lives. Obviously, she's not been hanging out at the Bear's Den.

Well, enough of this morbid bullshit. Let's get to the important stuff.

Rape. Five hundred will get me to the jail, buy Jennifer a drink, and if she's the one I think I remember from last night, maybe a dinner in Little Italy.

"Kelly!" I called out again.

21

I should tell you that we have this elaborate intercom system built into the phones, and I scream all over the place, because I've never figured out how to use the damn thing. The fact is, that since Kelly's desk is right outside my door, she can hear everything said in my office anyway, so there is hardly ever any reason to use the intercom.

"Yeah, I know," she hollered back. "Call the jail and ask them to bring what's his face up to the Bull Pen, and make sure he has his papers. What time are you going to go?"

"Name's Jefferson Wilkes. W-i-l-k-e-s," I spelled it for her. "Charged with rape. What's scheduled this afternoon?"

"Besides lunch with Dr. Wheaton at twelve-thirty," she replied, "Kim Steiner is coming in at two o'clock to answer Interrogatories for her accident case, but I can take care of that."

Kim Steiner, a secretary at the Baltimore field office of the FBI, was another little tidbit from the Bear's Den. She got rear ended on the Jones Falls Expressway by some drunk at two in the morning, shortly after the bars closed. When the case is over, maybe I'll take a shot at Kim and try to find out what bar the drunk was coming from. Probably a lot of business there too.

"There's a new case scheduled in at two-thirty, and another new matter scheduled for four-thirty," she read from the appointment book. "I'm sure I can handle the four-thirty. I'll set you up at the jail at three-thirty with the raper," she said with an air of authority.

"*Rapist*," I corrected. "I'll try to get back for the four-thirty appointment. Oh, and make a reservation for

22

me at Sabatino's; eight-thirty, for two." Just in case Jennifer turns out to be the one at the end of the bar, I thought to myself.

"I can handle the four-thirty for you, that'll give you enough time to see the raper and then go home to get dolled up for your date with what's her name. It's almost poetic," she laughed.

You could just see her eyes rolling toward the top of her head and the look on her face from the tone of her voice.

2

The Baltimore City Jail and Detention Center is located on the northeastern fringe of the heart of downtown Baltimore, about ten or twelve blocks from my office. It is a relatively modern looking square building with rows of barred windows and is topped with coils of razor wire. The comparatively new jail was built next to the Maryland Penitentiary, which by contrast was built at the turn of the nineteenth century of gray stone with two-foot thick walls crowned with towers, giving it the appearance of a formidable medieval castle. Armed guards are ever present walking along the top of the walls.

These are not very nice places. Just seeing them from the outside is scary enough to keep you from ever wanting to go inside, even as a visitor. As you enter the jail, you are assaulted by the noise and the stench. It's almost like walking into the Bear's Den, except that the Bears Den has a happy kind of noise. The jail noise is like a rumbling echo emanating from the bowels of hell. It stinks, not like the malodorous aroma in the Bear's Den from the stale cigarette smoke and stale beer, but a putrid kind of smell from the body odors of thousands of rank bad guys amalgamated with the Lysol disinfectant I think they must use for deodorant. It's a gruesome and brutal place.

The people here have legal problems too, but a lot worse than the folks at the Den. The prison population is a bunch of bad dudes; a real flock of assholes. The inmates aren't especially nice either. Not remotely akin to the people at the Bear's Den. You know what I mean?

All conversations are sifted through steel bars which are covered with wire mesh. This is truly a vile place. It's portentous to come here even knowing you're going to be on the good-guy side of the bars and that they'll let you out when you're ready to leave. They search your briefcase when you come in and require you to pass through a metal detector. Christ, they act like you're going to plunder the place and abscond with the prisoners. I hate this place. Can you imagine what it must be like to be imprisoned, or have to work in such a place?

"What can I do for you, Counselor?" asked the guard, as if there were really something he could do for me, or for that matter, that there could possibly be more than one reason for my being there in the first place.

I have to tell you that all lawyers hate being called counselor. And everybody in law enforcement and the courts always call lawyers "Counselor." They use the word like a term of derision. Why can't they call me

"Mr. West", or "Bruce", or "Mr. Counselor?" I don't call them "Correctional Officer." You know what I mean?

"I'm here to steal a fucking prisoner, asshole!" I thought to myself. I would have liked to actually say that, but there was genuine fear of the possibility that they might not let me out when I was ready to leave.

"I'd like to see Jefferson Wilkes," I replied in my most pleasant voice. "My secretary called earlier and arranged to have him brought up here to the Bull Pen."

The guard turned his head toward the holding cell and shouted, "Wilkes! Your lawyer's here."

What I've never understood is why this place is called the Bull Pen. This is the place they should call the Bear's Den. It smells like a place where bears, live . . . and eat . . . and shit. It's like a big cage about forty feet long and fifteen feet wide, divided down the middle by steel bars and wire mesh from the ceiling to the floor. There is a narrow counter with stools on each side. There's a narrow slot about an inch high and twelve inches wide through which you can pass papers. And last but not least, the people on the other side of the bars look, act, smell and sound like animals.

A smarmy looking weasel, about five foot eight, maybe a hundred and fifty pounds, who I guessed was in his mid twenties, swaggered over and took a seat on the stool opposite me on the bad-guy side of the bars. Actually, he didn't exactly take a seat. What he did was sort of propped his ass against the front edge of the stool with his legs spread, extended forward and locked at the knees. His hands were clasped behind his head with his elbows pointing East and West like a pair of oars sticking out of the sides of a row boat. He was leaning away from the counter, so at the very least we'd have to scream at each other to be heard above the jailhouse roar. I believe this was calculated to be a demonstration of *att-i-tude*.

He was dressed in a pair of what probably started out as black cotton pants that had been worn so much and laundered so often that they were now a washed-out, faded shade of gray. The fibers of the fabric were so stretched and limp that the pants had absolutely no shape. The fact that the fabric had not totally disintegrated was a tribute to the quality of goods produced by the Amalgamated Clothing Workers of America.

To top off the outfit, he was attired in a tee shirt, the color of which was no longer discernible, emblazoned with an illustration of a shiv protruding through a skull with blood running from its orifices, extolling devotion to some rap group.

The finishing touch to this *haute couture* was a pair of high-top basketball sneakers that appeared to be at least two sizes too big with untied laces. In short, the clothes, like Jefferson, had lived through better times, but they still delivered the message . . . baaad! It was love at first sight. I just knew I was really going to like this guy!

"Are you Jefferson?"

"Uh huh," he replied.

"Lean forward," I shouted. "Our meeting is supposed to be confidential, and I don't want everybody in this place to hear what we're saying."

Begrudgingly, he moved his hands from behind his head, crossed his arms over his chest, and leaned his elbows on the counter.

"I'm Mr. West. Bruce West. I'm a lawyer," I introduced myself and slid one of my cards through the slot.

"Uh huh," was his only response.

"Miss Dunn asked me to come see you."

"Who?" he asked.

"Miss Dunn. Jennifer Dunn," I repeated.

"Who dat?"

"The lady at Western Creek Apartments," I explained.

"I din' do it," he mumbled.

"You didn't do what?" I asked incredulously.

"To da lady at da potment."

"Christ! I thought to myself, this is really going to be fun! I was expecting a rocket scientist, but I ended up with a space cadet!

This was reminiscent of the time I came over to the jail when I was a young lawyer, fresh out of law school. I had gotten myself on the referral list from the Public Defender's Office. They would assign their overload cases to the young lawyers scratching around for business, and pay us on an hourly basis. I had been assigned three cases, and had already talked with the Assistant State's Attorneys handling the prosecutions before coming over to see the clients.

I had negotiated tentative plea bargains, which I had come to discuss with my new clients. After going through the same routine I just encountered to see Wilkes, I had the three clients lined up waiting to speak with me. I hollered out for Gregory Johnson. A young inmate took the stool in front of me.

"Greg," I said, "I've worked out a pretty good deal with the State's Attorney. You're charged with felony murder . . . murder during the commission of an armed robbery. The State will recommend a fifteen-year sentence with five years suspended if you will agree to plead guilty to second degree murder. How does that sound to you?"

"Sounds real good," he replied.

"Good," I said, "let me get some background information."

"You're twenty-five years old, married and have one child. Is that correct?"

"Dat ain right," he responded.

"Aren't you Gregory Johnson, 1351 West Lyndvale Street?"

"Nope, I be Antoine Jackson," he replied.

"Antoine Jackson?" I asked rather perplexed.

I looked through my files and pulled out Antoine's file. He had been charged with shoplifting. *Shoplifting*, for Christ's sake! Would you believe it?

"Antoine," I said. "You're charged with *shoplifting!* Why on earth were you so willing to accept a plea to second degree murder?"

"Sounded like a pretty good deal to me," he responded.

If the truth be known, he had probably committed a murder and robbery, but wasn't exactly sure for which crime he'd been arrested. I was young and inexperienced then.

W e had barely gotten started, but the way things were going with Jefferson, I was beginning to think I was talking to the wrong person.

"Hold it! Are you Jefferson Wilkes?"

"Uh huh."

"You work at Western Creek Apartments? Don't you?" I asked.

"Usta."

"What do you mean, used to?"

"Till Ah were 'rested."

"That was last night, wasn't it?" I asked.

"Un unh," he replied, expanding his vocabulary.

"Un unh? What do ya mean un unh? When were you arrested?" I demanded.

"Early dis mownin'," he said.

"Jesus, Jefferson!" I bemoaned out of near total frustration. "We're not doin' too good here. The clock's ticking and you're gonna run outa money soon! Let's start over."

"You're Jefferson Wilkes. You were arrested this morning. Up until you were arrested you worked as a maintenance man at Western Creek Apartments. The Lady who works there, Jennifer Dunn, she's the manager. You called her and asked her to get you a lawyer. I'm the lawyer she called. C. Bruce West. That's me. I came here to see if I can help you. You want me to help you don't you?"

"Uh huh," he muttered.

"Good, now we're getting somewhere."

"Ah din' do it," he blurted out.

"You didn't do what, Jefferson?" I asked impatiently.

"Wha dey sayin'," he replied.

"And what are they saying?"

"You know. To dat girl. Ah din' do it," he insisted.

Here we go again with the 'you know.' It's like contagious. You know?

"Do you have your papers?"

"Wha papers?"

"Your charge papers."

"You mean dese?" he asked, holding up a thick wad of totally crumpled papers.

"Yeah, Jefferson, those. Pass them through the slot to me." I rejoiced feeling, mistakenly as it turned out, that I might finally be getting somewhere.

"Ah don' think dey gonna fit through da hole," he stated, waiving the wad of papers in the air as if they were a trophy he'd just won in a public speaking contest, or an Oscar for worst performance by a bad actor.

"That's what I was afraid of! Slide a couple at a time through the slot," I suggested, trying to be helpful.

The Criminal Statutes are contained in Article 27 of the Annotated Code of Maryland. It is a book about two and one half inches thick and contains all of the deeds and misdeeds, which in the wisdom of our elected officials from the founding of the original thirteen colonies to date, constitute crimes against the State. From the appearance of the wad of papers in Jefferson's hand, he had been charged by the People of the Free State of Maryland with violating the entirety of Article 27, and probably the Ten Commandments as well.

"Are you sure you were arrested this morning?" I asked sarcastically.

"Yeah, why?"

"From the condition of these papers, it looks like you've had them about six months. What happened to them?" I asked. "I'm going to have to iron them out before I can read them."

"Ah dunno. Ah didn' have no good place ta keep um."

I tried to flatten the charging documents and smooth them out enough to decipher what crimes this innocent until proven guilty individual had been accused of having committed.

There I was with my yellow pad in its luxuriously soft, elegant lambskin case from Mark Cross and my Mont Blanc fountain pen ready to impress everybody, and not only wasn't he even slightly impressed, he wouldn't have known what they were, could have cared less, and so far he hadn't said a single word that was worth writing down other than uh huh.

"Jefferson, my man, they sayin' some nasty stuff 'bout you in these papers," I said. "Rape, Sexual Offenses, Common Law Assault, Assault with a Deadly Weapon, Nighttime Breaking and Entering of a dwelling house, Rogue and Vagabond. What do you have to say?" I asked, knowing full well what the reply would be.

"Ah din' do it!" he said matter-of-factly.

"Tell me about it," I said.

"Ain't nuffin' ta tell; Ah din' do it," he repeated.

"Help me, Jefferson," I pleaded. "You mind if I call you Jefferson?" I asked as an aside. "I need a little more to go on than just, I didn't do it."

"Ma frens calls me 'Slats,' he responded.

Don't even ask. Just let it go, I told myself. But, no, driven by some unexplained compulsion, I asked anyway, "Slats? Why Slats? Why not Jeff?"

"Ah dunno. Da's jus' wha dey calls me."

See? I knew not to ask!

"Okay, Jefferson, tell me why they sayn' all this stuff about you."

"Ma frens calls me 'Slats,' he repeated.

"Yeah, but we're not friends and I don't know you good enough yet to call you Slats, so I'll just call you Jefferson, okay?"

Once again I tried. "Now, tell me one more time why they sayin' all this stuff. Tell me what happened . . . say starting when you got off from work last night." Christ, I thought, I've only been here ten minutes and I'm already starting to sound like him.

"Well," he started, "Ah works at da Western Creek Potments . . . You know?"

Hot damn! This time I did know!

"Ahz da maint-nance man. So Ah gits off roun' six."

"In the evening?" I asked.

"Uh huh, and were just spacin' roun' wid some frens."

"Just spacin' round? . . . Where?"

"You know, man jus here 'nere; no place special. Jus signifyin' is all. Know what Ah mean?"

Christ he did it again. "know what I mean?" If I told him I didn't know what he meant, *(and I didn't)* he'd think I was stupid, or out of the loop.

"So you were signifying with some friends. What are their names?"

"One Ah be knowin' as Zippo, and his girfren . . . Ain't

33

zackly sure a her name; sompin' like Lukeshia, er Lakasha, er Luteshia . . . like dat, man."

Forget it, I thought to myself. I'll just pretend I know why his friend's nickname is Zippo, and not even comment about it.

"So there you are just spacing around and signifying . . . no place special, with Zippo and his girlfriend, 'till what time . . . approximately?"

"Till we split up when we git off da bus," he responded.

At the rate this guy's going, I thought, I'll be here so long they'll mistake me for a fucking inmate.

"Off the bus? What bus?"

"Numma 15," he replied.

Finally! Something to write! I began scribbling on my legal pad. *Call Mike, check on the Number 15. Route, Schedule, etc.*

"Where did you get on this bus?"

"Roun' Hampden somewhere. Ah ain't zackly sure."

"And where did you and Zippo and Luckshin get off?"

"Someplace near Tweny-Ninf Streek, Ah thinks."

See now we were starting to get someplace. He was starting to talk in words other than Uh huh. And I was getting some solid details. They were spac'n 'round someplace; got on a bus somewhere and got off someplace else, but he wasn't exactly sure. Specifics! The facts!

I continued my questioning, "So, then what happened?"

"Dey wen' up da streek dat way," pointing toward the far wall, like I'm supposed to know where dat way is. At least he didn't say know what I mean?

"An' Ah started to walk down Calvert Streek," he narrated.

"And where were they going?"

"Ah dunno, Ah guesses maybe home," he speculated.

"You know where they live? You'll be able to get me their real names and where they live and their phone number? So we can use them as witnesses."

"Ah ain't zackly sho, but uh huh, Ah get it fo' ya," he assured me.

"So they went home. What time was that?"

"Ah ain't zackly sure, but Ah guesses maybe 'roun three, three-thirty, maybe, er maybe four, four thirty, 'bout. Ah ain't zackly sure. Ah din' have no watch."

"But it was still dark, wasn't it?"

"Uh huh."

"Well, the papers here say these terrible things they are blaming you for happened about four forty-five in the morning. So would you guess it was pretty close to that time when you got off the bus?"

He replied with his standard answer, "Uh huh."

"Okay. You started to walk down Calvert Street from Twenty-Ninth Street, and where exactly were you going at four-thirty in the morning?"

"Ah were gonna see my wife."

"You're married? I was told you stayed at the apartments where you work?"

"Uh huh."

"Uh huh what? You're married, or you stay at the apartments?"

"Well, Ah were, but not zackly. She was like my fiancée," he said, "but not no more."

"How long have you been divorced, or separated, or whatever?"

"Roun' bout five years," he guessed.

"Do you have kids to support?"

"Not wit' her, un unh."

"What's her name?"

"Who?"

"Your wife, who you weren't married to, fiancée, who you were going to see at four-thirty in the morning. What's her name?"

"You mean LaDelle?" he asked.

"Does LaDelle have a last name?"

"Uh huh, were Harris, but Ah ain't zackly sure wha' she go by now."

"So where does LaDelle live?"

"Over near Warwick Avenue someplace."

"But you're not exactly sure of the address?" I asked incredulously.

"Well Ah knows da place when Ah sees it."

"Forgive me, Jefferson," I interjected, "but I just have to ask you this. Why, at four-thirty in the morning were you going to visit LaDelle who you've been separated from for five years, and whose address you don't know?"

He replied matter-of-factly, "Were our *anniversry!*" as if that made perfect sense.

"Your anniversary! You're telling me that you still celebrate your anniversary after you've been split for five years, at four-thirty in morning?" I asked in astonishment.

"Fahv-thirty," he mumbled.

"What, five-thirty?"

"Ah wou'na git dere till bout fahv-thirty," he explained.

"Jefferson, why in the hell would you go to see her at five-thirty in the morning?"

He proceeded to explain, "See, she wuks night shif' an Ah wuks days, so on'yist way we git ta see each uva be when she git off wuk."

"How were you planning to get from Twenty-Ninth and Calvert to Warwick Avenue. Warwick is on the other side of town," I said. *(Not the side where the Bear's Den group comes from.)*

This guy starts out in Northwest Baltimore, not far from the city limits. He travels to East Baltimore on a bus, not very far from the Bear's den, then starts to walk south toward the very same Baltimore City Jail, where it seems we both now reside, to get to a destination in West Baltimore. By that route, my best guess is he has to cover . . . minimum . . . twenty or thirty miles.

"Ah were gonna walk down Calvert Streek to Fayette Streek and catch the numma 8," he explained.

"Hold it a second." I noted on my legal pad, *"Have Mike check Number 8. Route, Schedule, etc."*

"Okay. So, then what happened?"

"Well, Ah walks a couple blocks down Calvert, and dere were dis guy ona porch," he began.

"What guy? What Porch?"

"You know, the porch dey say where it happen."

"What Guy?" I demanded.

"Dis guy. He be a white guy . . . sittin', you know, like on da side da porch, like dis li'l wall between da porch nex doh."

"What's his name?"

"How da fuck Ah spoza know dat?"

"So you never saw him before? you didn't know him? Can you describe him?"

"Yeah, he be dis white guy wida beard, kinda reddish beard, you know, on his face. He weren' wearin' no shirt, er shoes, er nuffin'. Ah mean, he had on like pants."

"And at four-thirty, quarter to five in the morning, he's just sitting out on the porch. What was he doing?" I asked in amazement.

"He axed me do Ah got a light? An so Ah went up onto da porch an' put down da flaers an' stop to gima light."

"Hold it! You put down the what?"

"Flaers. I done picked some flaers to take to Ladelle. I already tol' you it were our anniversry!" he said with a degree of exasperation in his voice. Like he was probably thinking, what is it with this honky?

"You picked flowers!"

I couldn't wait to get out of this place and tell somebody this story. He picked flowers for Christ's sake!

"Yeah, An you know what?" he asked.

"No. What?" I responded in a sudden frenzy of curiosity.

"He were smokin' a reefer!"

"Reefer!" I exclaimed, as if in total disbelief.

"Uh huh. Whatchu think a dat?"

"I think he was committing a crime," I said flatly. "You didn't smoke reefer with him did you?"

"No man, whachu think Ah am, man? Ah don' do dat shit." He was indignant.

Well, old Jefferson's not all bad ladies and gentlemen of the jury. He don't smoke reefer, I thought to myself.

"But he offer me some, an Ah say no, so he axed me did Ah wana drink," he continued.

"A drink!" I once again exclaimed in total disbelief.

"Uh huh, Man, you know, it be August da what? da six Ah guesses, *(I know, you didn't have a calendar, I thought to myself)* Ah ain't zackly sure, but, you know, it be hot, an Ah be sweatin' and thirsty, so Ah say okay."

"What kind of drink was he offering?"

"Neva foun' out. Cause as Ah walk in da house, it were real dark, an Ah taken a couple steps in and Ah hears dis loud screamin' . . . some woman screamin' verbal words out her mouf, 'he rape me! Hep! He rape me!' he related, demonstrating a little animation for the first time during our interview.

"Verbal words out of her mouth!" I repeated. "Then what happened?" I asked, urging him on.

"Well, he run out da house, an da cops runs right in, an dey tackles me onto da flo, and dey stan' on ma face wid his shoe on ma face. An Ah wants ta file charges for po-lice brutality!" he exclaimed all in one breath.

"Whoa! One thing at a time. Let's back up a little. You walked into the house. The white guy with the beard, did he open the door for you, or did you open the door?"

"It were already op'n. You know, da screen were prop op'n wid da li'l thing on da top, like da thing on da thing what make da doh close. An the front doh were op'n, so you could walk right through. Cause Ah guesses

39

it were real hot, it bein' like August . . . but Ah ain't zackly sure why," he rambled on.

I interjected, "so the cops ran in as the bearded guy ran out and they stood on your face. Did you get a look at the girl who was screaming? I mean, can you describe her to me?"

"Man, like Ah done aready tol' you; it were dark in ere; the cop he were stanin' on my face, and he were like pushin' my face into da flo. Ah couldn' see shit."

"Did the girl get a good look at you?"

"No way man, Ah keeps tellin' ya it were dark? The cop's standin' on ma face. Ma face be pointin' in a opp'sit drekshin, so she couldn' see me neeva," he emphasized.

"So, If they have a line-up, or if we make her identify you in court, she won't be able to identify you?" I asked.

"Ain' no way, man. Ah keeps tellin' ya dat!"

"Jefferson, you've been watching me write all this stuff down *(on my fancy Legal Pad with my fancy pen)*. Now, I'm going to summarize all this for you to make sure I didn't leave out anything important. Stop me if I got anything wrong. Okay?"

"At approximately four-thirty on the morning of August sixth, more than six hours after you got off from work, you were with two friends whose names you don't know, coming from no place in particular not far from where you work in Northwest Baltimore. You were traveling in an easterly direction to Twenty-Ninth and Calvert Streets where you then headed south to visit your ex-fiancée, LaDelle, whose last name you don't know and who lives on the west side of town, but you don't know her address. You've been split with

40

her for about five years, but you were taking her flowers for your anniversary. On the way, an unknown white man with a red beard, no shoes, no shirt, sitting on a porch smoking marijuana invites you in through an already open door for a drink of you know not what because it was very hot," I read from my notes.

I continued, "As you entered the house, a woman screamed rape; the man with the red beard, no shirt and no shoes ran out. The police ran in; tackled you and stood on your face."

"How am I doing so far?" I asked, and continued reading. "You've never seen the woman; don't know what she looks like. She doesn't know you; has never seen you before, and cannot possibly identify you. Is that about it?"

"Ah din' do it," was his only response.

"Here's the deal, Jefferson," I explained. "Since you didn't do it, we're going to have to go to trial and make the State of Maryland prove, beyond a reasonable doubt, and to a moral certainty that you did these horrible things they have written here on these papers. *(From what I've heard so far, they'd have no difficulty whatever doing that.)* That's going to cost about five thousand dollars in legal fees, plus the money I have to pay my investigator to track down witnesses, investigate the facts, dig up what he can on the lady who says you raped her, and get some information on any of the other prosecution witnesses."

"This is at least a thousand dollar story you've just told me," I explained, "but we'll just apply the check Miss Dunn has to the balance of my fee. What arrangements do you want to make for the rest of the fee and the expenses?"

"Ah gits da money soon as Ah gits outta here. Ha much is ma bail?"

"They haven't set bail yet; we'll have to request a bail review," I explained. "I'll do the bail review as a part of the five thousand dollar fee. How are you going to pay for the bail?"

"Ah dunno, but Ah gits it," he assured me.

"On the other hand, Jefferson," I began to explain," it seems like a total waste of money to me to pay bail and all this money for my fee and the investigator if you are going to tell a jury the same story you just told me."

"It be da truf man; Ah swear it," he retorted emphatically.

"Oh, I believe you, Jefferson. The problem is, I don't think anybody else will."

"But dat be wha really happen," he insisted.

"I'm sure it is," I said, suppressing my utter disbelief. "This place is full of people who didn't do anything; who told the truth, but nobody believed them. So, here's what we'll do," I went on. "Let's forget that I was here today *(Except for the fee part, of course)*. I'll come back, say in a couple of days. In the meantime, you think up a better story to tell me when I come back, cause, trust me Jefferson, nobody is going to believe this story."

"Ah ain' gonna lie, man. Da's da truf; da's wha' really happen," he insisted.

"On the other hand, maybe we could work out a quiet little deal with the prosecutor if he's one of my friends and it will only cost you about Fifteen Hundred."

"Ah ain' goin' fur no deals. Ah din' do nuffin'. Ah keeps tellin' ya." He was indignant.

"Okay, I'll talk to your boss, see if she can advance your bail money and some of the fee and investigative expense. Is there anybody else you want me to talk to about getting you out of here? Should I call LaDelle?"

"No man; she dunno nothin' 'bout dis. Ah don' waner knowin' ma biness," he confided. "Besides, Ah dunno her numma."

"But, don't you think she's been wondering what happened to you? Maybe she's wondering why you didn't show up with the flowers?"

"She din know Ah were comin'; it were gonna be a sprize!" he said dejectedly.

"Here's another one of my cards," I offered. "You might meet somebody in here who needs a good lawyer."

"If you think of something else, or a different story, call me. I'm going to keep these papers; take them home and maybe iron them so I can read some of the details. I'll be in touch."

"*Correctional Officer! Let me the fuck out of here,*" I screamed silently.

3

August in Baltimore is always hot and humid. It must have been one hundred ten degrees in the jail. When I came out, the sun was beating down to the tune of about ninety-two degrees and the humidity was hovering around eighty-nine per cent. You could actually see the heat rising in waves off of the asphalt paving of the parking lot. Still, compared to that Goddamn jail, it felt cool outside. I removed my jacket, loosened my tie and opened my shirt. I climbed into my fire engine red 500 SL, put the top down and turned the air conditioning to as cold as it would go.

The Baltimore City Jail and Detention Center is located not too many blocks east of the Mount Vernon Towers, the condominium building where I live. I can actually see my apartment building from the parking lot. Conversely, I have a view of the City Jail and the Maryland State Penitentiary from the windows on the east side of my apartment, but a great view of the Baltimore skyline and harbor from the windows on the south side. In fact, I can see my office building from the living room windows.

It was nearly five o'clock by the time I started to pull from the parking lot at the jail, so I called Kelly on my cell phone, to let her know that I decided to just head home instead of going back to the office. She answered on the second ring, "Mr. West's Office."

"It's me," I said. "No point in coming back to the office. What's happening?"

"Everything's under control," she responded. "I'm here with Mr. Martin now. He was your four-thirty appointment. I explained to him that you expected to be out of court by now, and apologized for you. He's very nice. We're almost finished here. Shall I refer him to Dr. Wheaton for treatment?"

"Only the best for Mr. Martin. Make sure it's convenient for him to get to Wheaton's office."

"Oh!" she exclaimed, "I almost forgot. The brief on the Bartlett appeal must be mailed tonight in order for it to arrive at The Court of Special Appeals in Annapolis before the deadline. I thought you were coming back to the office. Will you be able to take it to the post office tonight?"

"Can't you mail it?" I asked.

"It needs to go Certified with a return receipt, and I've really got to get home a little early tonight. How about if I drop it off at your apartment building on my way home. You could take it to the Main Post Office before you go to dinner with the raper's boss."

"Okay," I agreed. "Ask the doorman to send it up to my apartment, and it's *rapist*. Oh! One more thing, call Mike Richards and see if he's available to help me with this case."

By the time the conversation ended, I was already sitting in my parking space in the underground garage of my apartment building. I stopped at the front desk on my way up to the twenty-first floor to pick up the mail and mention to Hiram, the doorman, that my secretary was going to drop off a package. I slipped him a buck and asked that he bring it up when it arrived, as I would be going out early, and needed to take it with me. I think it's really neat to have a doorman named Hiram. It's almost as good as having a butler named Jeeves.

I love this building. It is a stately, twenty-two story structure in the Mount Vernon section of mid-town Baltimore. The condo employs uniformed doormen, and has around-the-clock security, concierge and phone answering services. It's convenient to the Jones Falls Expressway which runs north out of the city to Baltimore County and connects with the Baltimore Beltway which rings the entire city of Baltimore. Getting almost anywhere is only a matter of minutes. It is less than one mile from the heart of the city, and less than ten minutes from the Bear's Den. I could walk to my office if I had to, and can walk to many of the better downtown restaurants.

The condo which I've owned about five years is a large two bedroom and den with two and a half baths, an eat-in kitchen, and a huge living room and dining room. It was decorated with quiet elegance, in traditional furnishings by Alexander Baker, Baltimore's hottest interior decorator. He selected everything from the towels to the dishes. It exudes a feeling of comfort; an invitation to fall into the furniture and be enfolded by its warmth. It is perfect for a high-living, fast-moving man about town.

I walked through the door, and began stripping my drenched clothes, ending up almost naked before I got from the foyer into the living room. I threw another log on the air conditioning on my way to the kitchen to make myself a Stoli Crystal Gimlet with a twist of lime on the rocks in a snifter. I really don't like to drink, but a friend of mine always orders a Stoli Crystal Gimlet with a twist of lime on the rocks in a snifter. He also always sends it back because it never seems to be just right . . . too much of this, or too little of that. Anyway, I like the ring of it and think it sounds quite sophisticated to order a Stoli Crystal Gimlet with a twist of lime on the rocks in a snifter. So that's what I've been drinking. I always send them back too, just to keep up the tradition, except of course when I make one at home.

I took an inspection tour of the apartment to make sure everything was tidy and clean. After all, I had a date with the raper's boss, and one never knows what might happen. Anyway, this was the day for the cleaning lady and I thought I'd better check around, just in case. I've never met the cleaning lady. She always comes in after I leave for the office and leaves before I get home. I just leave the money for her on the dresser in my bedroom. She's an amazing cleaning lady. She always manages to get from the front door of the apartment all the way to my bedroom to get the money, then leaves without leaving any footprints in the carpet and without disturbing any of the dust. Were it not for the fact that the money was gone and the refrigerator completely cleaned out, I would never really be sure that she had been there. I don't complain though, first because I never see her to register my complaints, and second because it is so difficult to find reliable domestic help. I don't want to stir up any trouble.

Anyway, I could tell she had been there. The money was missing, the bed was made and the bathroom was presentable, adorned, as it were, with clean towels. Upon reflection of my mother's advice to always wear clean underwear because you never know what might happen, I decided to shower in the guest bath instead of messing up the master bathroom. After all, I did have a date with the raper's boss, and you never know what might happen. Know what I mean?

As I stepped out of the shower, I heard the door bell. It was Hiram with the brief that had to go to the Post Office. I threw on my robe and took the package from his extended hand, which after it was relieved of its burden, remained extended and almost got closed in the door. I had to remind him that I had already demonstrated my appreciation for bringing up the package before it had even arrived. Hiram is up in years, a little addled, a little deaf, and a little blind. But, he's a dashing figure in his red coachman's uniform and he is exceptionally pleasant. I was dripping water all over the foyer, and had no money in my bathrobe in any case. I placed the package on the table in the foyer so I couldn't miss it on the way out.

I flipped on the Six O'clock News to see if by chance Jefferson Wilkes' crime had made it to the big time. It's highly beneficial to one's career to handle a case of some notoriety. Even a bad result in high profile cases brings more work into the office. I thought for sure, "Slats" would get his name on television, but apparently nobody cared. I started selecting my wardrobe for the night's main event while I half listened to the news, and reminisced about the case of Lamont Crowell a couple of years ago. That was a high profile case, but I could never understand why.

It started out as a routine assault case. As I recalled, Lamont got pissed at his foreman down at the Westport Bottle Works and went after him with a knife, right there in the factory. The foreman got a few cuts and bruises, mostly from bumping into things in his efforts to flee from Lamont. If you can believe it, Lamont got fired from his job. The case really wasn't very complicated and because of its rather routine nature and the very low fee that hadn't been paid until about two days before the trial, I had not done much in the way of preparation. It was one of those kinds of cases that an experienced criminal lawyer could just try from the seat of his pants.

On the day of trial, Lamont and I walked over to the Criminal Courts Building from my office. When we arrived, there were people picketing the court house, carrying signs and chanting. The Eyewitness News Team as well as the news departments of the other network television stations were on the scene.

There were reporters roaming around with microphones and notebooks. It was a real media event.

Lamont and I pushed our way through the throng, into the court house and made our way up to the third floor for Lamont's assault trial. The hallway outside of the courtroom was packed with more sign carrying people, reporters and cameramen.

When I said to Lamont, "I wonder what's going on?" He replied, "They're here for me."

"What do you mean, here for you?"

"They're my people. Protesting about them firing me," he replied.

"Are you kidding me!" I remembered saying. "I'm not prepared for this kind of event."

Next thing I remember, some reporter had a microphone stuck in my face asking me what I thought was going to happen to Lamont. I, at that moment was hardly concerned about what was going to happen to Lamont. I was more concerned with what was going to happen to me. I had no idea that so much attention was being focused on this case. I was forced to retreat to one of the stock responses you pick up from watching television and movies. "I don't believe in trying my cases in the press. We'll just have to wait until the verdict is in before I will comment." I pushed my way into a packed courtroom where one might have reasonably expected sanity to prevail. But there was to be no sanity that day.

Without a commentary on the state of the Maryland judiciary, I will simply say that the genius who was playing Judge for a Day, filling in for a Circuit Court Judge who was otherwise occupied, normally tried cases in Civil Court at the Magistrate's level. He really had never actually conducted a serious criminal trial, which this had suddenly become.

Here was a courtroom packed with reporters, an unprepared lawyer, a less prepared judge and a courthouse surrounded by protesters. Was I happy? In the now famous words of Jefferson Wilkes, "Un unh!"

Well, the case proceeded, and with the questioning of the first witness, very quickly plunged from a bad scene to a three-ring circus; me in the center ring. The prosecutor questioned the first witness, who happened to be the victim's sister-in-law, leading her through a series of objectionable questions and answers. My trial strategy has always been to let a prosecutor ask whatever he pleases, without raising objections, unless absolutely necessary. Then, when it's my turn to cross-examine the witnesses, I try to lead them to a recantation of everything to which they had just testified. Except that wasn't to be in this case. Every time I asked a leading question of a prosecution witness, which is the only proper way to cross-examine, the prosecutor objected and Super Judge sustained the objection. Every time I objected to a leading question asked by the prosecutor of one of his own witnesses, which is not permitted, I was overruled. With a courtroom full of the press, this was hardly an enhancement of my blossoming reputation. Usually when situations strike rock bottom, they can only get better. Not that day. With each of the State's witnesses, it just got worse.

During the lunch break, Lamont asked me how I thought it was going. I told him that the best thing he could do was flee the jurisdiction of the court and take me with him, because if it got any worse I would probably end up with him . . . *in jail.* Oddly enough, Super Judge, after allowing the prosecutor to lead the witnesses through a new rendition of *"Friday the 13th; Freddie's Back"* and having refused to permit me to cross-examine a single witness, decided in his infinite wisdom that there was insufficient evidence, and found Lamont not guilty. I was astonished. Lamont and the press thought he got off because of my brilliant representation. I didn't then, and to this day, still don't understand why Lamont got off. Lady justice, although blind as a bat, and probably deaf and dumb as well, does in fact, wield a mighty sword.

I selected a pair of freshly laundered, rather faded, tight-fitting Levi 505's, a little frayed at the cuff, but only one cuff, a white linen long sleeved shirt and a pair of black ostrich cowboy boots topped off with an Ermenegildo Zegna blue blazer slung over my shoulder. I really wasn't sure that Jennifer was the one I remembered. I couldn't tell how tall she was because the only time I saw her, if indeed it was her, she was sitting on a bar stool. Although I think and act like I'm over six feet tall, I'm only about five ten depending on whether you measure before or after I get a haircut. Under the circumstances, the added height of the cowboy boots couldn't hurt, I thought.

I fastened the strap of my Cartier tank watch, fished around in my briefcase for the crumpled piece of paper with Jennifer's address, and headed out the door.

As I turned off the Jones Falls Expressway onto westbound Northern Parkway, about three quarters of the way to the Western Creek Apartments, I remembered the brief on the table in the foyer by the front door which I had placed there so I wouldn't forget. I didn't actually forget. I remembered it was there, unfortunately after I had gone too far to return for it.

4

The Western Creek Apartments are located very close to the Baltimore County line. Not that many years ago, the neighborhood was quite affluent. A lot of single-family homes were built in the Fifties surrounding the apartment complex. The apartments were originally built as up-scale rentals for empty nesters who no longer wanted the responsibility of maintaining large homes. The area which had been predominately Jewish because it is within walking distance of the numerous synagogues on both sides of Park Heights Avenue, has changed considerably in the last twenty years or so. Now the area is a mixture of very religious Hasidic Jews and middle-class African-American schoolteachers, professionals and businessmen.

I pulled into the apartment complex which consists of seven or eight three-story brick buildings and searched for the address on the crumpled piece of paper, 2201-A. I was grateful that apartment A was on the first floor. The sun had drifted toward the horizon, but the thermometer was still stuck at around ninety degrees. I don't think I could have made it to E, or F.

I rapped gently on the door, which opened instantly as if the person on the other side were waiting there in anticipation of my arrival. There stood Jennifer. I wish I could tell you that before me stood the most beautiful creature ever to set foot on the face of the earth, but we are all influenced by the good traits of others. Having not too many hours earlier been exposed to Jefferson Wilkes, I simply cannot tell a lie. Jennifer was quite pleasant looking, but a long way from beautiful. She was about five three, shoulder length, straight, honey blonde hair, blue-eyed, soft, pleasant looking face, slim, and not much more than a hundred pounds. She was dressed in a pair of navy blue gabardine slacks and a white cotton blouse, top button open, but no cleavage showing. Her navy blue pumps with the spiked heels made her even taller. I was right about the cowboy boots.

"Hi! I'm Bruce," I said, never at a loss for words. She smiled showing a row of fairly straight teeth, with just a trace of an overlap of the two front uppers. It has been my experience that women with overlapping front teeth are exceptionally responsive sexually. Just an offhand conclusion based on no particular scientific study, other than my observations of a representative sampling of the numerous women who have been in and out of my life since I reached puberty. She also displayed a dimple in each cheek when she smiled.

"I know who you are. I'm Jennifer." She invited me in while she gathered her bag and a light sweater. As she returned to the living room where she had left me standing, she handed me the check for five hundred and twenty-five dollars.

"Do you still want to take me out for a drink?" she asked. There was a slight lilt to her voice, which was throaty, deep and resonant, yet only slightly above a whisper. It was a clever test to see if I had any interest in her now that I had the money.

"Actually, I've made a reservation for dinner at Sabatino's in Little Italy, if you'd like to join me for dinner."

Again, she just smiled. It was a hard smile to describe. She had heart-shaped lips that turned up a little at the corners when she smiled. There was a twinkle . . . No, more like a glint in her eyes. It wasn't what might be described as a sweet smile, more like a sensuous, slightly mysterious, I have a secret you don't know kind of smile. There was a message there, but not easily read. I couldn't quite put my finger on it.

"I'd love to," she responded.

She hooked her arm into mine and we headed out the door.

I opened the car door for her and as she slid in she commented, "Nice car."

"Thanks," I responded.

As I pulled out of the parking lot, I began to explain about the package that I'd forgotten to take. "I really didn't forget it on purpose," I explained. "I left it right by the front door and realized I'd forgotten to take it when I was practically at your place. I have to stop by to pick it up, but if you're even slightly apprehensive about my intentions, you can wait in the car while I run up and get it. It'll only take a minute."

She just smiled one of those smiles and said, "I'm not worried, I'm a black belt. I can handle myself." She chuckled. And I was quite sure she could. She seemed very self-assured for a woman her age, which I guessed to be in her middle twenties.

The top was still down on the car, and we were cruising down the Jones Falls Expressway at about sixty. It was a bit difficult to carry on much of a conversation with the wind whipping around the open car. It took less than fifteen minutes for the journey from her apartment to mine.

As I was pulling into the underground garage, I said, "If you have no objections, we can have a drink at my place. Our reservation is for eight-thirty and we have a little more than an hour. It only takes a few minutes to get to the post office from here, and the restaurant is just around the corner from the post office. I'll only be in the post office long enough to drop off the package and pay for the postage.

"That'll be great," she replied. "How long have you lived here?"

"Just about five years."

We made our way to the bank of elevators. As we stepped into the elevator, she pointed her finger at the row of buttons and asked, "What floor?"

"Twenty-one."

"Mmmm," she responded. The button lit up under her touch.

We reached the twenty-first floor, the doors opened and I ushered her into the apartment. Trying not to appear too defensive, as if this were all a contrived plot to snare little Miss Muffet in my web, I immediately pointed out the package I had left on the table.

"Nice place," she said as we entered the living room.

"What would you like to drink?" I asked, playing the perfect host.

"What are you having?"

"I think I'll have a Stoli Crystal Gimlet with a twist of lime on the rocks in a snifter." *(Slick!)*.

"Sounds good," she said. "Me too."

She followed me into the kitchen and watched while I prepared our drinks. I hoped she didn't know you're supposed to send them back. We clinked the Baccarat crystal snifters ever so lightly, raised our drinks in a toast, and sipped without a word being spoken . . . She gave me another one of those indescribable smiles.

She began the conversation by asking me about Jefferson.

I did what lawyers do best, ask questions. "Tell me what you know about him."

"Well, I only moved down here from New Jersey about three months ago when I separated from my husband. A friend got me this resident manager's position a couple of days before I left home. It was the only way I could have moved out. They provide me with the apartment as a part of the job. So," she continued, "I've only known him about three months. He was working there when I arrived. But, he's been working at the complex for about a year and a half. He does a good job. He's dependable and the residents seem to like him."

"Do you know if he's married?"

"I'm quite certain he's not. Like I told you, he's also provided with an apartment as a part of the job, and he definitely lives alone."

"Do you think he has a drug or alcohol problem?"

"I'd have noticed it if he did," she said. "I haven't seen any indication of it. Why?"

I summarized Jefferson's story and asked if she believed it.

"It is rather bizarre, isn't it?"

"Well, I've not had an opportunity, to really get into it. I'm making arrangements with my private investigator to check a few things out for me. Tomorrow, I'll arrange to get a copy of the police report, and spend some time trying to read the tome of charging documents I picked up from him today. I think he rolled them up and used them to swat flies. They are so battered and crumpled, I'm going to require a forensic scientist to restore them to a readable state."

"How long do you think he's going to have to stay in jail?" she asked.

"That's another thing," I explained. "I need to request a bail review hearing. I believe they'll set bail, but the amount will depend to some degree on any prior criminal record he may have. He is charged with a serious offense, you know?" *(There I'm starting to get even, you know?)*

"We really need him at work. What can I do to help get him out?"

"He'll probably need about twenty-five hundred dollars to pay a bondsman to post bail. It might also be very helpful if you appeared at the bail hearing to tell the judge of his character, and explain his importance on the job. How do you suppose he'll be able to come up with the bail money?"

"I'll talk to my boss. He'll probably agree to help him."

"There's another problem," I said. "This is a serious case and is going to cost about five thousand dollars to defend, plus I'd estimate at least a thousand for the investigator. I just can't go into court with a case like this, without at least some investigation and a thorough preparation. Do you think your boss is going to be willing to spend that kind of money?"

"I doubt it," she responded.

"Do you know if he has any family that can help him?"

"I'm not sure, but I really don't think so," she replied.

"I have to tell you, that I find his story too incredible to believe. It seems a shame to waste so much money for such a weak defense. I mean, I can't allow this man to take the witness stand and tell the story he told me. That would be an act of malpractice, for God's sake! Does he trust you?" I asked.

"I'd like to think so."

"Well, let's concentrate on getting him out of jail. He'll be able to earn some money to pay for his defense. Then, we'll have to wait and see what develops, but if it doesn't get better than it appears now, maybe you'll be able to talk some sense into him."

"Just keep me informed," she said.

"I think we'd better go," I said, looking at my watch.

"Nice watch," she commented.

"Thanks." I handed her the sweater and oversized purse and started for the door.

"I won't need this bag, will I?" she asked holding up her purse.

"I was planning to take you to dinner. I wasn't expecting you to pay."

"Then, I might as well just leave it here." She smiled as she tossed it back onto the chair.

Now, in the normal course of human events, the only person in a room full of people who knows if a guy is going to get laid is the woman he's with. But not tonight. Obviously, Jennifer was planning to return to the pad after dinner. I was beginning to understand the smile. We headed out the door and walked to the elevator.

"You forgot the package," she exclaimed.

"I'm afraid my mind is on other things."

She gave me another one of those Goddamn smiles, as she pushed the button for the elevator.

I returned to the apartment and retrieved the package, glancing into the living room to see if I had just imagined the bit with the purse, or if it had really happened. There it was . . . lying in the chair . . . sort of smiling at me.

The elevator had arrived by the time I returned. She hooked her arm in mine and down we went. I wheeled the SL out of the garage and headed downtown to the Main Post Office. Coincidentally, it is on Fayette Street, the same street as the *numma 8 bus*. I signaled to make a left turn into the parking lot, but had to wait for an oncoming bus. A number 12 oncoming bus, not the number 8 Jefferson said ran on Fayette Street to Warwick Avenue. I pulled into a parking space near the main entrance.

"Do you mind waiting in the car or do you want to come in?" I asked.

"I'll wait."

There was an armed guard at the door. I winked at him and said loudly enough for her to hear, "Do you mind keeping your eye on my car? You needn't worry about her. She's a black belt."

I looked back. She was smiling that smile.

After mailing my package, we drove the very few blocks from the main post office past the old Shot Tower on Front Street. Built in 1828, it was the tallest structure in the United States until the Washington Monument was built in Washington, DC, after the Civil War.

I turned onto Little Italy on Pratt Street and drove past the Flag House which was the 1793 home of Mary Pickersgill. She's the lady who sewed the first American Flag in 1813. That flag flew over Fort McHenry during the Battle of Baltimore in 1814 and inspired Francis Scott Key to write the Star Spangled Banner. It is a neighborhood of tiny, brick row houses with white marble steps lining both sides of the very narrow streets. These are the legendary white marble steps for which Baltimore is known.

Another interesting feature of these houses is, that although they are made of brick, during the early Fifties, a horde of siding salesman were unleashed on the inner city and they convinced ninety percent of the homeowners to cover their brick houses with Formstone. The product was a plaster like material colored to imitate stone and applied using a form that gave it the appearance of flagstone. It is puzzling, to say the least, why anyone would cover a brick house with imitation stone, but you can't say enough for the quality of the product, the houses look the same today as they did when the stuff was first applied.

The homes are occupied by the descendants of the early Italian immigrants who settled near the natural deep-water harbor where the City of Baltimore was founded and grew. There are at least four authentic, family-run Italian restaurants on every block.

It was really my lucky night. Jennifer didn't send back the Stoli Crystal gimlet with a twist of lime on the rocks in a snifter. Then there was the routine with the purse. I snagged a parking space right in front of the restaurant. Finding any parking space in Little Italy is nothing short of a miracle. Finding one in front of the restaurant is the mother of all miracles.

As usual, the very small waiting area of the restaurant was jammed and people were spilling out onto the sidewalk waiting for tables. I wormed my way through the teaming masses to announce my arrival to the Maitre de in the hope of getting my name on the waiting list, despite the fact that I had a reservation. Reservations at Sab's were just a formality, not to be observed. Besides the hopefuls that had reservations, there were those who just showed up because they were regulars, or knew somebody who knew somebody that could get them a table. For all the good it usually did me, I was a regular.

"Hi Mr. West!" Nick exclaimed. "Good to see you."

Nick is the owner of Sabatino's. He remembers everybody's name and never fails to make you feel like a long lost cousin. This particular restaurant is a favorite and is always over-booked. There are two chances of being seated by nine for an eight-thirty reservation . . . slim and none.

"Come with me. I have your table waiting."

I tried not to show any expression of surprise, or suffer cardiac arrest. "Thanks, Nick," I said very nonchalantly, as if I not only expected this kind of treatment, but was accustomed to it.

"I'm impressed," she said.

Can I get any luckier? I mused silently. Nick took us to a table in the Zone 8 room. Let me explain. Pikesville is in Zip Code 21208, commonly referred to as "Zone 8." Remember, I already described some of the people who live in Pikesville. Among their other attributes, these people dine out regularly, are good tippers, like to see and be seen, except, of course, on the nights reserved for the Bear's Den. The room where our table was situated is in the center of the restaurant. It has mirrors at eye level which allow even those patrons seated facing the wall a view of everything going on in the restaurant. Everyone seated in this room can see everybody, and be seen by everybody. Nick always puts the Pikesville crowd into this room. Thus, it is affectionately called the Zone 8 room. I assume he puts me in this room because I used to live in 21208, and once a Zone 8, always a Zone 8.

"What wouldja like ta drink?" asked Camille. Camille has been a waitress at Sab's for as long as I can remember. All the waitresses wear name tags on their black vests, but she's been there so long that everyone knows her.

"Let's have one of those gimlet things," said Jennifer.

"Nah, they don't make them right. I always have to send them back." The fact was that I didn't believe I could handle another one. The way the night was going, I needed to stay in full command.

"Let's have a bottle of wine instead," I suggested.

"Good," she responded.

"Red or White?"

"You pick," she directed.

I selected an expensive bottle of California, Silver Oak, Cabernet Sauvignon. A flavorful, full-bodied red with low tannins. I swirled the wine in my glass, sniffed it, took a little sip, swished it around in my mouth and nodded my approval to Camille. You would have thought I knew what the hell I was doing. I looked at Jennifer. She was wearing one of those smiles. I think this one was a smile of approval.

Camille poured two glasses. We raised and tipped them toward each other and took a sip.

"Nice wine," she commented.

The wine was a nice compliment to Sabatino's Bookmaker Salad. The salad, named, I suppose after the bookmakers who, in addition to the zone 8'ers, patronize the restaurant, is a variety of lettuces, tomato, hard-boiled eggs, cucumber, olives, radishes, celery, hot peppers, assorted Italian antipasto meats, cheese, shrimp and just about anything else you can think of to put in a salad, and some things you wouldn't think of, smothered in Sab's secret-recipe salad dressing. A Bookmaker Salad with an order of garlic bread to dunk into the dressing is a meal in itself, but not to appear cheap, I ordered the salad and garlic bread, which we shared and veal Parmesan with a side of angel hair pasta in marinara sauce which we also shared, and couldn't even finish.

There was no rush to get out of there. I already knew what was going to happen, or at least I thought I did. The dinner conversation was uninspiring, mostly small talk about my current marital status, or absence thereof, and about her bad marriage, recent separation and escape to restore some sanity to her life. She confided that she hadn't been dating since she arrived in Baltimore. She had been having a hard time meeting people. The night we met at the Bear's Den was her first encounter with the place. She claimed to have left alone, which would be quite unusual. She must have hit it on a bad night. She mentioned her car being in the shop. Something to do with the exhaust system. Maybe her vibrator was broken too, I thought. I began to wonder if she weren't just using me. She apparently thought I'd be easy, what with the purse routine and all. Among her other traits, she was obviously very perceptive.

One trait did surface, though, over dinner. This petite, soft-spoken, young lady was tough as nails under the facade. There was a lot more to her coy little smile than was readily apparent. I was left with the distinct impression that she was not somebody to mess with.

She could definitely handle herself. If you catch my drift. *(I didn't want to say, know what I mean?).* For a skinny little thing, she could also pack away some food and booze.

We drained the bottle of wine, and ordered coffee to top off the meal. She was pleasant enough company. She displayed good manners, was fairly intelligent, and as I said, not at all unpleasant to look at.

I paid the check, left a generous tip for Camille, and thanked Nick for taking such good care of us. As much as I hated to give up the great parking spot, we climbed into the SL. I looked over at her and asked, "Are you really a black belt?" This time she just laughed out loud.

For whatever reason, I drove more slowly than usual back to the apartment. Instead of taking the expressway, which would have avoided a lot of traffic lights, I used the surface streets past the old Fish Market and warehouses that had been restored and converted into restaurants and nightclubs. Since she was relatively new in town, I thought she might enjoy a little tour. The city of Baltimore actually predates the American Revolution by a couple of hundred years. There is a lot of history in this city. I pointed out some of Baltimore's many historic monuments and headed toward Harbor Place. I asked if there were anywhere else she might like to go. She responded by sort of curling up on the seat and saying, "Let's just go home."

She'd spent less than an hour in my apartment and was already referring to it as home. This was not a good omen, as omens go!

5

We had taken about three steps into the living room. Jennifer put her arms around my neck and whispered softly in my ear, "Thank you." She flicked her tongue under my earlobe, drawing it between her lips, gently nibbling on it. I could feel her breath in my ear. Just as suddenly, she glued her lips to mine, her tongue hungrily searching, darting, licking and nibbling my lower lip. She placed her hands against my chest under my jacket and with one deft maneuver, slid it back over my shoulders pulling it down toward the floor where it fell in a heap, sleeves turned inside out. With her lips still pasted to mine, she unbuttoned my shirt, pulling it too back over my shoulders and downward toward the floor. The sleeves of the shirt, like the jacket, had turned inside out but would not slide to the floor because the cuffs were still buttoned, effectively hog tying my arms to my sides. She began running her long fingers through the hair on my chest lingering over my nipples and sliding her hands down my belly toward my crotch.

I was seized by instant pangs of severe pain. You will recall I was wearing tight fitting jeans. There was simply no room in those 505's for the rampant erection that was desperately struggling to slash its way out. As she reached the waistband of the jeans, I sucked my stomach in to aid her with the button, but she needed no assistance. With great dexterity, she unfastened my belt, unbuttoned the jeans and unzipped my fly. I got the impression that she had prior experience. In one motion, she pushed the jeans down to my knees, where they wedged against the tops of my cowboy boots, immobilizing my legs. My arms were pinned to my sides, and now my legs were disabled. *(The cowboy boots weren't such a good idea after all!)* I was trapped and at her mercy, though I readily admit I did absolutely nothing to dissuade or otherwise discourage her. I wondered if she'd learned these moves in karate school.

She placed her forefingers into the waistband of my jockey shorts, and nimbly lifted them over my erection, sliding them down to my knees on top of the jeans. The pain was replaced by a surge of pleasure the moment Big Jim leapt to freedom.

Her hands were now gently caressing my engorged member. She slid to her knees in front of me and began rubbing my penis against the soft skin of her cheek. Ever so imperceptibly, she flicked her tongue over the head and finally, after what seemed like an eternity, took me into her mouth, her hands in the meantime moving skillfully over my testicles and stroking the shaft. I resigned myself to my fate and became determined to withstand this torture for as long as possible without uttering a single word of complaint.

Little sounds began emanating from deep in her throat, causing subtle vibrations against my ready to explode member. It was difficult to tell at this point who was enjoying this more. I struggled with this frenetic insanity until I could hold out no longer. In a moment of religious fervor, I began to shout, "Oh God! Oh my God!" I prayed over, and over. As I stiffened, she felt the seismic contractions, the precursor of an imminent volcanic eruption. She engulfed me as I exploded in a violent fury of vibrating ecstasy. Though I was already deprived of my senses, she continued to manipulate me with her lips and tongue. My knees started to buckle and I thought I would collapse atop the heap of clothes on the floor. I had to beg her to stop. No way she could've acquired these skills in any karate class. Maybe she studied with Linda Lovelace.

Slowly she raised herself to a standing position. Sometime during the affray, she had managed to kick off her shoes, but otherwise, was still fully dressed. She stood before me, never taking her eyes from mine, and with calculated and deliberate movements, slowly began to unbutton her blouse. First the sleeves, then down the front. She let the blouse fall crumpled to the floor behind her. She reached behind her back and unfastened her bra, shrugging it off so that it too landed on the floor. She unbuttoned the waist of her slacks, pulled the zipper down and let them slip to the floor beneath her. Then demonstrating extraordinary agility, she slipped her panty hose along with her bikini panties over her hips down to the floor and into the pile beneath her feet.

In the meantime, I was busy trying to extricate myself from my bonds. I managed to get the cuffs of my shirt unbuttoned, allowing it to drop to the floor on top of the jacket. I pulled up my jockeys and the jeans enough to free my legs, which still hadn't fully recovered. My knees felt like rubber . . . barely supporting my hundred and sixty-five pounds. She now stood naked before me; her smile was the only thing she was wearing. She was a natural blonde; her breasts were small and firm, I guessed about thirty-two B, with pert little, pink, stiffened nipples pointing toward the ceiling. She had flawless skin; butter-like to the touch.

"Nice bod!" I commented.

All of this for just a dinner. I can't imagine what might have happened if we had also gone to the movies.

Restricted as I was by the partially removed jeans, waddling like a penguin, I took her by the hand and led her into the bedroom. She stripped down the bedspread, top sheet and blanket and nudged me gently onto my back on the bed. She set about expertly removing my cowboy boots.

"Nice boots," she said.

She pulled off my jeans and jockey shorts, then curled up next to me and began attempting to revive my dead penis. Surprisingly, it wasn't long before she breathed new life into it. She mounted me like her favorite Pinto pony, digging her knees into my flanks, and sucking me into her. She began gyrating ever so slowly, clutching my penis with her vaginal muscles. She pressed her pubis into mine. She leaned forward, brushing her nipples across my chest, pressing her lips to mine and swirling her tongue deep into my mouth. She reached back and caressed my balls with her fingertips. It took a little longer this time, but she didn't quit until the assigned task had been completed to our mutual satisfaction. I tried to think of ten Jewish men I knew for a minion to say Kaddish *(the traditional Jewish prayer of mourning)* for my dead dick. We disengaged and I plunged into the unconsciousness of critically needed sleep.

I was raised from the abyss of my peaceful sleep by the roar of Victoria Falls cascading into the gorge of the Zambezi River. My eyes were bombarded by the rays of the sun screaming through the slats of the walnut Venetian blinds that covered my bedroom windows. It took a few minutes until I realized I was in my own bed. The running water, I discerned was the sound of the shower.

My mind began to refocus on the preceding night's gambol, and I quickly checked between my legs to see if my shriveled member had regained consciousness. It didn't look too promising. I glanced at the clock. To my dismay, it was only six-thirty in the morning. Why would anybody, especially me, be up at this ungodly hour, unless, of course, one had a very early tee-off time? With great difficulty I agonizingly removed myself from the bed and stumbled into the kitchen for a glass of juice. The living room looked like Sarajevo after a day of Serbian shelling. Clothes were strewn over the floor in silent commemoration of last night's revelry.

By the time I had poured two glasses of juice *(I told you I was considerate)* and returned to the bedroom, Jennifer was stepping from the shower dripping wet, making absolutely no attempt to cover herself with the towel. Although I didn't think it possible, to my surprise I began to get aroused. You can't imagine the relief at discovering that my dick was still alive and well. She was standing there in the bathroom adorned only in her smile, towel wrapped around her head. I guess she didn't want me to see her with wet hair. It seemed like the perfect opportunity to get even . . . Do unto to her what she had done unto me.

I sauntered into the bathroom, placed my hands around her waist and lifted her slightly so that she was sitting on the edge of the vanity. Delicately, I began to lick the water from her neck, slowly moving down to her breasts, tenderly flicking my tongue over her succulent nipples. I lingered there for a while; then began working my way down her belly. I lifted her legs so that they were draped over my shoulders, spreading her wide and nestled my face into the muskiness of her sex. I penetrated her with my tongue and manipulated her clitoris between my tongue and my teeth, sucking and gently pulling it between my lips until she erupted into a frenzy of convulsive spasms. I sucked the honey from the deepest recesses of her womb and continued until she pleaded with me to stop, pushing my head away.

"I've got to get ready for work," she protested.

"But what are we going to do about this?" I pointed, with pride, to my stiff penis.

She took it in her hand and gently began stroking me. She stopped long enough to apply a glob of Jergen's Lotion to the palm of her hand, from a small bottle which she must have had in her purse. She wrapped her hand around my very much aroused member and began massaging me until she brought me shuddering to a fit of orgasmic delight. As I was about to come, she turned me toward the open shower and directed the pulsing ejaculations against the wall.

"There," she said. "Think that will hold you until tonight?"

I assumed she was planning an encore performance, but I wasn't sure that I wanted to, or for that matter, if I'd be able.

I climbed into the shower and let the streams of hot water beat against the remnants of my ravaged and spent body. I adjusted the showerhead and directed the stream against the wall to rinse off the fruit of the Jergen's Lotion hand job that had begun to slither down the tiles.

When I emerged from the shower, Jennifer seemed to have plotted the entire day's activities. She informed me that she would drop me off at work and then take my car to her apartment development so I wouldn't be inconvenienced and have to go out of my way to take her home. If I needed my car during the day, she'd leave work and return it. I protested that it would be no problem for me to take her home, but she insisted that it would work out better her way. Just as I had observed, this was a tough little cookie; she would have her own way. End of subject! Period!

6

The elevator doors opened. Kelly looked up from her desk and exclaimed, "What happened? Were you in an accident? My God you look awful!"

"Actually, I feel pretty good. A little weak in the knees, but pretty good."

"What are you doing here so early? It's only eight-thirty."

"Lots to do," I proclaimed and headed into my office. Neither of us could ever remember a time when I had gotten to the office that early.

Kelly followed me soon after, bearing a cup of steaming coffee. I looked at her with a puzzled expression.

"I can't hassle you this morning," she said sympathetically. "Last night must have been awful." She was being obviously sarcastic.

Kelly had prepared the Wilkes file and placed it on my desk. I removed the notes from my briefcase and began dictating. I called her into my office.

"We need to get the police report on the Wilkes case," I told her. "I'd like to arrange for a bail hearing today if possible. Have you reached Mike Richards?"

"Give me a break," she responded. "You asked me last night at five to call him and it's only eight forty-five now. I'll call him at nine when he gets into his office."

"Oh, and call the MTA. Find out what buses run from Hampden to Twenty-Ninth Street, also from Fayette and Calvert to Warwick Avenue; see if they'll mail us copies of the bus schedules for those lines. Also, call the State's Attorney's Office and see if you can find out who will be prosecuting the Wilkes case."

"What was he like?" she asked.

"I think he's a lying scum bag. His story is totally incredible; total bull-shit!"

"What was she like?"

"Who?" I asked coyly.

"The *raper's* boss."

"They're a good pair," I responded. "He runs around raping strangers, and last night the *raper's* boss raped me."

"How awful it must be for you! Should I try to get you an appointment at the Rape Crisis Center?"

"I'm going to try to handle this alone." I laughed.

I handed her the check from the Western Run Apartments, which Jennifer had thoughtfully made payable to me, to add to the deposit. "Now, get out and leave me alone. I have to deal with my emotions," I kidded.

I began reading, with some degree of difficulty the badly battered charging documents I had taken from Wilkes. He should have also been charged with assault and battery of the papers. According to the statement of charges, and the witness statement, the victim, Marianne Krenshaw, was in bed asleep in a second floor bedroom of her home in the Charles Village neighborhood of Baltimore City, when sometime between four-thirty and a quarter to five in the morning she was awakened by a black male standing over her with a sharp pointed instrument pressed against her throat. She screamed; the intruder threatened to kill her if she didn't remain quiet. Her assailant then pulled down the covers on the bed and raised her nightgown. He began to stroke her and said that he did not want to hurt her; he just wanted to make love with her. The assailant then undid his pants and got into bed on top of her. As he was about to force himself into her, the phone rang. She convinced him that the ringing phone would wake her roommate and suggested that he allow her to answer it.

Remember, this is after four o'clock in the morning. Who the hell would call someone at that ungodly hour?

I continued to read in disbelief. He agreed that she could answer the phone and walked out of the bedroom with her into the hall where the phone was situated, holding what appeared to be a screwdriver to her throat. She picked up the receiver and said "Hello." It was her next-door neighbor who had heard her scream. The neighbor asked if everything was okay. She responded, by saying "No."

The neighbor then asked if she should call the police, and the victim said, "Yes."

As incredible as it sounded, she then hung up the phone and was forced to returned to the bed by her assailant, who once again attempted to force himself on her.

The statement went on to relate that a police car had arrived and the intruder saw the blue lights flashing through the window. He began cursing her. He screamed, "You called the police, you bitch!" and fled from the room, down the steps and into the living room. His pants were unbuttoned and unzipped, and down to just above his knees. Marianne followed him down the steps and ran to open the locked front door to permit the police to enter.

The first police officer into the house chased the suspect into the dining room where he tackled him to the floor. There was a Phillips-head screwdriver on the floor near where the suspect was captured.

I recalled with fond memory the assault I endured last night, and formed a picture in my mind of my trying to run down a flight of steps with my jeans down around my knees. I began to chuckle out loud.

Well, I pondered the two stories I now had about the events leading to the arrest of Mr. Wilkes. This, I thought was starting to get interesting. I wondered what really happened.

M y phone was boiling over, but Kelly didn't seem to be answering it. I raised the receiver and said, "This is Mr. West. Can I help you?"

"Hello Mr. West," Kelly responded. "Your door was closed and you were in there giggling to yourself. I didn't know what you were doing in there, so I decided to use the intercom."

"You figured out how to use it?" I asked in astonishment.

"The *raper* is on the phone."

"*Rapist!*" I corrected.

"What's the feminine of rapist?" she asked.

"*Rapess*, I suppose."

"Well, she's on line one."

"Hi, Jennifer, what's up?"

"I have good news and bad news," she announced.

"Tell me the good news first."

"My boss is willing to go the twenty-five hundred for Jefferson's bail."

"What's the bad news?"

"That's all he'll pay. He won't help with the legal fees or the expenses. But it's not all bad."

"Why not?"

"He said he would make regular deductions from Jefferson's pay and send payments to you. Will you take payments?"

"My usual installment plan is one hundred percent down, no monthly payments," I replied. "But I'll ask Kelly and my landlord if I can pay them in installments. It might work out."

"Oh, I have some more good news," she said.

I wasn't sure I could handle any more good news.

"The repair shop said they could deliver my car to me. They're located right up on Charles Street, a couple blocks from your apartment. So, they're going to deliver my car to your apartment building and you won't have to take me to pick it up."

Just how lucky can one person be? I was truly relieved to hear this.

She continued, "I decided to pick up some stuff for dinner. I'll bring it down when I return the car. We can stay home all night." Again she referred to my apartment as home!

"I'm not sure I can handle a repeat of last night's performance," I said. I was sure she was smiling that smile.

Kelly buzzed me on the intercom again. I put Jennifer on hold. "Did you find a new toy?" I asked. "Why can't you just holler like you usually do?"

"This is more professional," she said. "Mike is on the line."

I got back to Jennifer and told her I had to take an important call and that I'd see her later.

"Michael, my man! What's happening?"

"You tell me," he said.

"I need some help with a case. I'll fax you a summary of the facts, but I need a run-down on any prior criminal record for a Jefferson Wilkes. I'd also like to see what you can find out for me about a Marianne Krenshaw."

I gave him the information he would need to track down these people and told him there would be more.

Mike Richards is an unlikely private investigator with a very mysterious past. He was in law enforcement in Boston some years ago, maybe the CIA, or the Secret Service. He's always been evasive about his past. Maybe he was in jail; who knows? He's about six feet tall, lanky, maybe 170 pounds and bald except for heavy fringes of curly black hair around the edges. He sports a luxurious mustache and wears those funny little, round, wire-rimmed glasses. He's probably a reformed hippy throwback from the Sixties. He could easily pass for an absent-minded college professor. Nobody could ever guess what he does for a living. Perhaps it's his deceptive appearance that makes him so good at what he does. I've never seen him when he didn't display an infectious, broad grin. *(I should introduce him to Jennifer; they could smile at each other and try to figure out what's hidden behind the smiles).*

Mike and I have worked together on many occasions in a wide variety of cases. He investigated the witnesses in a drug distribution case, and uncovered a dirty DEA agent, who threatened to kill both of us. I had little doubt that the putz was capable of carrying out his threat. Unknown to the drug agent and me, Mike had decided to wire himself with a recorder. In the elevator of the Federal Office Building, Mike pulled the recorder from under his shirt and played back the conversation, which had been recorded, for posterity.

One of his best pieces of work, though, was in a divorce case. My client was certain that her husband was running around, but couldn't prove it. He often traveled on business, and she believed he was screwing around when he was out of town. She was desperate and prepared to pay any price to catch him. She informed me that her husband was scheduled to go to Chicago the following week and she was certain it would happen in the Windy City. I put her in touch with Mike, who asked where the husband would be staying in Chicago. She didn't know and her husband refused to tell her. Mike suggested that she look through his wallet for anything that might have the name of a hotel, or some address in Chicago.

Following his advice, at the first opportunity, she searched through her husband's wallet and found a slip of paper with a phone number. In addition to the phone number it said "Wednesday 12:00." She relayed this information to Mike who recognized the phone number as a hooker he knew named Kathy.

He called Kathy on the pretext of providing a little dalliance for an out-of-town client and asked if she was available Wednesday at noon. She was very apologetic, and suggested a different time. Mike promised to check with his client and call her back. He gathered up a witness and our client, and on the appointed day, took them to Kathy's apartment building where he gained entry by sliding in behind a deliveryman who had been buzzed through the locked door. They secreted themselves in the stairwell opposite Kathy's apartment and somehow filmed old faithful as he entered, and again as he left after having his way with dear little Kathy.

What really pissed the client off was that he was smiling when he left Kathy's. She said that was the first time she could remember ever seeing the bastard smile.

I had the sheriff serve the poor son-of-a-bitch with the divorce suit as he stepped off the plane upon his return from Chicago. While he was away, armed with the incontrovertible evidence of his infidelity, my client cleaned out their house and moved.

M y reverie was interrupted by the Goddamn intercom again. This time Kelly informed me that Marvin Lewis was going to be the prosecutor in the Wilkes case, and that he was on the phone if I wanted to speak with him. Marvin is a talented lawyer who wasted ten years of his career defending criminals as the head of the major felony division of the Public Defender's Office. He handled just about every capital murder, drug dealer, rape and arson case in Baltimore City over that period of time.

Then he switched sides and joined the State's Attorney's Office, where he has been wasting more of his time for about six years. I think he has stayed with these government jobs believing that they will one day lead to a judgeship. He'd be a good judge, too, but I doubt he has the political clout to gain an appointment. His biggest problem is his tendency to get carried away with his cases. He brings a passion to the courtroom as if every case involved him personally. We have a great relationship both in and out of the courthouse.

"Word has it you're *persecuting* one of my best clients."

"Which case is it?" he asked.

"Wilkes," I responded. "Jefferson Wilkes."

"I'm going to put that piece of shit in the gas chamber."

"You'd be killing an innocent man, Marv."

"What do you mean innocent?" he protested. "We caught that son-of-a-bitch in the victim's house. A couple minutes sooner we'd have had pictures of him fucking her."

"I'm telling you he's innocent, Marv. He swears he's telling me the truth. Anyway, before you have him executed, I need to get him out on bail."

"No shot. I'm going to ask for a minimum hundred thousand dollar bail."

"Come on, Marv," I pleaded. "His boss needs him at work and will vouch for him. Besides his boss is a cute little blonde and I want to impress her. I think I might be able to get in her pants."

"Twenty-five thousand. That's the best I can do."

"How about asking for ten thousand and letting me argue for a recognizance bond."

"You've really got balls, but I'm telling you, I'm going to fight it."

"We're supposed to be friends, for Christ's sake. If I don't get her pants it'll be your fault."

"West, you're incorrigible; how's ten o'clock Monday?"

"That's good," I thanked him.

If I could get bail set at ten thousand dollars, Wilkes would only need about eight hundred to pay the bondsmen. That would leave seventeen hundred to apply to my fee and Mike's investigation.

"Kelly!" I called out.

My phone rang. "Yes," she said over the intercom.

"Why can't you just holler like old times?" I asked.

"It's not civilized," she responded. "What did you want?"

"I've forgotten. You see? If you'd have just yelled back, I . . . Oh, yeah! See if you can get the *rapess* on the phone."

The intercom light came on and the phone rang. I pressed the intercom button and there was Kelly. "Line two," she said. I was starting to get the hang of it. I pressed the blinking light for line two.

"Me again," I said. "If I can get a low bail for Jefferson, do you think your boss would mind allowing me to apply the difference between the bail and the twenty-five hundred dollars toward my fee and expenses?"

"I wouldn't think he'd mind, but I'll ask him and let you know tonight."

"Thanks. See you later."

I couldn't believe how much had already been accomplished and it was just approaching lunchtime. I arranged to have lunch with my friend, Jack Hughes. Jack is a defense lawyer. He defends the taxicab owners against personal injury claims. Socially we're close friends. In business, forget it; getting money out of him is like squeezing blood from a rock. He honestly believes that anyone who would ride in a taxicab is guilty of an assumption of the risk and doesn't deserve one cent no matter how badly they might be hurt.

Too bad I didn't have my car. It was a nice day and I could have headed out to the golf course. The last time I was up so early, I had stayed up all night. The days are just too long this way. I vowed never to get up that early again.

7

ennifer called from her cell phone to advise that she was parked and waiting for me in front of my office building. This is just great, I thought. She's taken over my car and is moving in on me one piece of clothing at a time. We're now into the second day of a one-night stand and she's referring to my apartment as home. Shit!

It was like a nightmare. I pictured myself standing at the altar, 505's down around my knees, arms pinned to my sides by my shirt. Jennifer next to me, standing naked; a towel around her head and of course wearing that evil smile. It came to me. That's it! Evil. The smile is evil.

The preacher asks if there is anyone who knows of any reason why this unlikely couple should not be joined in matrimony, and not one son-of-a-bitch opens his mouth in protest.

By the time the elevator reached the lobby, I was pissed-off at the world.

There she was sitting in the passenger seat of my car where everybody I knew could see her with that evil smile on her face. On the little ledge behind the seats were two brown paper bags from the Giant Food Market. As I eased myself into the car, I saw what appeared to be a black nylon sportsac on the floor of the passenger seat. It was embossed with the Nike logo on its side. An arctic chill coursed up my spine. Christ, I thought, how the hell do I extricate myself from this? Not that it was so bad, but there was still Laura and Lisa and Kathy . . . and Shirley . . . and Sharon . . . and Debbi . . . and Liz and a host of other women whose company I had been enjoying. I wasn't ready to give any of them up, and to be quite candid, there's not enough time to spend two nights in a row with the same person. It's just not fair to the others. I decided to explain that to Jennifer. She'd understand, I thought.

I guided the SL home through the ten blocks of traffic, thankful that Jennifer's car would be repaired and returned today. Tomorrow is golf day, and I need the car to get to the country club. Wednesday is also Bear's Den night, and I would need my car to get there. And since one never knows what might happen at the Den, I would also need my apartment, just in case something did happen.

Jennifer broke the silence by telling me that her car had in fact been repaired and had already been delivered to the condo garage. I started to feel better already.

"George said it would be okay if I left it overnight," she said. "I gave him a five dollar tip."

"Generous," I responded.

George! For Christ's sake! Now she's on a first name basis with the garage attendant. She's like a male fucking animal, I thought to myself. She's laying down a scent everywhere I go, and on everything I own, staking a claim to her territory. Next, she'll be lifting her leg on my office. At least she leaves little doubt about her intentions. First she leaves her purse, and now she's leaving her car.

"What's in the bags?" I casually asked.

"Chicken, greens for salad, some rolls, desert. Do you like chicken?"

I didn't care what was in the grocery bags. I was more interested in the nylon Nike sac, but didn't have the balls to ask.

"Do you think we'll have time to eat?" I teased as we pulled into the garage and I wheeled into my assigned parking space.

She responded with that vexatious smile.

I reached into the back and lifted the grocery bags. She grabbed the Nike sportsac.

"Let me take your briefcase," she offered. "I have a free hand."

As we got into the elevator, I said, "Hit L, I'll get my mail."

"I have your mail. I picked it up for you when I was here earlier to get my car."

"Anything of any importance?" I asked testily.

"I don't know," she responded. "I just picked it up. I didn't look at it."

My mail too!

As we walked down the hall to the apartment from the elevator, my thoughts focused on the Nike bag. I was sure she had handcuffs and whips in that thing. I could see myself handcuffed naked to the bed. Jennifer standing over me with that evil smile; a prisoner in my own apartment. If I try to escape, she'll give me a karate chop and break my legs. She'll kill the other three guys in my foursome who come looking for me. I must warn Kelly! Suddenly Jennifer's face mutated into the image of Kathy Bates. It was a parody of *Misery*.

I raised my leg and balanced the grocery bags on one knee while I struggled to turn the key in the lock and turn the knob to open the door. There was no chance I was going to suggest that Jennifer open the door, for fear of never getting my keys back. I entered the kitchen from the foyer and set the grocery bags on the counter. She continued through the apartment into the bedroom with her bag full of torture devices. Moments later she returned to the kitchen and said, "I put your briefcase and your mail next to your desk in the den. Is that okay?"

"Thanks," I replied. At least it was still *my* briefcase, *my* mail and *my* desk, I thought.

"You don't need my help in here do you?" I asked, hoping she'd say no. I hate kitchens.

"Why don't you get comfortable and then make us a couple of those gimlets?" she suggested.

Could this really be happening? I asked myself. "Good idea," I responded, thinking this would give me an opportunity to prowl through the sportsac.

I went back to my bedroom to change clothes. My unbridled imagination began to eclipse reality. I wondered if I should lock myself in. The fucking Nike sportsac, with which I had become obsessed, was sitting on the floor next to the chair. Do I dare?

I stripped to my jockey shorts, hung my suit in the walk-in closet and explored my wardrobe for attire best suited to the circumstances. Perhaps something slightly kinky to go with the handcuffs and whips? Should I wear something easy to get out of? Or something that would present a formidable challenge to remove? Maybe I really should look in that sportsac before I decide. Jeans and cowboy boots were definitely out of the question!

I settled on a pair of lime green, Ralph Lauren pleated shorts, a yellow Polo shirt, with a little green polo player embroidered on the front, and a pair of Bally, ecru colored, doe-skin, kiltied loafers. No socks. She couldn't pin my arms with the Polo shirt, and the shorts would drop with little encouragement. Thus clad, I cast a last glance at the little bag of horrors and returned to the kitchen where Jennifer was busily engaged in a demonstration of her culinary skills.

"Sexy," she said, casting that smile at me as I entered the room.

I created a Stoli Crystal Gimlet with a twist of lime on the rocks in a snifter for her; but nothing for myself.

"Not drinking?" she asked.

"I'll open a bottle of wine for dinner and have a little of that. Any preference?" I asked.

"You're the wine expert."

I selected a bottle of Bordeaux Blanc de Blancs which had been chilling in the fridge for God only knows how long. Actually, I was surprised to find it was still there considering the cleaning lady had been there yesterday. Oh my God! Could it only have been yesterday?

"I couldn't find any candles," she said.

"Do you expect the lights to go out?"

"Never know," she responded.

"We'll just dim the chandelier in the dining room. I don't think I have any candles."

"Dinner will be ready in a few minutes. Why don't you set the table?" she suggested.

The dining room table is four feet wide by nine feet long. If a site were needed for a re-enactment of the Last Supper, the table could easily accommodate everyone and leave a seat for Elijah. I gave a fleeting thought to putting a place setting at each end of the table. Instead, I set two place mats across from each other at the end of the table closest to the kitchen, wrested two five piece place settings of Limoges china and two Baccarat crystal water and white wine goblets from the china closet and arranged them on the table with two place settings of Christofle sterling silver flatware. Candles would have been nice, but what the hell! I placed a linen napkin next to each dinner plate, and went into the kitchen to fill a silver pitcher with ice water. I filled the two wine glasses, inserted the Gheorghe Zamfir Love Songs CD into the stereo, and dimmed the lights.

I stood back to survey the setting. Enchanting. Romantic. *Major mistake!* I had staged a mood of passion, instead of revelation. It was too late for a switch to K-Mart paper and plasticware.

Jennifer exited the kitchen balancing a silver tray

with a platter of chicken, grilled on the Jenn-air range, a bowl of tossed green salad, and some mixed vegetables. In addition to the other serving pieces, some of which I didn't even know I had, she found the bread basket which she had filled with warmed rolls. She placed the tray on the table, then pushed one setting to the head of the table, next to, instead of across from the other. *(Definitely should have used paper plates!)*

"Nice music," she commented. "Very romantic."

I prayed for divine intervention. Jennifer filled each dinner plate with a chicken breast and portion of mixed vegetables. After filling the salad plates and placing a warm roll on each bread plate, she returned to the kitchen and brought out two different bottles of Lite Salad Dressing, and a container of soft margarine. She sat next to me, folded her napkin into her lap and raised her wine glass.

"Cheers," she said with a smile.

Let me tell you, the kitchen was not one of her better rooms. Her accomplishments there paled by comparison to the expertise she demonstrated in the living room, or for that matter, in the bedroom. And how could I forget about the JLHG in the bathroom. In those rooms, on the Budweiser Scale of one to ten, she was a seven maybe reaching for eight. Measured on any scale, her culinary wizardry ranked zero. Oh! The Budweiser Scale? That's how many Clydesdales it would take to dislodge me from her crotch.

The dinner conversation centered around the day's events in Jefferson's case. She told me that her boss didn't care how the twenty-five hundred dollars was applied to Jefferson's account.

"The check's in my purse. Remind me to give it to you," she said, as if there might be even a remote chance I would forget.

I related the details of the charges against Jefferson. I told her about the bail hearing scheduled for Monday explained the necessity of her being there to demonstrate her support as Jefferson's employer. Otherwise, the conversation, like the night before, was somewhat less than exciting. The mood of the evening, inspired as it were by the amorous atmosphere I had inexplicably created, blended with the wine, all but one glass of which Jennifer had consumed, was not conducive to an honest disclosure of my intentions toward her, or of the part she would fill in the scene with Laura and Lisa and Kathy . . . and Shirley . . . and Sharon . . . and Debbi . . . and Liz and the others.

Although I knew she had to be stopped before she staked out the entire territory, given the time, circumstances and mood of the moment, not to mention the unknown contents of the black Nike fucking sportsac, my basic instincts dictated that a full disclosure of my intentions had to wait until another day.

After a dessert of delicious lemon meringue pie, which she had purchased in the bakery department of the Gucci Giant *(the Giant Food chain has an expensive gourmet supermarket in Zone 8, nicknamed "the Gucci"),* and coffee with a shot of Kalua, Jennifer began to clear the table. I already told you how much I dislike kitchens, but my aversion is even greater after dinner than before. I asked if she would mind my taking a shower while she destroyed the evidence of dinner.

"That's fine. I don't mind," she responded.

I went into the bedroom, leaving her to the task of cleaning the kitchen. I carefully folded my clothes and set them on the chair in the bedroom, next to the bag full of torture devices. Adopting an air of optimism, I assumed that my worst fantasies, would be no more than a trick of my too vivid imagination, and I could wear the shorts and shirt another time for golf. Seized with irresistible curiosity, I casually lifted the suspect sportsac by the handles, joggled it up and down once or twice, and returned it to the floor. It was nearly weightless and nothing in the sac made a jiggling sound like one might expect from handcuffs. However, there still lingered the possibility that she had leather or nylon straps which could be just as effective as handcuffs.

I stepped into the shower and luxuriated in the spill of the steamy water, and stared at the wall where only earlier this morning clung the product of the JLHJ. *(Jergen's Lotion Hand Job)*. I was drawn from my reverie by the sudden awareness of a rush of cold air created when Jennifer opened the shower door and slid into the shower with me. Her breasts were pressed against my back, her pubis rubbing against the cheek of my ass, her hands were wrapped around me, searching. Almost immediately, she found what she was searching for, and as if swept by a singular motion, we evacuated the shower, toweled off, and leapt into bed. Did I mention that I was aroused, and that all system were go, each component functioning and eager to perform? That's legalese for I had an erection.

This time I was the aggressor. Jennifer lay on her

back, head on my shoulder. We kissed and I stroked her buttery skin, my hands moving lightly over her body molding her breasts, delicately grazing her nipples. I caressed the insides of her thighs lightly brushing her pubic hair, moving my hand upward between her now spread legs, covering her sex with my palm. I pressed the heal of my hand gently against the pubic bone, while at the same time inserted my finger between the lips of her vulva, gingerly massaging her clitoris as I rhythmically withdrew and reinserted my finger.

My mouth was working at her breasts, licking, nibbling and sucking her nipples. She thrust her hips upward against my hand forcing my finger deeper into her. She was climbing the ladder of sensations. First she began to moan, then quiver. The quivering heightened and she began to writhe. The writhing gave way to spasmodic contractions of the vaginal muscles clutching at my finger until suddenly she convulsed into a throbbing orgasm.

While she was still coming, I rolled on top of her and drove myself deep into the flooded recesses of her womb, ground my pubic bone against hers, then very slowly withdrew until only the very tip remained in her. Gently I partially inserted and withdrew, each time making circular motions to rub the head against her clitoris. I penetrated a little deeper each time until I was completely engulfed by her. I withdrew again very slowly, then with one sudden, violent thrust, I buried my penis to the hilt, again and again pumping her in a frenzy of motion until I brought her to a second orgasm and exploded with her into euphoria.

I rolled off and lay next to her silently for a few minutes before I slipped out of bed and tramped into the kitchen for a cold drink. When I returned, she had fallen comatose, not even a twitch, lying spread eagle on her back, completely and invitingly exposed. It was only ten forty-five. I am not into necrophilia, so I pulled the covers over her, *(not over her head, just up to her neck)* and went into the den to flick through the television channels. I settled on Show Time and watched *Emmanuelle Goes To Tokyo*.

8

Jennifer and I spent most of the weekend together. I played golf on Saturday morning. Jennifer had to work most of the day, which suited me just fine. I needed a long nap Saturday afternoon to recover from all of the physical activity of the last couple of days.

She returned to my apartment at seven. We had a drink, then drove out to Michael's in Baltimore County, across the street from the Timonium Fair Grounds, to indulge in the best Maryland crab cakes in town. Michael's is a very happening bar and restaurant, frequented by a lot of very good-looking young people. The bar is huge and always packed. The noise level is deafening, but the restaurant is separated from the din of the bar. Their specialty is an eight ounce crab cake made with all jumbo, lump backfin crab meat. A crab cake, seasoned curly fries, apple sauce and a beer, is a feast fit for a king. That and steamed hardshell crabs are among the reasons that Maryland is known as The Land of Pleasant Living.

Sunday was a lay-around day. We stayed in bed late, and engaged in some serious physical activity in the morning. Jennifer walked around the corner to the convenience store and picked up some bacon, eggs and bread. I was amply supplied with Taster's Choice coffee and orange juice. After a late breakfast, we watched the final round of the golf tournament on television. Somehow, between the end of the tournament and the time that the delivery guy showed up with our salad and pizza, we managed another quicky on the sofa in the den.

Jennifer had to be at work early the next day, so we hit the sack before the Eleven O'clock News. I dozed off before the weather report, but regained consciousness long enough to turn off the TV with the remote. Jennifer was sound asleep. My last waking thought was this is really getting out of hand; I need to deal with this decisively.

The alarm detonated at eight A.M. Except for me, the bed was otherwise deserted. There were no sounds drifting from other rooms, no smells, as in fresh brewed coffee wafting through the air. I was alone; it was peaceful. Jennifer had obviously gotten up and left without waking me. I just lay there, in no particular rush to remove my body from the bed and played out the day's schedule in my mind.

Jefferson's bail hearing was scheduled for ten; I figured I'd get there about nine-thirty and talk with him before the hearing. I guessed I'd be out of there by eleven; make an appearance at the office for an hour and then head out for lunch with Jerry Sanders. Jerry is a lawyer whose office is in the same building. He and I have been having lunch together every Monday for the past five years. We go to the same restaurant, sit at the same table, order the same meal and exchange war stories about our practices. It's become a ritual.

I hadn't considered where, or with whom I'd have dinner. After dinner plans would also have to played by ear.

I stumbled from the bed to the kitchen. Poured a glass of orange juice and brewed a fresh cup of *Taster's Choice* with the instant hot. When I returned to the bedroom, I noticed that the black *Nike* sportsac *(the one filled with instruments of torture)* was gone. This discovery awakened me to the recollection of the last few days, and the disagreeable chore that lay at hand. I subscribe to the tenet, that to overcome adversity, you must stare it in the face and confront it head on. And that's what I decided to do.

I rehearsed my lines in the shower, play-acting both parts, carefully avoiding eye contact with the JLHJ spot, which for the sake of simplicity, I have decided to christen the *J Spot*.

"Jennifer," I'll say. *"I've had a great time with you over the last few days."*

"It was fun for me too," she'll say.

"I hope we'll be able to be together again soon," I'll continue.

"You mean I'm not going to see you tonight?" she'll ask disappointedly.

"Actually, I'm really busy for the next few days," I'll say. *"Prior commitments, you know."*

"Will I be talking to you until then?" she'll ask.

"Why don't I call you later in the week?" I'll say. *"See what we can work out for one night next week."*

"Was I that bad?" she'll respond angrily.

"Are you kidding?" I'll exclaim. *"You are the greatest!"*

"Then why are you treating me this way?" she'll demand.

"Well, you know I've been single and very socially active for five years now. I've been seeing a lot of super women during that time, many of whom I still have warm feelings for and see on a somewhat regular basis," I'll tell her.

"I'm totally unsuitable and presently unprepared to consider anything remotely related to any kind of steady or permanent relationship."

Then, I'll say, "But I'd really like you to join my harem."

"Fuck you!" she'll say and slam down the phone.

There, that was easy, wasn't it?

I can't do this over the phone, I thought. This is something that should be handled compassionately, in person, in a public place. I'll have lunch with her one day this week and handle it that way, I decided.

"You chicken shit, asshole!" I thought. you're just procrastinating and looking for excuses.

I chose a pair of medium gray Zanella slacks, a blue striped, button-down shirt, red and blue paisley tie, and the blue blazer. The very same blue Zegna blazer. Even if you looked closely, you couldn't tell it had been through a war only two nights before. I stuffed a red pocket square into the breast pocket of the jacket, and headed for the court house.

My first stop was the holding cell in the court house basement to see Jefferson.

"I'm hoping to have you out of here later today," I told him. "Hopefully, the bail will be under Twenty-five thousand dollars. Your boss has agreed to lend you the bail money. How's that sound?" I asked.

"Sound good to me," he said.

"I need to know about your prior criminal record," I said assuming that he had a prior record.

"Have you been convicted of any crimes?" I asked.

"Ah were in a li'l *alteration* couple years ago."

"What kind of *altercation*?" I asked supposing that's what he meant.

"Me 'nis dude hadda beef," he replied.

"About what?"

"Don' zackly 'memba. He say stuff 'n den Ah say some stuff."

"They arrested you for saying *stuff*?" I asked incredulously.

"Well, Ah had dis knife," he replied, "for self de-fense! You know?"

Maybe it really was an *alteration*, I thought. He probably altered the guys face with the knife.

"How bad did you defend yourself?" I asked somewhat sarcastically.

"Watcha mean?"

"How bad was the guy cut up?"

"Not too bad. He were on'y ina hosp'al maybe a week, is all," he responded.

"So you were convicted of assault with a deadly weapon?"

"Think dat maybe be wha' it were," he speculated.

"How much time did you serve?"

"A year," he replied.

"That's all? You were only sentenced to one year?"

"Got fahv, but foh be 'spended."

"Are you still on probation for the four years that were suspended?"

"Dat be over now."

"What else?"

"Cain't zackly 'memba, but, Ah thinks dat be all."

"No other sexual offenses?" I asked.

"Un unh."

"Any armed robberies or burglaries?" I probed.

"You means befo' Ah were twenty-one, er affta?"

"Since you were eighteen," I corrected.

"Oh yeah! Once Ah got caught borrowin' a frens T.V. from outta his house."

"When was that?" I asked.

"Dat be 'bout couple years 'go too, Ah thinks; ain' zackly sure."

"How'd you get caught?"

"Ah were set up," he asserted.

"Who set you up?"

"Ah dunno, cause nobody seen me. It were snowin' out and his house be rat nex' doh."

"Maybe they followed your footprints in the snow," I suggested.

"Das wha dey sayed, but how dey know it be ma footprints, see whad Ah mean? Ah were set up."

"How much time did you get for that?"

"Probation."

"*Probation!*" I exclaimed.

"Uh huh, da dude din' wanna tesify."

"Why not?" I questioned in disbelief.

"Mussa bin skeered," he conjectured.

"Of what?"

"He be da dude Ah had da beef wit."

"When you get out, you'll be going back to the apartments won't you?" I asked.

"Ah guesso," he said.

"What's the address there?"

"Wacha mean?" he asked.

"Jefferson," I said. "This was an easy question. I haven't gotten to the hard ones yet. *What—is—the—ad—dress?*" I asked emphasizing each syllable.

"Ain' zackly sure da zact nummas," he said.

"But you knows it when you sees it!" I said mockingly.

I'm not one to question the Lord's greater plan, but why, I asked did you create anyone this stupid; and why dear God, why, did you sic him on me?

J ennifer was seated on the bench in the first row, just behind the rail that separates the court room spectators from the trial tables. I smiled at her; she nodded back and smiled. This was not her evil smile. This was like an . . . official smile. The kind one would bestow on a passing stranger with whom there had been brief eye contact. I wondered if she read my mind when I showered this morning.

Marvin Lewis was standing by the prosecutor's table fending off a horde of lawyers who all needed to go first because of other pressing appointments, other appearances in other courts, or funerals they had to attend. But, none of the others had an important lunch engagement at noon.

"All rise. The Superior Court for Baltimore City, Criminal Division is now in session. The Honorable John Polis presiding. Silence in the Court!" bellowed the bailiff in his most officious voice.

The Judge, resplendent in his black judicial robes seated himself behind the ornately carved bench which rose several feet above the heads of the court personnel seated at desks beneath him.

"Listen for your name, or the name of the case in which you are involved, and step forward when you hear it called. You may all be seated," thundered the bailiff.

"Good morning, Ladies and Gentlemen," said Judge Polis. "Mr. Clerk, call the first case."

"The People of the State of Maryland versus Jefferson Wilkes!" he announced. "This is a bail hearing, Your Honor."

"Mr. Lewis," the judge nodded toward the prosecutor.

"Good morning, Your Honor," Marvin said. "Mr. Wilkes was apprehended in the very early morning hours of August sixth, inside the victim's house. The charges against him are First and Second Degree Rape, Attempted Rape; First, Second, Third and Fourth Degree Sexual Offenses, Attempted First Degree Sexual Offense, Common Law Assault, Assault with a Deadly Weapon, Burglary of a dwelling house, Rogue and Vagabond, *(and the Ten Commandments)*" he read a list of the charges. "The State by a prior understanding with defense counsel has agreed to request that bail be set at a minimum of twenty-five thousand dollars, Your honor."

"Mr. West," the judge nodded now in my direction.

"Good morning, Your Honor," I began. "I asked the prosecutor to request a *maximum* bond of twenty-five thousand dollars, not a *minimum* in that amount. The fact is, Your Honor, that to set bail at such a high figure, would effectively deny my client his freedom, and restrict his ability to help defend himself against the grievous charges of which he is wrongfully accused." I continued, "He is a poor man who works hard every day at what can best be described as a menial job and for meager wages. He has been so employed for nearly two years at the same job. His immediate supervisor is here in court today to tell Your Honor of Mr. Wilkes' trustworthiness and dependability." I turned and directed the judge's attention to Jennifer.

She gave him a new kind of smile. She has a smile for all occasions, I thought. The judge nodded and returned Jennifer's smile.

"Your Honor!" Marvin interrupted. "Mr. Wilkes has prior convictions for similar offenses; we caught him inside the victim's house. He represents a real and present danger to the community if he is released on bail."

"Forgive me for objecting, Your honor," I interrupted. "Mr. Wilkes is not here to be judged today on the merits of this case. He has not been convicted, and is not awaiting trial for prior offenses. I must, most respectfully, remind the Court, that the only purpose for this hearing is to determine the extent of the security required to assure Mr. Wilkes' future appearance for trial."

"In fact," I continued, "if, indeed, as Mr. Lewis has indicated, my client has been previously convicted of anything, that speaks to the fact the State faces no risk whatever that Mr. Wilkes will fail to appear for trial. The record speaks for itself; he showed up for trial the other times."

"Further," I said, "If Mr. Lewis truly felt that Mr. Wilkes were a threat to the community, or that there was some serious question of his future appearance in this court, he would have asked for at least a one hundred thousand-dollar bail."

If looks could kill, I would have fallen dead on the spot. Marvin glared at me and muttered under his breath, "I hope you choke on your lunch!"

"If there's nothing further?" said Judge Polis, "Bail is set at fifteen thousand dollars. The defendant is remanded to continued custody until bond is posted, after which time he shall be subject to the reporting requirements of Pre-Trial Release. Thank you, gentlemen. Mr. Clerk call the next case."

I told Jefferson we'd arrange for his release, and instructed him to call me the next morning.

I left the courtroom with Jennifer, reminded of the unpleasant task that still lay before me.

"I've got to stop in the office for a few minutes," I said to her. "I'll arrange for Jefferson's bail. He should be out this afternoon. I have a previous lunch engagement with another lawyer at noon, and I have previously made plans for tonight," I said.

"When will I see you?" she asked.

"How about an early lunch tomorrow around eleven-thirty?"

"Where?"

"I'll meet you in the lobby of my country club. It's not very far from your office. We can grab a quick bite."

This way, I thought, I can do the dirty deed, get it over with by twelve-thirty, and as long as I'll already be at the club, slip in a quick round of golf.

I gave her the directions, and took off for the office.

On my way from the elevator to my office, I instructed Kelly to arrange for Jefferson's release. I ran through the mail and returned several phone calls. It was almost twelve and time for my Monday lunch with Jerry.

"I'm out of here!" I announced. "If there are any emergencies you can't handle, tell them my funeral is tomorrow morning at nine forty-five. I should be back by two; my cell phone is on if you need me."

9

I was right on schedule as I headed North on the Jones Falls Expressway. The closer I got to The Delta Pines Country Club, the more I wished it were tomorrow and the coming events were already history.

Tomorrow is Wednesday, and Wednesdays are special. Wednesdays are for golf and good companionship with fellows well met. I don't really know what that means; I've read the expression in books and may have heard it in the movies. But, I like the sound of it; it's . . . it's slick! Yeah, like a Stoli Crystal Gimlet with a twist of lime on the rocks in a snifter. *Slick!*

Wednesday nights are special too. The Den always hosts new people on Wednesday nights. On the other hand, Tuesdays, it seems are no fun at all. At least not this Tuesday.

As I pulled under the canopy of the Delta Pines Country Club, I glanced at the Cartier. The little hand was on the XI and the big hand was reaching for the V.

The Delta Pines Country club is an elegant, members only, private golf and country club, which caters to about four hundred families. It boasts a magnificently manicured eighteen hole golf course, tennis courts, swimming pool, health club with sauna, steam and whirlpool, fully equipped gym, five restaurants, from a formal dining room to a casual outdoor grill and everything in between. It's members can take golf, tennis, swimming, or exercise lessons from the various professionals on staff. They can get a massage a haircut, or a manicure.

A member can also have lunch with a woman he's had an affair with and tell her he wants to dump her. This was one of the privileges of membership of which I was about to partake.

I rushed past the lobby and through the door with the brass plate that read "Gentlemen's Locker Room." I quickly changed into Friday night's green and yellow Ralphie dinner attire which had conveniently been left on the chair in my bedroom, pulled on a pair of matching green golf socks, and ran back up to the lobby in my stocking feet, carrying my golf shoes in my hand so as not to leave spike marks in the hardwood floors, or kill myself skating over the marble entrance foyer. As I emerged from the locker room, Jennifer was just walking through the front door.

"Super place," she remarked.

"Let's eat outside," I suggested. "It's a beautiful day, and the service will be quicker."

"Good," she said, "I really have to get back to work."

We walked outside, stopped so I could put on my golf shoes, then proceeded through the gardens to the outdoor grill overlooking the swimming pool. They serve a variety of sandwiches in addition to the grilled hamburgers and split, grilled kosher hot dogs wrapped in baloney that spewed their aroma into the currents of air wafting about premises.

Jennifer eyed me from head to toe and said, "Haven't I seen you someplace before? The clothes; they look familiar."

"I usually wear this for sex," I said, "but today I'm wearing it for golf."

As we entered the grill, I explained, "It's self service."

"What do you recommend?" she asked.

"I'm having a hot dog with mustard and relish. The hamburgers are real good too."

We stood at the counter and watched while our food was removed from the grill and expertly guided into the rolls and onto paper plates. *Paper plates!* Perfect, I thought. But can I really rush through this? Suppose there's a scene in front of all these people I know? Maybe this isn't the right time, or place. Oh shit! This is getting worse by the minute.

Jennifer led the way to an empty wrought iron table off to the side of the walled patio. The table she selected was protected from the sun by an overhanging branch of a red-leafed Japanese Maple tree.

We began to eat when suddenly, it was Jennifer who broke the silence. "I have to tell you something, and I'm not sure how to start," she blurted out.

"What is it?" I coaxed. Immediately, I thought the worst. *She's got some kind of sexually transmitted disease. Oh, Jesus. Maybe she's going to tell me she's pregnant! Nah; she couldn't possible know that this soon.*

My frightening thoughts were interrupted. "I hope you'll understand," she said.

"I'll try." *Yep, I thought; that's got to be it. VD, pregnant, or both. Oh shit!*

"The last few of days have been wonderful. I've had a great time," she said. "And I really like you a lot."

"Me too," I agreed.

"But, I feel like I'm being swept off my feet," she continued. "And I don't think I can handle it at this stage of my life."

"Do you mean . . . "

"This is tough enough. Don't interrupt me. Let me finish." She continued, "You know I have only recently escaped from a really bad marriage. I just don't think I'm ready for any kind of commitment, or permanent type relationship right now."

"You mean you're not going to see me anymore?" I protested.

"Oh, I hope we can get together again soon," she responded. "But, I need time to let it cool down. Maybe we can get together sometime next week. I hope you understand."

"I do. I really do," I said. *Son-of-a-bitch This is worse than I thought!*

We finished eating in silence. She rose from the table and said she had to get back to work; then extended her hand to me, with a smile. A different smile; not at all like the other smiles. She really had a smile for all occasions. After all the passion, she was offering a fucking handshake. I said I'd call her next week.

This wasn't how I rehearsed it. Where the hell does she come off dumping *me*, I thought. This will be a day of infamy that will live in the hearts of men for eternity. Jesus, is this depressing.

Despite having been given the gate, I put my mind to the immediate task of chasing the little white ball around the golf course, and with some degree of success, I might add. I won three dollars, so the day wasn't a total loss.

On the journey home from the country club I was devastated at the depressing prospect of dining alone. I needed a live dinner companion. My ego was mortally wounded and in desperate need of some tender loving care.

When I got home, I foraged through my address book in search of the perfect dinner consort, and selected four excellent choices; none were available for dinner. How utterly depressing!

The pizza with mushroom's, olives, capers and smoked-salmon was a chapter out of Wolfgang Puck. Dining alone wasn't all that terrible. I didn't have to talk if I didn't want to. I didn't have to listen. I didn't have to be polite. I could've even picked my nose, or farted if I wanted to. After dinner, I stripped off my clothes and got into the shower. Instead of washing away the memories of an unpleasant day, I found myself face to face with the *J Spot* and the nostalgia it kindled of that delirious moment in my former life.

I searched my closet for the appropriate hunting

113

attire, dressed and took off for the Celebrity Lounge, a few blocks up the street, where perhaps a new life, a new love, a new adventure, or a new client awaited.

10

several months had passed since Jennifer blew me off. I saw her a few times after the Delta Pines lunch, but the conversations were uninspiring and most of the excitement and passion had disappeared from the sex.

However, you know what they say about moss on a rolling stone. Well, like a stone which gathers none, I made sure that I kept rolling to insure not only that no moss would gather, but that all of my essential parts would remain well oiled and in perfect working order. After the devastation of that infamous lunch, I mustered my resources, pulled myself together and managed to suffer through a series of rather insignificant, but not wholly unsavory trysts.

In the meantime, as if being all but terminated by Jennifer weren't enough of a blow to my ego, Laura, Lisa, Kathy, Liz and the rest of the West harem ladies also seemed to have taken a powder at the same time. Laura just plain disappeared; moved and left no forwarding address. Lisa got engaged to some other guy without so much as a by your leave. Kathy got a new job in the Big Apple and moved to New York so she could be nearer to her new boyfriend whom she met one evening when I was otherwise involved in one of those insignificant trysts. Shirley ran off with some tycoon in the plumbing supply business.

One day while on her way back to work from lunch Liz met a construction worker who whistled at her as she walked past a construction site. She is going to live with him because, by her account, he has great buns. How can anybody argue with that kind of logic?

The good news was that Sharon was still around. The bad news was that she was offered a job in California. The worse news was that she was accepting the offer and was moving to Los Angeles.

Oh! I almost forgot about good old Jefferson Wilkes. Actually, I would have liked to forget about him altogether. Like all my girls, it seemed as though Jefferson had also taken a powder and left no forwarding address.

Now the picture was complete; everyone had deserted me and disappeared from my life. I hadn't seen Jefferson since his bail hearing. He had called me the next day as I had requested and scheduled an appointment which he failed to keep. He did tell me, and I know you're not going to believe this, but Zippo and Lukshin, if they ever really existed, had also left town and were nowhere to be found. I figured that they flew the coop with Laura, but I didn't mention that to Jefferson. And, wait. This next piece of information is going to just blow you away. LaDelle,

THE SWORD OF JUSTICE

the former fiancée, wife, girlfriend, or whatever, who we were going to surprise with flowers for our anniversary at five-thirty in the morning . . . *gone!* Dropped straight off the face of the earth same as Zippo, Lukshin and Laura and all the rest. *Moved,* no forwarding address, and forgot to give Jefferson, or anybody else her new phone number. If Mike Richards couldn't find her, then she had either departed the earth, or never existed in the first place.

I had called and left messages for Jefferson several times to reschedule his missed appointments. He never posted for any of them. The last time I tried to reach him, he, like all of the others before him, had just simply taken a flier. I tried to trace him through Jennifer, but he had quit the job and disappeared. Of course, he never repaid the money owed to his boss. Needless to say, he never gave me another dime toward my fee, or for Mike, whose bill was pushing a thousand dollars. Mike tried to track him down through Pre-Trial Release. It came as no great surprise, that they were also looking for him for having failed to report each week as required by the terms of his release pending the trial. The address and phone number he had given them was his grandmother's house, and even she didn't know where he could be found. We left messages at all of his known haunts. We put the word out on the streets that we needed to speak with him. All of our efforts came to naught.

During the course of his investigation, Mike uncovered some revealing information, but most of it was damaging to Jefferson's defense. For starters, Jefferson's past criminal record was quite a bit more extensive than he had disclosed. This information most certainly would be used against him by the prosecutor to destroy whatever little bit, if any, credibility he might have had, assuming that he ever shows up for his trial.

One interesting little tidbit that Mike learned from Jefferson's grandmother was why he was nicknamed *Slats*. It seems that when Jefferson was a little boy, he used to sit at the window and peak through the slats of the blinds to watch the other kids on the street. He never wanted to play with the other kids. He preferred to hide from sight and watch rather than participate. Grandma thought he was just shy. She raised him practically from an infant. There had been no male presence, or influence in his life. He never had any contact with his father. In fact, according to his grandmother, nobody even knew who his father was.

Jefferson's mother was a crack addict and gave birth to him when she was just fifteen years old and still living at home. She abandoned him shortly after he was born. She went out one night, got locked up, and just never returned for him. She had apparently spent several years in jail. She did make some effort to take responsibility for her child, but on each occasion, she left her young son alone and unattended while she went out on drug binges. His grandmother had to fight tooth and nail with her daughter just to keep her away from Jefferson.

Finally, the Department of Social Services gave

custody to the grandmother when Jefferson was just a tyke of about four years old. She did the best she could under the circumstances, but didn't really have firm control over Jefferson, and he started getting into trouble when he was about twelve years old. She blamed it in part on the bad neighborhood they lived in, but she couldn't afford to move. It wouldn't have mattered anyway. When you're on welfare, no matter where you move, it's still going to be a bad neighborhood. She lost contact with her daughter years ago, and didn't believe Jefferson had seen her in a number of years.

Mike's investigation of Marianne Krenshaw, on the other hand, revealed that she might just as well have been nominated by the Pope for sainthood when one compared her life with Jefferson's past. Okay, she wasn't a virgin, but Mike could discover only one romantic involvement that lasted about a year and a half. She had lived with her boyfriend at the very address where the rape occurred. She was a college graduate with an advanced degree in social work. She was employed by the State as a social worker in, of all places, the Department of Corrections. She had an excellent work record, was popular at work, and well liked by her friends and neighbors.

I took stock of my dilemma. Being jilted by Jennifer was one thing. The girls deserting me, I could handle. Jefferson's disappearance wasn't the first, or last client who would disappear. But that son-of-a-bitch didn't pay me, and that could not be tolerated, not under any conditions, no way, no time, not ever. That truly pissed me off. Actually, at this point, I hoped he never showed up again. I'd cut my losses and spend my time more profitably on other cases.

The other thing that really bothered me was the prospect of Sharon moving to California. Of all the women in my life, she was the one with whom I was most comfortable. Just the prospect of not having her around was depressing. She had the potential to replace my mother, but my stars must have been out of alignment.

I filed a motion to have my appearance stricken as counsel of record in the State vs. Jefferson Wilkes. There was a hearing before Judge Polis, who was unsympathetic to the best argument I could muster, without of course complaining that I hadn't been paid enough money. The only way out of the case was if another lawyer entered his appearance. I couldn't find my client. How was I going to find him another lawyer?

We had completed as much of the preparation as could be done without the cooperation of the client. I had obtained the incident report filed by the police officers who responded to the scene. I got copies of all written statements given by witnesses and had obtained the crime lab reports. I found among the documents that I had gotten from Jefferson in the jail, a receipt for the personal possessions taken from him at the time he was booked on the day of his arrest. Interestingly, among the items listed was a Phillips-head screw driver. The very same one, I supposed, that was itemized on the evidence list. And how's this for a zinger? *Flowers.* They actually found flowers on

THE SWORD OF JUSTICE

the porch wall. Was he really headed to LaDelle's with flowers?

Mike had taken photos of the victim's house and her street. Our discovery motions had been filed and answered. I objected to the failure of the prosecution to produce certain reports and other forensic evidence. A hearing was held, without Wilkes' presence, and the State's Attorney's Office was ordered to make the forensic lab reports available for my inspection. Without a client, there was little else to do until the trial which was scheduled in two weeks.

There was one positive thing that had come from all of this. I had virtually mastered the intercom system. It rang. It was Kelly. No surprise really; she was the only one in the office who would be using it to ring me!

"You won't believe who's on the phone."

"Who?"

"The rapist," she replied. I had mastered the intercom; Kelly had mastered *rapist*.

"Which one?"

"Wilkes," she said.

"Tell him I left town with his witnesses and his wife-girlfriend—fiancée, and didn't tell anyone my new address."

I pressed the other lit button on the phone. "Wilkes! where the fuck you been, man?"

"Ah been roun'," he said.

"I've had everybody I know looking for you."

"Wha fo'?" he asked as if he were surprised.

"For my fee. For your defense. For your trial which is in two weeks," I said. "And there was one other reason."

"Wha' dat?"

"I forgot. Oh," I said, "I just remembered."

"Memba wha?"

"You need to get a new lawyer."

"Whachu mean?"

"I mean you didn't finish paying me, I'm not going to court with you."

"Ahz gonna pay ya, man."

"It's too late, Jefferson, there isn't enough time to prepare your defense."

"You cain' do dis ta me," he protested.

"I'm doing it, watch me."

"Youz da bes'; Ah ont wan' no uva lawya."

"Your trial is less than two weeks away. How the hell do you expect me to prepare with so little time left. And besides, when were you planning to pay me, before or after you're convicted?"

"Ah be tryin' to get money fo' ya."

"If you don't have the money and don't get in here tomorrow," I said, "forget it!"

"Ah be dere," he said. "Wha' tam?"

"Ten thirty," I said. "And Slats; don't be late!"

I pressed the intercom button and dialed twenty-two. "Put that asshole down for ten-thirty tomorrow. What are the odds he won't show?"

"Which asshole?" Kelly asked.

"The rapist asshole," I responded.

Did he show up at ten-thirty the next day? How about the day after that, or even a couple of days later? Nah!

November ninth. It was the three-month anniversary of the day I got discarded by Jennifer. It, by some quirk of fate and no doubt as a part of the Lord's greater plan, also happened to be the date scheduled for the trial of the State of Maryland versus Jefferson Wilkes.

Unfortunately, Jefferson posted at nine forty-five, as I was about to stroll over to the Criminal Courts Building to advise the Court of the disappearance of my client.

"Your trial starts in fifteen minutes."

"Ah knowz," he said.

It's good that you didn't wait till the last minute to help prepare your case! You have my money?"

"Un unh, but ahz gonna git it."

"Sure you are, Jefferson," I said sarcastically, "but I was kinda hoping it might be sometime during my lifetime."

"Ha come ya doan calls me Slats no mo'?"

"Cause we ain't friends no more," I said irritably. "Listen," I went on, "When we get to court, you tell the judge you don't want me as your lawyer any more."

"Why not?"

"Because you don't want to be in jail for the rest of your life. That's why," I said in my most sarcastic, son-of-a-bitch voice.

"Whyz ah gonna be in jail fo da res' a ma life?"

"Because you didn't pay me. Because I'm not prepared. Because you have no defense. Because you're going to get convicted."

"Ah don be needin' no de-fense. Ahz jus gonna git up dere an tell em da truf, is all."

"That's the other reason," I said.

"Dayz gonna b'leave me."

"You think so?"

"Jesus be ma widness!"

"I don't think so."

"How you mean?" he questioned.

"You never gave me his address, I didn't issue a subpoena for him to appear and testify in your behalf. And anyway, he's probably disappeared like everybody else in your case."

"You da bes'," he replied with a big grin on his face. "You gonna git me off." He must have thought I was just kidding.

"Listen, Slats," I said in my most confidential tone. "If you tell the judge you want a new lawyer, he'll probably agree to a postponement and give you time to find one."

"But ah don' wants no uva lawya."

"Then why don't you let me work out a plea bargain for you?"

"Wha' fo'?" he asked indignantly, "I din' do nuffin'."

"Last chance, Jefferson. Let me out of this case, or I'm going to get you the maximum sentence, and you'll never figure out how I did it."

"Why you wanna do dis ta me, man?"

"Because you stiffed me for my fee, and you're going to ruin my reputation."

"How ahm gonna do dat?"

"Because people will remember me as the lawyer that got Jefferson Wilkes sent to the guillotine for a non-capital offense." I thought there's an appropriate punishment. He probably wouldn't notice that his head was missing.

We were on Fayette Street rounding the corner toward the courthouse. The very same Fayette Street where the number 12 bus runs, and not the number 8 that Wilkes was going to take to visit LaDelle.

"Okay, Jefferson, you walk the rest of the way to the courthouse yourself. When you see me, don't come near me. Don't speak to me inside or outside of the courthouse. Find some black guys your age among the spectators, and sit with them. When they call your case, stay put. Don't stand, don't raise your hand, don't answer, don't blink, don't come forward. Just sit there as if they called somebody else's name. Remain there until I tell you to move."

"Why you gonna treat me dis way?"

"You said the victim couldn't identify you because it was dark, and the cop was standing on your face, didn't you?"

"Mmm hmm," he said. He learned a new word, I thought.

"Well, I want to see if the victim will be able to pick you out and identify you."

"Gotcha," he said.

You sure did, I thought. You got me!

11

We made our separate ways into the courtroom, where the first order of business was a conference in the judge's chambers to discuss the trial procedures, and for a last ditch effort to resolve the case with a plea bargain. There was no chance of a plea; Jefferson was adamant about his innocence. The judge asked us for an estimate of how long the case would take to conclude.

"One hour, Your Honor," I responded.

"Three days," said Marvin.

"Slight difference of opinion, Gentlemen," said the judge.

"We are demanding an in-court identification," I said. "My client is certain the alleged victim will be unable to identify him. That shouldn't take more than a couple of minutes, Your Honor."

"The victim has his face burned into her memory for the rest of her life, Your Honor. She will identify him without the slightest hesitation. We will need two days to put on our witnesses and the third day for closing," Marvin argued.

"Mr. West?" said the judge questioningly.

I just shrugged my shoulders and replied, "He always says that, Your Honor."

Once again, I attempted to remove myself from the case, but the judge would have none of it.

The judge assigned to the case was His Honor, Judge Abraham A. Bliss, the son of Hungarian immigrants, Yale law degree, former State's Attorney, fifteen years in private practice, ten on the bench. A highly qualified and very fair jurist who demanded the best from both sides. If his past as the City's chief prosecutor created a bias against the accused in a criminal proceeding, it has never shown from the bench. He also has little, or no sense of humor and is an opinionated, straight-laced, no-nonsense, radical right-wing conservative jurist. I was stuck. This was not going to be any fun.

As a part of my strategy in the trial of most criminal cases, I ask that the witnesses be sequestered. By barring them from the courtroom, they cannot hear, and therefore not have their testimony influenced nor tainted by the testimony of the other witnesses. The judge granted my motion as a matter of right and we moved to the selection of a jury.

This is one of the most critical elements of a trial. The success of many cases often rests squarely upon the characteristics of the jury. You start off at a distinct disadvantage, knowing little, or nothing about the pool of jurors, except what you see and sense from the answers they give to the questions asked by the judge. *Voir dire,* as it is called in legalese, is a series of questions asked by the judge and the lawyers to determine the competency of the potential jurors and to ferret out any bias or prejudice against the accused.

It's true that in very high profile cases with clients who own money pits, a lawyer can hire specialists to delve into the backgrounds of the entire jury list and build a profile for the perfect jury. But in the real world, with the vast majority of clients like Jefferson Wilkes, there isn't enough money to pay the lawyer's fee, much less to hire experts. This is the kind of thing that supports the notion that true justice can be bought if you have enough money to buy a defense by a *dream team.*

Jury selection is considered by many to be an art form, but it's really little more than an exercise in common sense and a basic understanding of human nature. Human beings have certain quantifiable traits. For example, people have a natural instinct for survival. We have a natural affinity for people most like ourselves. There is a somewhat natural, self-imposed separation among people by race, national origin, sex, ethnic background, religion, culture and class.

This thing we call human nature accounts for the ethnically divided neighborhoods we find in almost every major city of the world . . . the Little Italy's, the Chinatowns, the Barrios . . . people seeking out others most like themselves. Common sense dictates, that among many other factors to be considered when selecting a jury, an effort be made to get people on the jury who will most likely identify with the client. We try to select people of the same race, the same national origin, the same ethnic background, the same sex, age and religion, and as many other common traits as possible. Naturally, the more like the client each juror is, the better the chance that the jurors will view the case from the client's perspective.

On the other hand, the prosecutor of a criminal case seeks to select jurors who are either most like the victim, or unlike the defendant, in the belief that they would more than likely decide against the accused. The perfect example of what I'm telling you, was the famous Rodney King trial. But for the twelve jurors on the panel, the rest of the world was dumbfounded by the verdict. Look at what the defense lawyers did. They had Caucasian policemen for clients who were accused of beating a Black man. Indeed, the beating had been video taped for the world to see. Because of all of the attention focused on the case in Los Angeles, the defense lawyers were successful in having the trial removed to a virtually one hundred percent Caucasian, rural, conservative, middle class community. One of the principal concerns of the citizens of Simi Valley is their safety and protection from the criminal elements. Not one person in that county could identify, nor sympathize with Rodney King. The defense was all but guaranteed a jury favorable to the defendants.

As you know, it worked. The white police officers were acquitted. The verdict was a reflection of that community's collective psyche. Rodney King was not like them; he was different in every respect. He was therefore, in the collective attitude of the citizens of Simi Valley, to be feared, to be disliked, to be dismissed and the kind of person from whom they needed police protection.

Ideally, in the Jefferson Wilkes case, the most favorable juror would be an inner-city, unmarried, black, male, laborer in his middle twenties to middle thirties. That is if you wanted Jefferson Wilkes to be acquitted.

Having already made up my mind to screw Wilkes like he screwed me, I looked at the jury list which had been given to me by the court clerk. After a cursory perusal, I noticed only six male names on the list, all in their fifties. It got worse. There were only four black people on the entire panel. There was no chance of selecting a favorable jury. This was going to be easy.

Judge Bliss began reading the standard *voir dire* questions. No panel member knew any of the parties, witnesses who would testify, or the attorneys. None were related to a police officer. No panel member would give greater weight to the testimony of a police officer simply because he was a policeman. No panel member would admit to being prejudiced against black people. A surprising number of the potential jurors had either themselves been victims of a crime, or members of their families had been the victims of a crime. Those potential jurors were challenged for cause, and eliminated from the panel.

And so it went through a long and arduous series of questions. Of course, only someone who really doesn't want to serve on a jury would ever admit to being prejudiced. Without exception, they proclaimed their willingness to judge the case solely on its merits, and proclaimed their open-mindedness. With so few pre-emptive challenges permitted, and after those who were challenged for cause were dismissed, the culling process took relatively little time. The black members of the panel were so far down on the list, there was no chance of eliminating enough of the others to reach their names.

Forgetting for the moment that this rapist, son-of-a-bitch stiffed me, with so few favorable jurors on the panel, the best we were going to get was the worst we could possibly get. Twelve white women, over the age of fifty. How fitting, an all white, female jury for the trial of a black man accused of raping a white woman. What possible chance did Wilkes have of an acquittal? *(Goodbye Jefferson Wilkes!)*.

And so the stage was set for the conviction of Jefferson Wilkes. It was like playing Monopoly. He landed on Chance and picked the card that says, *Go directly to jail. Do not pass GO. Do not collect two hundred dollars.*

The jury of twelve citizens, tried and true, was selected. Two alternate jurors were also selected, who would hear all of the testimony and see all of the evidence, but would not take part in the deliberations, unless one of the original twelve jurors, took ill, died of boredom, or otherwise became incapacitated and unable to continue serving on the jury. The selection process took less than two hours and the jury was impaneled before lunchtime.

The judge announced that we would break until one-thirty for lunch and have opening statements when the court session resumed. I told Jefferson to be sure to be back before one-thirty. Deep down I hoped he would take off and I'd get off the hook. But, like everything else that was going on in my life, the son-of-a-bitch showed up like a bad penny after the lunch break.

M arvin was seated at the trial table with the victim. Slats was buried in one of the back rows of the spectator section of the courtroom. I was parked at the defense table, the court reporter was positioned at her steno machine. The court clerk was seated at his desk below the Judge's bench, and the jurors were seated in the jury box. Everyone rose as Judge Bliss took the bench. The baliff announced that the Superior Court of Baltimore City was now in session, and directed that everyone be seated.

"Mr. Lewis, do you wish to make an opening statement?" queried judge Bliss.

"I do, Your Honor."

"Very well, you may proceed."

The prosecutor approached the jury box and began his opening statement.

"Good afternoon Ladies. The case you are about to hear involves the sexual assault of a young woman in the early morning hours of this past August the sixth. The State will prove through its witnesses and the evidence that the victim of this crime was assaulted in her own bedroom by an intruder who broke into her home in the middle of the night, crept up the steps in the darkness and into her room, where he threatened her life with a sharp weapon and raped her.

The State will prove that the defendant is the person who committed this heinous crime. The defendant was apprehended inside the victim's home by the police who interrupted the crime while it was in progress. This is an open and shut case. I'm certain that when you have heard all of the witnesses and seen all of the evidence, you will have no choice, but to find the defendant, Jefferson Wilkes, guilty of all charges. Thank you for your kind attention."

His opening was short, sweet, to the point, deadly; *an open and shut case!*

"Mr. West, do you wish to make an opening statement?" asked the judge.

"Thank you, Your Honor," I replied as I stood and approached the jury box.

Intellectually, I wanted to see Wilkes burn for this offense. I felt like he was lying to me. His story was total bullshit. He was stupid and unreliable, and he stiffed me out of my fee which was the worst part. But, these human frailties I've been telling you about, the instincts that comprise what we call human nature are often so overpowering that they easily overcome intellect. A soldier, for example, who is pissed-off at his sergeant, still fights like hell and shoots to kill when the enemy comes charging through the front lines.

As much as I disliked Jefferson Wilkes, and as furious as I was about not being paid, I was seized by an uncontrollable force of human nature; the killer instinct took hold, and winning became paramount. It was the most important thing. It was everything. No! Not everything; *it was the only thing!*

133

I began, "If it please the court, Your Honor, Ladies of the jury, I truly wish this were an open and shut case. We could all just go home now. But I don't share Mr. Lewis's predictions for the outcome of this trial. The reason I don't is because this trial is taking place in America. Open and shut cases only occur in places like Russia and Romania, not in America.

Our laws are fairer than in those other places. In America, the accused, in this case Mr. Wilkes, comes to this courtroom presumed to be innocent of each and every one of the charges leveled against him, and he remains innocent throughout this entire trial, until the very moment that the twelve of you reach a *unanimous* decision of *guilt beyond a reasonable doubt and to a moral certainty*, which I am confident you will not do. That means, if just one of you cannot decide on his guilt, he will remain innocent. I seriously doubt that once you have heard the witnesses and reviewed all of the evidence you will all agree on his guilt. Actually, I believe that you will all agree that he is innocent."

I continued, "The State of Maryland, is represented by the prosecutor, Mr. Lewis. His job is much more difficult than mine, because he is charged with an awesome responsibility; no, it's more than just a responsibility, it's a legal duty . . . Well, it's even more than a legal duty . . . he has a very heavy burden to prove to you *beyond a reasonable doubt and to a moral certainty*, that an innocent man in fact committed these crimes.

I have emphasized, and will continue throughout these proceedings, to emphasize the phrase, *beyond a reasonable doubt and to a moral certainty*. In this country, this is the standard against which a finding of guilt must be measured."

No one was sleeping yet, so I continued, "My job on the other hand is much easier. First, because I have an innocent man for my client. He comes before you today as innocent as the day he was born. Secondly, my job is easier because I don't have to prove *anything*. As a matter of fact, I don't even have to produce a single witness. The entire burden of proving every aspect of this case is Mr. Lewis's job."

My job is so easy, I thought, that my innocent rapist, son-of-a-bitch client didn't think I was entitled to be paid!

"I'm not going to comment at this time about what happened, or didn't happen, or what evidence you will hear, or what you will observe over the next several days. Let's just see what Mr. Lewis can prove *beyond a reasonable doubt and to a moral certainty*.

Mr. Lewis is not the only one in this case who has an awesome responsibility." I pointed my finger at two jurors, one in each row, and then swept my hand to embrace all of them. "You, *each* of you, also has the awesome task of sorting out the evidence and unearthing the truth.

I'd like you to promise me that you will perform the awesome task imposed upon you by the oath of office you took as a juror. You have pledged to be open-minded, to listen carefully to all of the evidence, and to observe closely the manner, attitude and demeanor of the witnesses.

Pay very close attention to the evidence presented, but focus even more closely on the evidence that *is not* presented. At the conclusion of the presentation of this case, examine what you have seen and heard. Examine what you *did not see* and what you *did not hear*. Ask yourself, are there any questions about important issues in this case that have not been answered to my complete satisfaction by the State? Do I have any lingering doubt about any issue? Is there a reasonable doubt about whether or not Mr. Wilkes committed these crimes?"

I let a moment of silence pass before I continued, just for dramatic effect. "I predict that your answer will be *yes* to each of these questions.

Can I live with my decision to imprison this man without having all of the answers? I predict that your answer to this question will be *no*.

If this case were open and shut as Mr. Lewis would have you believe, we would have to put the sword of justice into its sheath and surrender our rights to a totalitarian, or despotic government."

This is Academy Award stuff, I thought. Encouraged, I bellowed on in an oration which would have gotten me top honors in drama class.

"But, the sword of justice has no scabbard. And as long as it is unsheathed, it must be wielded to defend that which is the just due of the people it protects. It is a two-edged sword. It protects all people equally, both the victims and the accused."

I thought to myself as I returned to my seat at the trial table, if bullshit could fly, this place would be an airport!

12

At the conclusion of the opening statements, Judge Bliss instructed the State to call its first witness.

"The State calls Miss Marianne Krenshaw," Marvin announced.

Marianne Krenshaw, a relatively young Caucasian woman, approximately five feet three inches tall and at least twenty-five, or thirty pounds overweight, rose from the trial table and came forward. She was sworn by the bailiff and took the witness stand.

She was wearing no makeup, not even lipstick and had a hairstyle that could only have been accomplished by Toro . . . the lawn mower, not the hair dresser. She was wearing what I think might be described as a house dress; something one might wear when dusting, or cleaning house, which from the looks of her, I doubt was a task she often performed. She wore rather thick eyeglasses, and was somewhat disheveled in her dress and overall appearance. She displayed no apparent interest in fashion. One less charitable might describe her as a slob.

At first sight, and I know this was a very uncharitable thought, one might give pause to ponder the mystery of why anyone, even Jefferson Wilkes, would have a desire to have sex with this woman. The paradox was, in and of itself, a near perfect definition of reasonable doubt. Of course, rape is not a sexual act. It is an evil manifestation of anger and hatred . . . a misguided exercise of power gained through terror. Although totally inexcusable, in reflection upon Jefferson's life and relationship with his mother, I could readily understand what might drive him to so vile an act of aggression.

"Miss Krenshaw, state your name and address for the record, please," Marvin began his questioning.

She responded hesitantly as if she were afraid to disclose her address, which was already generally available to anyone interested, since it was a part of the police report which was accessible to the general public. She gave an address in the Charles Village section of Baltimore.

Charles Village is a neighborhood north of the center of town, and just south of The Johns Hopkins University Undergraduate School campus. Believe it or not, it is very near the Bear's Den.

The area was developed as country homes for wealthy urban residents when it was still considered suburbia; it was annexed by the city in the late 1800s. The houses are rather opulent row homes of quite generous size. They boast large covered front porches separated by three-foot high masonry walls, set back perhaps fifteen or twenty feet from the sidewalk. The house where the crime was alleged to have occurred was one that was elevated approximately five steps from ground level.

The neighborhood attracts young professionals and career oriented people who are starting out with limited budgets. The houses afford an opportunity to acquire a spacious residence in a conveniently located area at a relatively moderate price.

"Miss Krenshaw, are you employed?"

"Yes."

"Where?"

"The State of Maryland, Department of Corrections, Juvenile Services Division."

"What do you do there?"

"I am a social worker."

"Do you have special training as a Social worker?"

"Yes, I have a masters degree in social work from the University of Maryland."

"I direct your attention to the early morning hours of August sixth, and ask if you will tell us what, if anything unusual happened that morning."

She began to relate her side of the story. "I had gone to bed around eleven-thirty. I had been out with some friends and got home about ten-thirty. When I came home, I remember watching the Eleven O'clock News before going to bed. I checked the doors, both the front and the back, and went to the second floor into my bedroom."

"This was the night of August fifth, correct?"

"Yes. I was awakened between four-thirty and four fourty-five in the morning, by a black man standing over me with a sharp instrument pressed against my throat. I was startled and instinctively screamed as loud as I could."

"And tell us what happened next."

"Well, he told me if I made another sound, he would kill me."

It was here that my mind drifted back to my first encounter with Jefferson Wilkes and the raper's boss. I struggled to refocus my attention.

"Did he say anything else?"

"He said he really didn't want to hurt me, he only wanted to make love to me."

"Forgive me for asking this, but did you want to make love with him?"

"*Of course not!*" she protested emphatically. "He wasn't intent on love he was attempting to rape me."

"Then what happened?"

"He unfastened his belt, unzipped his fly and dropped his pants. Then he removed the covers and climbed onto the bed over me."

She began to break up, but bravely continued. "He raised my nightgown and wedged his knee between my knees forcing my legs apart. He began to fondle me and then attempted to force himself inside of me."

"What were you doing during this time?"

"I was struggling and crying and begging him not to hurt me. Pleading with him not to do this to me."

"Were you afraid?"

"He had a weapon to my throat. He threatened to kill me. I'm very happy to be alive. I really thought I was going to die. Of course I was afraid!"

I expected Marvin to follow up on the fondling with

more detailed questions. So far, her testimony wasn't legally sufficient to prove any of the more serious sexual offenses, only the assault. I made a note to avoid any mention of the fondling.

"Please continue with what happened next," Marvin encouraged her.

"The phone rang. I asked him to let me answer it so it wouldn't wake up my roommate. I tried to reason with him that he would have a problem if she woke up. He said, 'okay,' and got off of me."

"Did you answer the phone?"

"Well," she responded. "The phone is located out in the hall. I had to get out of bed to answer it. He followed me into the hall."

"Who was on the phone when you answered it?"

"It was Linda, my next door neighbor. She had heard my scream."

"What did you say?"

"Linda said . . . "

I was about to object. If the victim testified to what someone else said, it would be hearsay. But I figured they'd produce Linda anyway, so I just let it in.

"Linda said she heard me scream and asked if I was okay? I said, 'No.' She then asked if I wanted her to call the police. I said, 'Yes.'"

"Then what happened?"

"I hung up the phone and he forced me back into the bedroom and back into the bed."

Marvin interrupted, "How did he force you?"

"He had me by the arm and kept the sharp object pressed against my neck," she responded.

I made a note: *How was he holding his pants up?*

"Please continue." Marvin went on.

"He pushed me onto the bed and again climbed on top of me. As he did before, he forced himself between my legs, and attempted to push himself into me."

"Were you able to see the person who did this to you?" Marvin asked.

"Yes."

"Did you know this person?"

"No."

"Did he have permission to be in your house?"

"*No!* I never saw this man before in my life!" She was emphatic.

"Would you recognize the person who assaulted you that night if you saw him again?"

"I can never forget his face," she replied.

"Now, Miss Krenshaw, look around the courtroom carefully. Do you see that person in this courtroom?"

"Yes."

"Will you point him out, please."

Well, I thought, this ought to end it right here. Jefferson said it was dark, his face was turned the other way and the cops were standing on his face. So she can't identify him, and that will be that!

Without hesitation, she pointed toward the back of the courtroom. "The black man in the third row from the back, on the right hand side of the courtroom, my left. Seventh seat in from the aisle," she said, pointing directly at Jefferson Wilkes.

So much for, "It were dark; she never saw me." *Goooodbyyyye, Jefferson.*

Judge Bliss looked to the seat just pointed out by the witness, and said, "Sir, please stand."

142

Jefferson remained seated and just looked around without acknowledging that he had been pointed out, or that he had just been addressed by the judge. At least he follows some instructions.

I rose and turned toward the back of the courtroom. "Mr. Wilkes," I said. "Please step up here and have a seat at the trial table."

He stood, pointed to himself and with a puzzled expression on his face, mouthed the word, "*Me?*"

I shook my head up and down slightly. He came forward, making a great show of apologizing to the other spectators whom he had to crawl over to get out to the aisle. He came forward and slumped into the chair beside me at the trial table.

Marvin removed several photographs from the thick Manila folder on the table in front of him and walked toward the witness. He handed the first one to Miss Krenshaw and asked if she could identify the photograph. She removed her glasses to look at it and responded that it was a picture of the staircase that led from her living room to the second floor of her house. Marvin then showed her several other eight by ten glossies, and asked what they depicted.

They were photos of her dining room, her bedroom with particular emphasis on the bed, and the area of the living room near the front door.

None of these photographs had previously been submitted for my examination pursuant to my discovery motions. Further, the prosecutor had not yet laid sufficient foundation for their admission into evidence. However, he did not attempt to offer the exhibits into evidence. He handed the photographs to me for my examination.

They were obviously taken by the police department crime lab unit. Each had an official-looking seal stamped on the back with other identifying notations made by the police photographer. The photograph of the staircase, depicted broad, curved steps, and a wooden curved banister which terminated at the foot of the steps in a rounded balustrade. Draped over the banister was what appeared to be an extra-large man's sweat shirt, stenciled, **U of M Athletic Dept**. On the floor in front of the base of the balustrade, lay a pair of men's tennis shoes, my best guess, about size twelve.

The picture of the dining room showed a corner of the floor. There was a camera tripod lying on the floor in the corner and a Phillips-head screwdriver lying on the floor not far from the tripod. The ball of dust in the corner, along with Miss Krenshaw's physical appearance would bring one to the inescapable conclusion, that she was indeed a slob.

The photo of the area near the front door, depicted an iron radiator of the type found in older homes that utilize hot water heating systems. The radiator was covered by a tin shelf straddled across the top.

The bedroom scene was a real piece of dramatic photography. I doubted that it would win any Pulitzer Prizes, but if there were a Name This Photograph Contest, I might have called it, *"The Desecration of Marianne's Bed."* If left to the imagination, there's no telling what one might conjure having happened in that bed. Anything from the Battle of Hastings to a scene from Jennifer and Bruce on the eve of the JLHJ.

Marvin offered the photographs to be marked for identification only. He then produced a plastic bag containing a Phillips-head screwdriver with a yellow Lucite handle. "Can you identify this?" he asked, holding up the exhibit.

"Yes, that's the weapon he held to my throat."

He offered the screwdriver into evidence as the first State's Exhibit. I objected. No foundation had been laid for the introduction of this piece of evidence. No chain of custody had been established. It was, after all, one of millions of similar screwdrivers. There was no evidence that this particular screwdriver was, in fact, the one that had been used as a weapon, nor that it was even recovered at the crime scene. The judge sustained my objection. Marvin then had it marked for identification only.

"I have nothing further at this time," Marvin announced.

"Mr. West," said Judge Bliss, "Your witness."

That's odd, I thought. I could've sworn I read somewhere in the original police report that she was transported to Union Memorial Hospital. Why would he not have wanted the jury to hear about the results of the examination. He didn't ask her anything about her injuries. I made a note on my legal pad. *Hospital?*

Lawyers must tread very delicately down the path of the cross-examination of an innocent crime victim. If the victim is attacked too aggressively, too much sympathy is generated with the jury. So I decided to take a low-key approach to Miss Krenshaw. What I hoped to get was some clue as to who red beard, no shirt, no shoes was. You remember . . . the white guy with the beard on his face, no shoes no shirt, on the porch smoking reefer at four-thirty in the morning.

I had to try to lay some foundation for Jefferson's absurd story, and even though she had identified him, I had to try to cast some doubt on the events and the identification. The only remote chance of success in this case was to create reasonable doubt where none really existed.

"Miss Krenshaw, I see that testifying here is a very traumatic and somewhat unpleasant experience for you. Would you like to take a short break? I'll ask Judge Bliss for a recess if you'd like."

What a nice guy; so sympathetic; so considerate. Those ladies of the jury are going to just love me.

"No, I'm okay," she responded. "I'd prefer to continue, and just get it over with."

"I'll try to be brief then," I promised, brevity not being one of the traits of most lawyers.

"You told us that you had been out with friends the night before the incident you have described. How many friends were you with?"

"There were four of us," she replied.

"Were you out on a date with a male friend?"

"Well, there were two men and two women."

"But not a date, Miss Krenshaw?"

"Not in the ordinary sense, no."

"What is the ordinary sense of a date?" I asked.

"Well, it wasn't like we were paired off. I mean, there were just four friends who went out to dinner."

"Two men and two women?" I asked.

She rejoined with, "Yes, but not like you're thinking."

"Who paid for dinner?"

"We each paid our own way."

"Now, of the two men, which one had a beard, the one with you or the one with the other woman?"

Marvin vaulted from his chair and shouted, "I object! There is no testimony about anybody with a beard."

"Gentlemen, approach the bench," said Judge Bliss. "Mr. West, what's this about a man with a beard?"

"Your Honor," I pleaded. "The defense has reason to believe that a bearded individual played a very significant role in this case. The accusations against my client are very serious and have the direst of consequences if he is convicted. Even though this is an open and shut case as Mr. Lewis would have us believe, I ask the Court's indulgence and request a little latitude on this issue."

Judge Bliss granted me the latitude I requested and overruled the objection. He turned to the witness and instructed her to answer.

"Neither of them had a beard," she replied. *So much for that, I thought.*

"You said you got home about ten-thirty and retired at about eleven-thirty. Did any of the people you were with come into the house with you?"

"No."

"Then you were alone in the house?"

"Yes."

"When you went upstairs for the night, did you turn off all of the lights downstairs, or did you leave a light on for your roommate?"

"I don't recall."

"You testified that you have a roommate. Is this roommate a male or female?"

"Female."

"But she wasn't at home when you came into the house at ten-thirty, isn't that correct?"

"I believe she came home after I was asleep."

"But you were not really sure what time she arrived home, were you?"

"No," she responded.

"So at the time you told your attacker that you didn't want to wake your roommate, you really didn't know if she was home, isn't that correct?"

"Well, I assumed she was home at quarter to five in the morning."

"How did you determine what time it was when you were awakened by this intruder?"

"I looked at the clock."

"Where is the clock in relation to the bed?" I asked, knowing full well where it was. I had seen it on the table in the photograph.

"On the night table next to the bed."

"So if you're lying down, you'd have to partially sit up and turn sideways to see the clock wouldn't you?"

"Well, I guess I would, yes," she replied.

"This man was standing over you with a sharp instrument at your throat. You didn't sit up to look at the clock while that was happening did you?"

"No."

"He was standing next to the bed on the same side as the clock radio, wasn't he?" I guessed.

"Yes."

"So you really didn't know what time it was, did you?"

"Well, I knew it was late, and I knew my roommate was at home," she retorted.

"Oh, how did you know that?" I asked.

"I assumed she was . . . but now I remember," she exclaimed. "When I went into the hall to answer the phone, I noticed Marlene's door was closed and then when I walked back into the room from the hall, after I answered the phone, I could see the time on the clock radio very clearly."

"So, you actually learned the time, and the fact that your roommate was home *after* you said the phone might wake your roommate, isn't that so?"

"Yes, I suppose so, but under the circumstances, I

would have said anything to buy some time and get him away from me."

"Besides the clock radio, what else was on the night table next to your bed?"

"Do you mean like the picture of my parents?" she asked for clarification.

"Yes, and what else? Like your watch, or rings, *(or teeth in a glass I thought)."*

"There's a vase on the night table and a lamp," she said.

"I notice that you wear glasses. You don't sleep with them on, do you?"

"No," She acknowledged, "they were on the night table too."

"Neither you nor your attacker turned on the lamp next to your bed, correct?"

"No. It was not turned on."

"Now you screamed. I guess you must have screamed pretty loudly?"

"Yes, I did."

"I believe that you testified that your neighbor, Linda, heard you scream through the thick fire wall between the houses?"

"Yes, that's what she said on the phone."

"How long do you think it was between the time you screamed and the time Linda called you?"

"I guess only a couple of minutes."

"How many times would you estimate that the phone rang before you were able to answer it?"

"I would say about eight or ten times."

"And how long do you think it was from the time you hung up the phone to the time the police arrived."

"It wasn't very long. I'd have to guess maybe about three . . . not more than five minutes, but it seemed like an eternity," she asserted.

"While all this was going on. The screaming, The phone ringing, the conversation in the hall, where was your roommate?"

"She was in her room."

"And where is her room in relation to yours?"

"Across the hall."

"So we can have a better picture of the scene, can you describe this hall where you had to go answer the phone?"

"You come to the top of the steps into a hallway. There are two bedrooms. One on either side of the hall; mine is on the right, my roommate's is on the left. At the end of the hall is a bathroom."

"The phone is located in the hallway between the two bedrooms, then?"

"Yes."

"Is it against the wall closest to your room or closest to your roommate's room?"

"Closest to hers."

"When you went into the hall to answer the phone, you didn't turn on the light in the hall did you?"

"No."

"During this entire episode, did Miss Howell come out of her room?"

"No."

"Didn't she hear you scream?"

"No. I guess not"

"Do you think she could hear the phone ring ten times?"

"Maybe she was so sound asleep it didn't wake her."

"She obviously then didn't hear the conversation either did she?"

Marvin was finally on his feet objecting. "The witness can't possibly know what someone else could hear."

"Objection sustained."

"I suppose she didn't hear him curse you for calling the police either, did she?"

"Object! Same reason."

"Sustained."

"She wasn't awakened by your subsequent screams that he raped you, either, was she?"

"Apparently not, but its a real old house, and the walls are pretty thick," she explained.

"I object, Your Honor, and ask that you direct Mr. West not to ask questions of this witness about what someone else could or couldn't hear."

But it was too late. The point had already been made.

"The point is well taken Your Honor, sorry!"

"Which do you think are thicker, the walls between the rooms in your house, or the walls between the houses?"

"I would guess the walls between the houses."

"Do only the two of you live in that house?" I asked.

"Yes," she replied.

"How long have you lived there?"

"A little more than two years."

"Has your present roommate lived there with you the entire time?"

"No. Someone else lived there with me before her. She's only been there about six or seven months."

152

"Oh! Who lived there before?" I asked, knowing full well that it had been her boyfriend.

"My boyfriend used to live there with me, but he moved out about seven months ago."

"How long had he lived there?"

"About a year and a half."

"And do you still see him?"

"Yes, we're still friends."

"He still has a key to the house doesn't he?" I was guessing.

"Well, yes he does, but he hasn't used it. I mean, he has it only in case of an emergency, like if someone needed to get in if I'm away or something like that."

I wondered if he has a red beard! I won't ask. I'll let the jury wonder about that too.

"Where does he live now?"

"In Catonsville," she responded.

"Now Miss Krenshaw, please forgive me if my questions seem too personal or embarrassing. I hope you'll understand. You testified that at least twice, and I'm going to try to quote you, *he tried to force himself into me.* From the way you phrased that, are we to assume that he never penetrated you?"

"He kept losing his erection," she said, blushing.

"So then at no time did he have intercourse with you? Is that correct?"

"Yes."

I noted on my legal pad, *"NO RAPE!!"*

"Would it be fair to characterize the activities in the bed as a struggle?" I asked.

"Yes, but I was afraid of being stabbed. I wasn't about to become involved in a violent struggle."

"But, nevertheless a struggle, right?" I insisted.

"Yes, I did what I could to resist him physically, but was hopeful that I could somehow talk him out of it and not be hurt."

"But you weren't frightened enough by the threat to just lie there passively and let him penetrate you without any resistance, were you?"

"I was afraid to scream again. Surely your not suggesting that I wasn't frightened," she shot back.

"Well, what I'm getting at is, you didn't just lie there passively and let him have his way with you. You did offer resistance, didn't you?"

"Yes, of course I did. That was like an automatic reaction."

"You weren't physically injured, where you?"

"No, thankfully, I wasn't."

"Now, I'm curious about what happened when you went to answer the phone. He was on the bed with you, with his pants down. Were they down to his knees, or down to his ankles, or just open at the fly?"

"Well sort of just above his knees, I think. I could feel the buckle of his belt against my thigh."

"When the phone rang and you got out of bed, he walked with you to the hall, correct?"

"Yes."

"Where were his pants when he walked into the hall with you? Still down to just above the knees?"

"He was holding them up around his waist with one hand. He still had the screwdriver in his other hand."

"You stated that he led you back into the bedroom by the arm, while holding the screwdriver at your neck.

How was he able to do this and still hold his pants up?"

"I don't know," was her only response.

"Okay. He sees the blue flashes of the lights on the police car reflecting up from the street through the window and onto your bedroom wall. You said he jumped up and started cursing you for calling the police. Was he struggling at that time to get his pants pulled up so he could run?"

"Yes."

"And this struggle with his pants occurred while he was still in the bed, correct?" I asked.

"Partly," was her response.

"So he jumps out of the bed and runs down the steps to get away. You testified that you followed him down the steps and ran to open the front door to let the police in, correct?"

"Yes."

"Is that when you were screaming that he tried to rape you?"

"I was screaming for help, yes"

"You didn't turn on the lights when you ran down the steps did you?"

"No, I don't think so."

"Earlier, you testified that you locked both the front and rear doors of the house. Would you describe, if you can, the kind of lock that's on the front door of your house?"

"It's one of those locks that you have to turn a knob to unlock the door. The lock is mounted on the surface of the door."

"So if you close the door, it locks automatically, doesn't it?"

"Yes."

"You don't have to use a key to unlock the door from the inside do you?"

"No."

"You do not know for a fact that your roommate locked the door when she came home, do you?"

"The door was locked when the police arrived. I had to turn the knob on the door to release the lock so they could get in."

"But you don't know who locked it do you?"

"Well, I know I locked it, and I assume that Marlene locked it after she came home."

"But you're really not certain that your roommate locked the door when she came home, are you?"

"No. I'm not one hundred percent absolutely certain. Only reasonably sure," she retorted angrily. "Who else would have locked it?"

"Do you have any hobbies?" I asked.

Marvin was out of his chair objecting. Judge Bliss waived us up to the bench.

"Mr. West, is there some relevance to that question?"

"Well, Your Honor, Mr. Lewis had Miss Krenshaw identify and describe some pictures which I'm certain he's going to attempt to introduce into evidence. My question goes to something revealed in one of those photographs which I consider quite relevant to the case. I can wait until he attempts to introduce the photographs, and then recall this witness if you would prefer."

"I'll withdraw my objection for now," Marvin conceded.

"You can answer the question," I said.

"I like to read, and I bowl," she responded.

"How about photography? Is taking pictures something you do as a hobby?"

"I take pictures, but I wouldn't call it a hobby," she offered.

I asked Marvin for the photographs and showed the picture of the dining room to the witness. "So, the camera tripod in this photograph belongs to you?" I asked.

"Yes, it does."

"Why was it lying on the floor?"

"It had been broken."

"Had you been trying to fix it?" I inquired.

"Yes," she exclaimed. "My father was over and tried to fix it the day before."

"What was wrong with it? Did one of the screws come loose?"

"One of the legs was unstable," she responded.

"And the screwdriver on the floor," I pointed out, "That was what your father used to fix it with, isn't it?"

"I think so," she replied.

I retrieved the bagged screwdriver, walked over to the witness and said, "Now, Miss Krenshaw, doesn't this look like the same screwdriver as the one on the floor in this picture?"

"Yes," she replied.

"Is there anything about this particular screwdriver that would help you distinguish it from millions of other similar screwdrivers?"

"No," she said.

"So you can't say for sure that this is, in fact, the very same screwdriver that was used as a weapon, or for that matter, that was found in your dining room, can you?"

"The Judge, the jury, the witness, the prosecutor and anyone else who had not yet fallen asleep, was certain that I was trying to prevent the screwdriver from being introduced into evidence. Quite to the contrary. I was trying to force them to establish that this tool was the one used by Marianne's father to repair the camera tripod. I wanted to establish that this screwdriver was already in the house. That Jefferson had not carried it with him and had not taken it inside. This screwdriver was listed on the receipt for Jefferson's property and I wanted to show that it wasn't his.

To be guilty of the Rogue and Vagabond charge, the State would have to prove that he was in possession of burglary tools before he got into the house. I suppose if you stretch the definition of burglary tools, the Phillips-head screwdriver could be considered as such. I also wanted to establish that Jefferson did not enter that house with the intent to use a weapon for any purpose. If he went in at someone's invitation for a drink, as unbelievable as that might be, he wouldn't need anything that could be used as a weapon.

Next, I removed from my file, Mike's photograph of Marianne's street and asked if she would describe the picture for the jury. She said, "It looks like the street I live on."

"Is your house pictured in this photo?"

"I believe so," she responded.

"You believe so, but you're not sure?" I asked.

"Well, the houses are all identical on the outside and it's hard to read the house numbers on this photograph," she declared.

"Do you know anyone that has a red beard?" I asked.

"Larry Warner, my next door neighbor. He's Linda's husband. He has a sort of a red beard." *(I wanted to ask, "On his face?")*

"Thank you, Miss Krenshaw."

"Any redirect, Mr. Lewis?" asked Judge Bliss.

"A few questions, Your Honor," he replied.

M arvin took the dining room picture to the witness stand and showed it to Marianne. "When you went to bed that night, was the screwdriver on the floor in the dining room as pictured here?" He asked, pointing to the screwdriver in the picture.

She removed her glasses to look at the picture and responded, "The last time I remember seeing that screwdriver, it was on the top of the radiator in the front hall near the front door."

Marvin fished through the pictures he had offered for identification, locating the one of the radiator, and asked, "Is this the place you last saw the screwdriver?"

"Yes. That's the place."

Well, we've just proved that the screwdriver was in the house before Jefferson. It wasn't his. There goes the rogue and vagabond charge.

"Were you able to see the defendant clearly during the course of the attack on you?"

"Yes."

"Even without your eyeglasses?"

"I'm myopic. I need the glasses only for seeing at a distance. You may have noticed that I have to remove them whenever I look at something close, or to read," she said.

"Were you able to see him clearly in the dark?" Marvin asked.

"Well there's enough light in the room from the street lights outside that shine through the window in my bedroom, and there is a night light in the bathroom at the end of the hall where the phone is, which casts enough light to be able to see in the hallway."

"I have nothing further, at this moment," said Marvin.

"Anything further, Mr. West?" asked Judge Bliss.

"Just a few questions on re-cross, Your Honor."

"You have curtains on your bedroom window, don't you?" I asked.

"Yes, but it's still not totally dark," she replied.

"At what distance do you begin to require the glasses to see clearly?" I asked.

"I would say beyond three or four feet," she responded.

"Like to see the clock radio on the table from the door to your room? I have nothing further, Your Honor," I said without giving her a chance to answer the question.

Jefferson leaned over and whispered, "She be lyin'!"

"I think that's enough for today," announced Judge Bliss. Court will reconvene at nine forty-five, tomorrow morning. I admonish all of the witnesses and the jurors not to discuss the case with others, or among yourselves while court is recessed."

14

I ran to the office and caught up on the mail and phone calls. On the way, I was reflecting upon the course of the trial so far.

Despite the victim's educational credentials and her near flawless performance on the witness stand, I detected a distinct dislike of the victim by a couple of the jurors who seemed put off by her unkempt appearance. In particular, it seemed to me that juror number four, Thelma Cross, a retired librarian and Sunday school teacher who still plays the organ in church every Sunday actually made a face like someone nearby let loose with a silent fart. Maybe someone really did, but I'd almost be willing to bet she's the proverbial little old lady with the thirty year old car that only has ten thousand miles on it, accumulated from Sunday drives to church. She appeared to show discernible disgust over the idea of Miss Krenshaw's having lived with her boyfriend for one and a half years without being married. This was a devoutly religious lady, with old-fashioned ideals and a rigid set of values. My assessment was that the jury wasn't exceptionally sympathetic to the victim.

There was a message from Jennifer inquiring how the trial was going. I had thought about using her as a character witness. But, I struck that thought. Since Jefferson had quit his job without notice and all but disappeared, leaving his employer holding the bag for the better part of the twenty-five hundred dollars he borrowed, I thought the character testimony would do more harm then good.

The intercom rang. "I hate to interrupt you, but Irene Thompson is on the phone. It sounds important. She says she was involved in a fatal accident last night."

Despite my anxiety to begin my preparation for tomorrow's court session, I picked up the phone without hesitation. Fatal accidents pay a lot of bills. "Miss Thompson, Kelly told me you were involved in a fatal accident last night. What happened?"

"We were stopped at a red light and this truck ran right into the back of us. He hit us so hard that the whole trunk is squashed all the way up to the rear window."

"That's awful!" I exclaimed. "How badly was everybody hurt?"

"Real bad; we're just lucky nobody got killed."

"Nobody got killed! What do you mean nobody got killed? You said it was a fatal accident!"

"It was."

"How could it be a fatal accident if nobody got killed?"

"Whatchu mean?" she asked.

I told her to hold on while I got Kelly on the intercom.

"Kelly, take care of Miss Thompson. This was one of those fatal accidents where nobody got killed."

"What do you mean nobody got killed?" she asked. "How can it be a fatal accident if nobody got killed?"

"Have Miss Thompson explain it to you, I've got things to do." By the time I sifted through the mail and returned a few calls, it was after six.

I gathered up my file and left the office. On the way home, I was thinking past the examination and cross-examination of the neighbors and the police officers, and was contemplating my examination of the crime lab people and the forensic experts.

I spent the evening closeted at home with the crime lab reports and the test results from the FBI's forensic lab.

Nothing! There was absolutely no forensic evidence to link Wilkes to the crime. There were no identifiable fingerprints. No matching hair samples. No DNA matches.

So what if he had been caught with his pants down? There would be absolutely no reason for Marvin to call any of these people as witnesses. There was nothing positive to which they could testify. That's why he didn't provide me with the reports initially and made me obtain a court order to get them.

I made a note for the first thing in the morning to have Kelly prepare subpoenas for the crime lab guys and the FBI forensic lab technicians and get Mike to serve them immediately. I wanted these jokers in court tomorrow, but I didn't think the State's Attorney was going to call them.

C ourt was reconvened at nine forty-five on the button. The Jurors took their places, and Marvin called Miss Marlene Howell, Marianne's roommate. She was fairly attractive and presented a much neater appearance than Marianne. She swore to tell the truth, the whole truth and nothing but the truth, and gave her name, the same address as the victim, and stated her occupation as a registered nurse, employed at Doctor's Hospital, very near where the girls lived.

Marvin began his examination. "I direct your attention to the night of August fifth and the early morning hours of August sixth. Can you relate to us what you remember of that night?"

"That was the night my roommate, Marianne Krenshaw was raped in our house," she began.

There was no point in objecting. It was obviously an erroneously drawn conclusion. Marianne had already testified that she had not been penetrated. I'd deal with it in cross examination.

"What time did you get home that night?"

"I came home after midnight," she responded.

"And where was Marianne when you came home?"

"I wasn't sure at first when I got home, but when I went upstairs, her bedroom door was closed, so I assumed she had already gone to bed."

"What time did you go to bed that night . . . well, actually, that morning?" Marvin asked.

"I was really tired. I had worked a double shift. I went to bed as soon as I got home."

"When you got home sometime after midnight, was the front door locked?"

"Yes. I had to use my key to open it," she replied.

"After you got into the house did you lock the front door?"

"Yes, and I also checked the back door."

"Were both doors locked when you went up to the second floor?"

"Yes."

"At any time during that night, was your sleep interrupted?"

"Well, it was about five or five fifteen. Marianne came into my room and woke me. She told me what had just happened."

"Did you see the person the police arrested?"

"No. They had already put him into the police car."

"Did you allow anyone else into your home that night?"

"No."

"Did you give permission to anyone to come into the house?"

"Absolutely not," she emphatically replied.

"Your witness," Marvin offered.

I began my cross-examination. "Miss Howell, you indicated that you arrived home a little after midnight. Could you narrow that down a little more?"

"I suppose it was between twelve forty-five and one fifteen A.M.," she speculated.

"But couldn't it have been four, or four-thirty, or even a little later?"

"Oh no!, I'm absolutely certain it wasn't that late?" she insisted.

"What makes you so sure?" I asked.

"I never stay up that late. And besides, like I told that other gentleman, I had worked a double shift, and there's no way I could have been up that late. I would have collapsed," she protested.

"What time did your first shift end?"

"Three-thirty in the afternoon."

"So your second shift ended at . . . what . . . eleven-thirty that night?"

"Yes."

"Where had you been before you came home?"

"Out with my boyfriend," she replied.

"Out where?"

"If you must know, we went to the International House of Pancakes for breakfast."

"Do you go there often?"

"Yes, we go there a lot when I work the late shift."

"How late is the International House of Pancakes open?"

"I'm not really sure."

"Where did you go when you left the restaurant?"

"Alan brought me home."

"Alan is your boyfriend?"

"Yes."

"Describe your boyfriend, I mean his physical appearance."

"He's kind of tall, maybe six feet. He has blonde hair, blue eyes and weighs about one hundred and eighty pounds. Why?" she asked.

"Does he have a beard?"

"No."

"Did he come into the house with you when you got home?"

"No, I told you I was ready to collapse, I was so tired."

"Did he walk you up to the front door?"

"No. He stayed in the car and waited until I went into the house."

"How did you open the front door when you arrived home?"

"I used my key. The door was definitely locked," she emphasized.

"Before you could insert your key into the lock, wouldn't you first have to open the screen door, or was it already propped open?"

"That's not what I thought you meant," she said. "Yes, of course, I would first have to open the screen door."

"But you didn't have to that night, did you?"

"Well, you can't open the front door without first opening the screen door," she insisted, in evident frustration.

"You don't clearly remember actually opening the screen door do you? You think you did, and are just saying you did, because that's something you routinely do, isn't it?"

"Like I said, you can't open the front door without first opening the screen door."

"Is there a lock on the inside of the screen door?"

"Yes, but I didn't lock it if that's what you're driving at."

"Do you or Miss Krenshaw ever prop the screen open using the little device on the door closing mechanism?" I asked.

"Are you referring to the little sort of clip that slides on the rod that connects from the top of the door to the door frame?" she asked demonstrating with her hands.

"I believe we're both talking about the same thing. Do you ever do that?" I reiterated.

"Only if we're carrying things in or out of the house," she responded.

"What were you carrying into the house that night?"

"You mean like my purse?" she questioned.

"Were your arms full, like with laundry, groceries, or a large box?"

"No, Just my purse."

"Does your boyfriend also have a key to the house?"

"No," she replied.

"Okay. You unlocked the door with your key, checked both the front and rear doors to make sure they were locked and immediately went upstairs to bed. Correct?"

"That is correct."

"Did you turn out all of the lights downstairs before you went to bed?"

"Yes."

"Did you leave any lights on in the upstairs hallway?"

"None other than the small night light plugged into the wall in the bathroom at the end of the hall."

"I assume you brushed your teeth before you went to sleep, didn't you?"

"Yes, of course I did."

"And you removed your makeup and washed your face before you went to bed, didn't you"

"Yes," she sighed as if bored by the questions.

"Did you take a sleeping pill before you went to bed?"

"I already told you, I had worked a double shift and was so tired I didn't need any help falling asleep."

"You didn't open the door to Marianne's room before you went into your own room, did you?"

"No, I wouldn't do that. We respect each other's privacy," she scolded.

"So you don't know if she was alone, or not. Do you?"

"I assumed she was alone."

"That was just an assumption, wasn't it. You weren't positive, were you?" ·

"Well, no, I wasn't absolutely positive."

"You didn't hear the conversation between two men on the front porch did you?"

"No."

"You didn't hear Marianne scream during the night, did you?"

"No."

"You didn't hear the phone ring in the wee hours of the morning, did you?"

"No."

"You didn't hear a phone conversation that took place immediately outside of your door, either, did you?"

"No."

"You weren't disturbed by the activity of the policemen in the house, were you?"

"No."

"And you didn't hear your roommate screaming that she had been raped, did you?"

"No."

"But for the fact that Miss Krenshaw told you what happened to her, you had no first hand knowledge of the events that occurred that night? Isn't that so?"

"I guess that's so," she replied.

"You didn't hear anything, nor did you observe anything that night, did you?"

"No, Sir. I did not."

"As a matter of fact, you don't know for sure that a rape even occurred, do you?"

"Only what I was told."

"In fact, Miss Krenshaw didn't tell you she had been raped, did she?"

"Are you suggesting that we're making all of this up?" she demanded.

"I'm suggesting that you are assuming a great deal that did not in fact occur, Miss Howell."

"I have nothing further of this witness."

"I have a question or two for redirect, Your Honor," said Marvin.

"Miss Howell, can you give a reasonable explanation for your not hearing anything that night?"

"Well, I told you I was extremely tired, and maybe that plus the noise from my window air conditioner would have blocked out the sounds."

"Nothing further, Your honor," said Marvin.

"One more thing, Your Honor," I said.

"You didn't hear anything, maybe because you were so tired. Is that what you said?"

"That's what I said," she retorted.

"You didn't hear anything, maybe because of the noise from the air conditioner?"

"Maybe," she replied with a snippy attitude.

"Or, maybe you didn't hear anything because there was nothing to hear?"

"Yeah. Maybe. If you say so," she responded angrily.

The fact is, that as far as you know from your own personal knowledge, nothing happened at all, did it?"

She was hating me and it showed. The Agatha Christies were hating her and it showed. This was starting to be fun after all.

Again Jefferson leaned over and whispered, "She be lyin' too."

15

Marvin called Linda Tanner as his next witness. As she took the stand, I searched my notes to see who this person was. There was no Linda Tanner named on the State's list of witnesses. She was much more attractive than Marianne. If I had to rape somebody and had a choice, I thought, I would pick her over Marianne anytime. I requested a bench conference rather than object. We stepped up to the bench where in whispered tones, so as not to be overheard by the jury, I questioned the absence of the witness's name from the list. Marvin advised that this person was listed as Linda Warner, but that she continued to use, and preferred to be called by her maiden name. Judge Bliss asked if I had any objection to this witness being called. Actually he said, "Certainly you don't object to this witness, do you Mr. West?" To which I replied, "Of course not, Your Honor."

"Please state your name and address for the record."

"Linda Tanner," she responded, and gave her address which was next door to the victim.

"Are you employed?" Marvin asked, I suppose just to establish her credibility.

"Yes. I'm an accountant with the accounting firm of Joiner, Lancaster, Heath and Johnson."

I scribbled on my yellow pad, "*Accountant—JLHJ.*" I nearly missed the rest of her testimony.

"I direct your attention to the early morning hours of August sixth past. Can you tell us what, if anything unusual occurred that morning?"

"Yes. I was awakened at approximately a quarter to five in the morning by a blood curdling scream."

"How did you know what time it was?" he asked.

"I looked at the clock when I was awakened," she responded.

"What did you do when you heard the scream?" asked Marvin.

"I reached out and turned on the lamp beside the bed, then I looked over at Larry, my husband, to see if he had been awakened."

"Had he?" Marvin questioned.

"He was sitting up in bed, so I asked him if he had heard the scream too."

"Don't tell us what he said," Marvin interrupted. "That would be hearsay. But tell us what you did as a result of your conversation."

"We decided we should call next door to see if the girls there were alright, so I called Marianne on the phone," she responded.

"Marianne Krenshaw?"

"Yes. My next-door neighbor."

"Tell us what you said."

"I said, I thought I heard you scream. Are you okay? Marianne sounded upset and said, 'no.'" she continued without being prompted.

Judge Bliss looked down at me from the bench, and Marvin looked over from his table, both anticipating my objection to the witness's characterization of Marianne's state of emotion. But there seemed no point in raising an objection. First, my strategy is to object as little as possible. Second, the jury already heard what was said, and the judge's admonition to ignore it, would just reinforce it in their memories. So, I just let it pass.

She continued, unaware of the silent communication that had just taken place, "Then I asked her if she wanted me to call the police and she said, 'yes.' so, I hung up and immediately dialed nine-one-one."

"What happened next?"

"Larry and I got up, threw on some clothes and went out onto the front porch to wait for the police. It wasn't very long before the police arrived. They arrived almost immediately."

"What happened when the police arrived?" Marvin questioned.

"Well, it was somewhat confusing, but I seem to recall that a police officer jumped out of the first car to arrive on the scene and ran up the front steps to the front door. Marianne pulled the door open and the officer ran into the house. She was screaming for help and something about being raped."

"Is there anything else you can tell us?" asked Marvin.

"A couple of minutes after the police officers ran into the house, they came out half dragging and pulling a man whose hands were handcuffed behind his back."

"Did you get a good look at that man?"

"Yes. He's sitting right there," she indicated, pointing at Jefferson.

"Were you able to tell how he was dressed?"

"He was wearing dark clothes. They were in disarray. His shirt was hanging out of his pants. His pants were undone."

"What do you mean about his pants being undone?"

"They were unbuttoned. His belt was unbuckled and flopping around. His fly was partially unzipped?"

"I have nothing further of this witness at this time," Marvin advised.

"Your witness, Mr. West."

I began, "Miss Tanner, I assume you were quite sound asleep at four forty-five in the morning. Is it fair to say that you were jolted awake?"

"Yes. I was quite startled."

"You only heard one scream, isn't that so?"

"Yes."

"Since you were sound asleep and that single scream woke you, you weren't really sure who screamed or from what direction the scream came, were you?"

"Well, our bedroom and Miss Krenshaw's bedroom share a common wall. We have a window air conditioner in our bedroom, and it was running at the time. So, the only logical place it could have come from was next door. I don't believe I could have heard a scream from anywhere else."

"You testified that you looked over to see if your husband had been awakened and that he was sitting up in bed when you looked over. Is that correct?" I asked.

"Yes, he was sitting up in bed."

"So, you don't know how long he had been up, or what in fact woke him, do you?"

"I don't understand your question," she said.

"For all you know, he could have been up for an hour, but you had no way of knowing, since he was already up when you first awoke, right?"

"Anything is possible," she responded. "But we got in bed together so I assume he was still in bed at four-thirty in the morning."

"How long did it take you to determine where the scream came from, and to make the decision to call your neighbor?"

"I don't know. I heard the scream, sat up in bed, reached over and turned on the light, saw that my husband was awake and asked him if he'd heard it too. How long could that take?"

"That's what I'm trying to find out from you. Do you think it took two or three minutes?"

"I'm not sure, but I'd guess maybe two?"

"Okay then. Two minutes to do all that. Now how many times before that night had you called your neighbor on the phone?"

"I have no idea. Not too many."

"Did you know her number by heart, or did you have to look it up in the phone directory?"

"No, I didn't have it memorized, but I had it written down in my address book which was in the drawer of my night-table next to the bed."

"You indicated that you threw on some clothes, after calling the police. What did you throw on?"

"A terry cloth bath robe, she replied.

"And do you recall what your husband threw on?"

"I believe he pulled on a pair of trousers."

"Did you see him put them on?" I inquired.

"I don't actually recall," she said.

"So, he could have already had them on when you first noticed that he was awake."

"Do you mean that he might have slept in them?" she asked.

"If you didn't observe him put them on, you can't say with any degree of certainty that he was not wearing them already when you first observed him after turning on the light. Isn't that correct?"

"Well, I can't state that with certainty, but I've never known him to go to sleep with his clothes on, so I feel quite certain that he didn't sleep in them that night either!"

"Ah, but it was dark in the room when you heard the scream, wasn't it?"

"Yes."

"And when you turned on the light and looked over at your husband, he was already sitting up in bed, wasn't he?"

"Yes."

"And since you didn't observe him put his pants on, isn't it possible that he had gotten out of bed, put on his pants, left the bedroom, and then returned while it was still dark and gotten back into bed just moments before you were awakened by the scream and turned on the light?"

"I guess it's possible, but why would someone do that in the middle of the night?"

"Well, maybe someone would do that to say . . . slip out to the front porch for a breath of air, or to have a smoke. Don't you think that's possible?"

"I suppose anything's possible, but I seriously doubt that Larry did anything like that."

"What would you think if someone said they saw him on the porch before any of this happened?"

"I wouldn't think anything, because I am quite sure that didn't happen."

"Because of the drone of the air conditioner, I don't suppose you would have been able to hear any conversations that took place on Miss Krenshaw's porch, shortly before you heard the scream, could you?"

"Like I said, it's hard to hear anything over the drone of the air conditioner."

I leaned over to Jefferson and whispered, "Why were your pants open and your belt undone?"

"Dat happen wen da polices pull me up offa da flo. He grab me by da topuma pants and dey come undone den."

"You indicated that Marianne opened the door for the police officers, but it was dark and there were no lights on in Marianne's house, so you couldn't actually see who opened the door could you?"

"Well, I just assumed it was she who opened it."

"It was still very dark outside wasn't it?"

"Well the moon was out, the street lights were on, and we had turned on our front porch light," she said.

Damn it! I thought, now why the hell did you ask that question?

"You indicated that the police were half pulling and dragging someone from the house. Can you describe that in more detail?"

"I'm not sure I understand what you mean," she responded.

"Can you describe how the police officers were holding the person that was being half dragged and pulled?"

"You mean him?" She asked, pointing at Jefferson.

"Why? Were the police pulling more than one person out of Ms. Krenshaw's house?" I asked in surprise.

"No, no, there was only one person that I saw."

"Describe how the police officers were holding this person?"

"I'm not sure that I can."

"Let me rephrase it. At least one of the officers was pulling him by the waist of his pants, wasn't he?"

"Well, sort of. Yes."

"How many officers were sort of pulling and dragging him from the house?"

"Two."

"Was one of them behind him kind of pushing and the other in front kind of pulling him, or was one officer on either side of him?"

"They were kind of off to the side, one toward his back and the other toward the front."

"So, the officer to the left of the person being arrested had hold of the back of his pants with his right hand and was beside and slightly behind him, kind of pushing. Is that a fair description?"

"No. He was sort of ahead and pulling him."

"And the other officer was to the right and slightly behind the person being arrested, holding him by the back of his pants with his left hand and kind of pushing him then. Is that correct?"

"That's about how it was, yes."

"If you were standing on your porch facing the street, is Ms. Krenshaw's house on your right, or left?"

"Her house would be to my right."

"Well, isn't it true that with two police officers flanking the person they were arresting, your view of the person was blocked?"

"No. I observed them from the time they emerged from the house until they put him in the police car. As they progressed I was able to see him very clearly."

"Correct me if I'm wrong, but didn't you say that this person's shirt was out of his pants?"

"Yes, it was."

"It was a tee shirt, wasn't it?"

"Yes."

"So if the shirt was out, it would hang down outside of the pants and cover the waistband, right?"

"I'm not sure."

"Well, you can't see the waistband of my pants, can you? It's covered by my suit jacket, isn't it?"

"Yes, but his shirt wasn't as long as your jacket."

"But it was long enough to hang past the waistband of his pants wasn't it?"

"I suppose so."

"It didn't take very long for them to walk from the house to the car did it?"

"No, not very long."

"How long would you say; ten, maybe twenty seconds?"

"Oh, I would guess a lot longer than that."

"How much longer? A minute or two?"

"Yes, that would be more like it."

"Okay, let's do a little experiment. We'll watch the clock on the wall back there," I said nodding toward the clock on the wall at the back of the courtroom, "and you close your eyes and estimate how long it took for them to get from the front door to the car. Tell us when to stop counting the seconds. Start now."

She closed her eyes and everyone in the courtroom stared at the second hand as it crept slowly around the clock.

"Now," she said as she opened her eyes. Much to her amazement, the second hand had just reached fifteen seconds.

"Fifteen seconds. Does that surprise you?" I asked.

"It seemed much longer than that," she replied.

"So, in fifteen seconds, in the dark, with your view partially blocked by the police officer between you and the suspect, you are now suggesting that you were able to accurately identify the suspect and observe and describe minute details about the condition of his clothing?"

"I know what I saw," she said indignantly.

"And you saw that his pants were unbuttoned, his belt undone, and his fly partially unzipped, despite the fact that his shirt was hanging out and covering the waistband of his pants."

"Yes."

"What do you suppose was keeping his pants from falling down? His willpower, or your imagination?"

"I object to this badgering of this witness, Your Honor," Marvin screamed.

"Well, Mrs. Warner, or excuse me, Miss Tanner, you know that I doubt the accuracy of your observations don't you?"

"You can doubt them all you want. I remember what I saw."

"Won't you admit that you had a little help with what you saw and what you remembered from Mr. Lewis?"

"We discussed my testimony, if that's what you mean."

"And he sort of reminded you of the details to which you testified, didn't he? That's all I have, your honor," I said without waiting for a response.

Marvin was on his feet objecting. "Is Mr. West suggesting that the Prosecutor is guilty of suborning perjury, Your Honor?"

"It seems that he is suggesting that you may have suggested some of the testimony, but I think we all know that you didn't; did you Mr. Lewis?"

"Of course not, Your Honor. I didn't tell you what to say did I, Ms. Tanner?" he asked redirecting his question to the witness.

"I've never had to testify before, I didn't think it was wrong to discuss what I was going to say before I got up here and was made a fool of. I mean I would have been a nervous wreck if I didn't have a chance to go over what I would have to say," she responded guiltily. It wasn't wrong was it?"

I thought she was going to get hysterical, but the judge looked over at her and said reassuringly, "You did nothing wrong. Thank you for being kind enough to come forward and testify." Judge Bliss continued, "If there are no further questions, may we excuse this witness?"

Both Marvin and I voiced our agreement to dismiss the witness. I felt that I might have had some degree of success in casting a little doubt on her observations, and certainly raised the possibility, albeit remote, that there really was somebody *sittin' on da porch smokin' a reefer!*

16

"The State calls Doctor Laurence Warner," Marvin advised the Court.

The Bailiff escorted Doctor Warner into the courtroom. *Bingo!* Slightly graying red hair and beard.

The oath was administered, and Doctor Warner stated his name and address for the record. He is the husband of Linda Tanner.

"Doctor Warner, what kind of doctor are you?" Marvin asked.

"I am a psychologist. A PhD, in private practice."

"I draw your attention to the early morning hours of this past August sixth, and ask what if anything unusual you remember about that day?"

"I was awakened by the sound of a woman's scream," he replied.

"What time was it?"

"It was four forty-five in the morning according to my clock-radio."

"At the time, did you know who it was that was screaming?"

"What happened was my wife was also awakened and we decided that the scream had to have come from next door."

"What, if anything did you do then?"

"My wife called next door to see if they were okay."

"You said they, Doctor Warner. To whom are you referring?"

"Well, two women live in the house; Marianne Krenshaw and Marlene . . . I'm not certain of her last name."

"After your wife called next door, what happened?"

"As a result of the conversation she had with Miss Krenshaw, she called nine-one-one and reported what had happened."

"What did you do?"

"I put on some clothes and went downstairs to the front porch to wait for the police."

"Did you put your pants on after your wife called the police?"

"You know, I really am not sure. It could have been while she was calling them."

"Did you by any chance sleep in your pants that night?"

"Now, that I do know for sure. I definitely didn't sleep with my pants on!"

"At any time after you went to bed, but before you were awakened by the scream, did you get up, put on some clothes and go out for fresh air, or perhaps to smoke a cigarette?"

"First of all, I don't smoke. As I recall, it was quite hot that night and we had the air-conditioning running, so it would have been a lot cooler inside than out. So to answer your question, no. I didn't get up and leave the bedroom for any reason."

"Okay, so your wife called the police and you went out to the porch. When you got to the front porch, did you see anyone else?"

"No one else was there, except my wife; we went out to the porch together."

"How long would you estimate it took for the police to arrive?"

"I was amazed at the speed with which they responded. It seemed as if they had arrived almost as soon as we reached the porch."

"What happened when they arrived?" Marvin questioned.

"Two police officers ran up onto Miss Krenshaw's porch. The door was pulled open by someone inside, and they ran into the house."

"Do you know who opened the door for the police?"

"Well, I didn't then, because I wasn't able to see inside. It was still dark, and there were no lights on in the house that I could see, but I know now after talking with Miss Krenshaw," he responded.

"What happened after that?" Marvin asked.

"A few minutes after they ran into the house, the police came out with a black male with his hands cuffed behind him. They hauled him down the steps and into the police car."

"Did you see the man they brought out of the house?"

"Yes."

"Can you describe his attire?"

"Yes. He was wearing dark clothing. He was all disheveled. His shirt was hanging out of his pants. His pants and his belt were undone."

"Can you identify him?"

"He is sitting right there," he said, pointing directly at Jefferson.

Marvin looked my way and said, "Your witness."

"Doctor Warner, I'm slightly confused," I confessed. You live next door to Miss Krenshaw with your wife don't you?"

"Yes, I do."

"Just before you, a lady named Linda Tanner testified that *she* lived next door to Miss Krenshaw. Who is she?" I asked.

"She is my wife. She still uses her maiden name," he responded.

"Oh, I see, your name is Warner, but your wife's last name is Tanner."

"That is correct," he replied.

I figured I'd get as much as I could from the negative reaction of the jury to Linda Tanner's continued use of her maiden name. Twelve little Agatha Christie's on my jury. Prim, proper, old fashioned morals, old fashioned ideals and not in the least bit understanding or tolerant of newfangled lifestyles. They didn't like Marianne Krenshaw because she lived out of wedlock with her boyfriend, and they weren't going to be enamored of a married woman using her maiden name.

"What time did you go to bed the night before the events you've just testified to?"

"My normal time; around eleven-thirty, quarter to twelve," he replied.

"Since you retired at approximately eleven-thirty, did you hear, or were you aware of when Miss Krenshaw came home that evening?"

"I may have heard her, but I probably didn't pay any attention to it," he replied.

"Did you happen to hear or become aware of Miss Howell . . . Marlene . . . returning home for the evening?"

"I can't say that I did."

"And, I don't suppose you heard any part of the conversation between two men on Miss Krenshaw's porch before the scream, did you?"

"No."

"It was quite warm that morning, wasn't it Doctor Warner?"

"I think I already said that it was."

"Are you quite certain that you didn't go outside sometime during the night for a breath of air?"

"I'm certain that I did not," he retorted.

"You heard the scream; your wife, Miss Tanner, called nine-one-one and you threw on some clothes to go out to meet the police, is that correct?"

"Yes."

"What clothes did you throw on?"

"I pulled on a pair of pants," he responded.

"Anything else?

"Not that I can recall," he said.

"So you were wearing pants, but no shirt?"

"Correct."

"How about shoes and socks? You didn't throw on shoes and socks did you?"

"As I recall, no, I didn't."

"Da white guy wid a reddish beard, on his face, wid no shirt and no shoes." "It were dark; she never saw me." Two now famous quotations by Jefferson Wilkes.

"I would like you to focus your attention on the events surrounding the opening of Ms. Krenshaw's front door. Let's pretend we have a video tape of this event and we are going to show it to the jury in slow motion. I would like you to describe, step by step, each thing we will see in this slow motion film. For example: The police officers run up the steps, walk across the porch and reach out for the door. What happened next?"

"Someone pulled the door open."

"No. Before that didn't the police officer have to open the screen door?"

"Oh, yes. I see what you mean. Yes he opened the screen door."

"Did he just grab the handle and pull the door open, or perhaps the door was already open when he reached it?"

"To be quite honest, I can't be certain about that. I didn't pay that much attention to that seemingly insignificant detail."

"So you consider whether or not the screen door was propped open to be an insignificant detail?"

"Not significant enough for me to have noticed."

"I see. So would the question of whether or not the front door of the house was open or closed be any more significant in your opinion?"

"Well, I haven't thought about it."

"Yet, you seem to remember and give some significance to the fact that someone pulled the door open, don't you?"

"Yes, that's one of the things I saw and remembered."

"Couldn't that fact be fresher in your memory and seemingly significant because it was a part of the story that was told when the details of the incident were related to you by Ms. Krenshaw after the dust settled, so to speak, and it was discussed with the prosecutor in preparation for your testimony here today?"

"I suppose that's possible."

"Well, anyway, bottom line is, you are unable to say with any degree of certainty whether or not the screen door was propped open, correct?"

"Yes, I really don't remember that detail."

"So, then, it's highly possible that the screen door was in fact propped open, but you simply didn't pay any attention to that seemingly insignificant detail?"

"I suppose it's possible."

"Think back. Replay our slow motion film. Isn't it just possible that the front door was also open?"

"Anything's possible. But for whatever reason, I remember somebody pulling the door open."

"The pulling open of the door was part of the testimony that you discussed before hand with Mr. Lewis, wasn't it?"

"Yes."

"But whether or not the screen door was opened was not something you discussed, right?"

"No, we didn't discuss that."

"You stated that the police hauled him down the steps. Describe for us how he was being *hauled*."

"One officer had him by the arm and the other had him by the back of his pants. One was sort of pulling him along, and the other was kind of pushing him. But, they weren't being brutal if that's what you're getting at."

"Mr. Wilkes wasn't resisting the officers was he?"

"No."

"And the officers . . . you didn't mean to suggest that they were being brutal in any way did you?" I asked with a quizzical expression.

"No. I said that," Doctor Warner retorted somewhat confused.

"They weren't beating on Mr. Wilkes were they? I mean this was no Rodney King thing was it Doctor?"

"No. No." He sputtered.

"You didn't happen to video tape this thing did you?"

I leaned toward Jefferson and said in a whisper, "Is this the guy with the red beard on his face, no shirt, no shoes?"

"Ain' neva seed um befo' in ma whole life!" he said emphatically."

"Doctor Warner, before testifying today, you had an opportunity to meet with Mr. Lewis to review your testimony, didn't you?" I nodded toward Marvin.

"Yes, we reviewed my testimony."

"Did he tell you what kind of questions you could expect from me?"

"Well, he advised me that you would ask questions of me about my testimony, if that's what you're asking."

"And he made suggestions about how to answer my questions didn't he?"

"I don't think he could anticipate exactly what you were going to ask, so I don't know what you mean about telling me how to answer."

"Well, for example, he told you that if I asked a question that could be answered by simply saying yes or no, to answer with simply a yes, or a no, and not to elaborate. He did tell you that didn't he?"

Every lawyer advises his witnesses this way. It's like one of the first things you learn after you graduate from law school, and I know that Marvin is no exception.

"Yes, as a matter of fact he did," he responded somewhat amazed that I knew this. Now he's not sure how much I really know about his conversation with the prosecutor.

"And among the things you discussed was your description of Mr. Wilkes' clothing and his appearance, isn't that so?"

"We discussed that yes."

"But, I'll bet you never discussed how I might question the accuracy of your observations, considering it was dark, the events unfolded in a matter of seconds, and that your view of the activities was somewhat obscured by the position of the police officers in relation to Mr. Wilkes. You never discussed that did you, Doctor Warner?"

"No, actually we never went into that much detail."

"That much detail about what I might ask, you mean?"

"Yes."

"But you did discuss the details of your observations, didn't you?"

"Yes."

"For example, did you discuss how you were able to observe that the Mr. Wilkes' pants were undone, when his shirt which was hanging out was covering the waistband of the pants?"

"No we did not discuss that detail."

"And, I'll bet you've never given any thought to that detail either, have you?"

"Actually, no. I've not thought about it."

"And, you understand that I'm just guessing, but I'll also wager that you never discussed with Mr. Lewis, or anyone else, why if his belt was unbuckled, the button was undone and his fly was unzipped, his pants didn't fall down as he was being led from the porch to the police car. Am I right?"

"I must admit that I never thought about that."

There, that ought to be confusing enough. I'll just let it hang right there.

"I require nothing further from this witness, Your Honor."

"Very well. You may step down Doctor Warner. Thank you for your testimony. Please do not discuss your testimony with any of the other witnesses or parties involved in the case. Please call your next witness, Mr. Lewis."

17

Next to be called was Officer James Delaney. He was the first policeman on the scene. A very large, brutish looking, uniformed policeman, encumbered by all of the police paraphernalia hanging from his belt, made his way through the rear doors of the courtroom, and lumbered down the aisle to the witness box, where he raised his right hand and was sworn to tell the truth and all the rest of the crap they recite.

"Officer Delaney, were you on duty on the morning of August sixth?"

"I was."

"What was your assigned post?"

"I was assigned to patrol cruiser 1052, Northern District," he responded.

"While on duty that morning, were you dispatched to investigate a disturbance?"

"At approximately oh four forty-eight hours, we received a radio transmission to respond to 2627 North

Calvert Street to investigate screams believed to have come from that house."

"Where were you at the time you received that radio transmission?"

"Approximately three block away in the 2400 block of St. Paul Street."

"How long would you say it took from the time you received the dispatch to the time you arrived on the scene?"

"I'd estimate two or three minutes at the very most."

"Tell us what happened when you arrived."

"I was met at the front door of the house by a Caucasian female, later identified to me as Marianne Krenshaw. She unlocked the door and pointed toward the living room of the house. She was nearly hysterical, screaming, Help! He tried to rape me, or words to that effect."

"What did you do then?" Marvin asked.

"It was dark in the house, but I saw a person running toward the dining room. I identified myself as a police officer and told him to halt, but he continued to try to get away. I caught him in the dining room and brought him to the floor with a lunging tackle."

"What happened next?" Marvin prompted.

"I held him down on the floor until my partner, Officer Webster, came to assist me. We cuffed him and led him out of the house and into the patrol car."

"Did you take statements from persons on the scene?"

"Yes, statements were taken from Miss Marianne Krenshaw, Miss Marlene Howell, Miss Linda Tanner, and Doctor Laurence Warner," he read from his notes.

"As a result of these statements, what if anything did you then do?"

"I examined the premises, secured the scene and called for the crime lab to take prints and collect other evidence of the crime. I then arranged for Miss Krenshaw to be transported to Union Memorial Hospital to be examined and treated."

"As a result of your investigation, did you arrest and charge the defendant, Mr. Jefferson Wilkes?"

"I did."

"Officer Delaney, can you tell us what if anything you observed about the defendant at the time of his apprehension?"

"He was breathing heavily and sweating profusely. His pants were undone and his belt was unbuckled."

"Do you see the person who you arrested in this courtroom?"

"Sitting right there," he said pointing directly at Jefferson.

Marvin retrieved the baggie with the screwdriver, held it up for the world to see and asked Officer Delaney if he could identify it.

"That is the screwdriver I recovered from the floor next to Mr. Wilkes when he was apprehended. I tagged it with the tag you see attached to it, and I placed it into this plastic evidence bag."

I could have sworn it was a ziplock sandwich bag. Every day you learn something new.

"How did you handle it?" Marvin asked.

"I used standard police procedures for handling evidence, using a rubber glove to pick it up at the tip so as not to destroy any prints."

"After bagging the evidence what did you do with it?" Marvin continued.

"I turned it over to the crime lab technicians for further processing."

"I offer this as State's exhibit Number one, your honor," said Marvin confident that he could now get it into evidence.

The judge looked at me waiting for me to object, knowing that I would, but I decided not to. I had what I wanted and even if he still hadn't proved an unbroken chain of custody, I now wanted the screwdriver in evidence.

"I have no objection, Your Honor," I announced.

Then, feeling that he was on a roll, Marvin retrieved the photographs he had been unable to introduce before and showed them to Officer Delaney. He asked him if he was present when the photographs were taken, and to describe each one. He asked if each picture truly depicted the scene at the time of the occurrence on the morning of the offense.

When he offered them into evidence, I objected . . . on purely technical grounds. I objected before because I wanted to make sure that the crime lab technicians were required to testify, but I had subpoenaed them, and could call them as hostile witnesses.

Now I wanted to make a deal. I wanted to avoid having to pay Mike Richards to testify in order to get my picture of Marianne's street into evidence. Although it had virtually no evidentiary value, I really wanted to use it in my closing argument.

"What is the basis of your objection, Mr. West?" the Judge asked.

"The technician who took the pictures is required to testify as to the circumstances, and the technical particulars of the photographs."

"Approach the bench," Judge Bliss directed.

Marvin and I stood before the elevated bench. The Judge looked at me and said, "You mean like the lens settings, focal length of the lenses, F stops, and the like Mr. West," clearly indicating his irritation at my demands for this minutiae.

"With all due respect, Your Honor, I am entitled to require that; but, I'm willing to waive my client's right to demand that in return for a *quid pro quo*."

"I'm not making any concessions to this guy," Marvin interrupted.

"What difference does it make; it's an open and shut case," I challenged.

"What kind of *quid pro quo*?" the judge asked warily.

"I'll agree to let his pictures in, if he agrees to allow my picture in," I bargained.

"You mean that picture of Calvert Street?" Marvin asked in astonishment.

"That one," I said.

"Done!" he said in disbelief.

We returned to our places at the trial tables. He offered the photographs into evidence without my objection. They were marked by the clerk and received into evidence. Nobody but me saw the time bomb that was in those pictures waiting to explode.

"Officer Delaney, did you take fingerprints at the scene?"

"No, that was done by the crime lab technicians."

"That's all I have of this witness at this time."

"You may proceed with cross examination, Mr. West," said the Judge.

I handed him Mike's picture of Calvert Street, and asked, "Officer Delaney, can you identify Miss Krenshaw's house in this photograph?"

He studied the picture for several seconds and handed it back. "I can't be sure," he said. "All of those houses look the same from the outside, and I can't see the house numbers in that photograph."

"How were you able to pick out Miss Krenshaw's house when you responded to the call?"

"I shined my searchlight on the house numbers and located the address I was given. Also, Dr. Warner and Miss. Tanner were outside on their porch next door."

"But, if there were no numbers on the house and if no one were outside, you wouldn't have been able to determine which house to go into would you?"

"Not easily, no."

"When you reached the front door of the house was it still closed?" I asked.

"Yes."

"How about the screen door, was it still propped open?"

"Do you want to know if I touched the handle on the screen door, Counselor?"

They must have a special course for law enforcement officers on how to piss off lawyers . . . They all do that *counselor* shit.

"Yes. First, I'd like you to tell me if you did and then I'd like you to tell me if the screen door was still propped open, *Officer!*" I said sarcastically.

"The screen door was ajar and it wasn't necessary for me to grasp the handle. I was able to open the door by placing my arm into the opening and moving the door aside with my elbow like this," he said demonstrating with his arm the manner in which he opened the door. "This way I didn't disturb any prints on the door."

The door was not a jar; a jar is a glass container for jelly, I thought. Gotcha again! No fingerprints belonging to Wilkes on the door.

"Did you examine the screen door to determine why it was ajar and not tightly closed?" I asked.

"Yes."

"Won't you please share it with us, *Officer?*"

"The door keeper, that's the little round thing on the piston arm of the door closing device, had slid down and was blocking the arm from closing the door completely."

He wins the prize so far for the best description of a door closer on a screen door. I can just see it happening tonight. All the dear little ladies of the jury will go home from court and examine their screen doors.

"You couldn't tell from your examination of the door closer whether or not the door keeper you described was in a position to hold the door open accidentally, or intentionally, could you?"

"No. There is no way to tell that."

"So, you pushed the screen door aside using your elbow, being very careful not to disturb any prints, and then attempted to open the front door?"

"No. I never touched the front door. As I opened the screen, the front door was pulled open from the inside by Miss Krenshaw."

"So you don't know from your own personal knowledge whether or not the front door was locked at the time you arrived?"

"Miss Krenshaw said she unlocked it."

He knows he's not supposed to say what somebody else said. I wonder if he's just messing with me?

"So, then I was right. You don't know from your own *personal* knowledge if the door was locked. You only know what Miss Krenshaw *said*, right, *Officer*?"

"I only know what she said," he responded refusing to give any quarter.

"Well, you didn't administer a lie detector test to determine if she was being truthful, did you?"

Marvin jumped up shouting, "I object, Your Honor. He's badgering this witness!"

"I'm not badgering him, I'm trying to make him testify honestly and tell the truth," I cut in.

"Gentlemen, Gentlemen. Please!" begged the Judge. "Can't we conduct this proceeding like a trial, instead of a circus? Let's calm down and get on with this."

"You testified that you tackled Mr. Wilkes to the floor in the dining room. Will you describe to us how you tackled him?"

"I lowered my shoulder and threw my weight into the middle of his back and wrapped my arms around him at the same time wrestling him to the floor."

"Then you stood on his head to keep him down, didn't you?"

"No. I knelt over him with my knee in his back and held his head down with my right arm while my partner cuffed his hands behind his back."

"How much do you weigh?"

"Two twenty-five."

"Ever play organized football?"

"Played for Poly," he said proudly.

Polytechnic Institute was an all-boys technical high school that had a football rivalry dating back more than one hundred years with Baltimore City College, another all-boys college preparatory high school. I, of course, had gone to City. This guy was really starting to piss me off.

"Mr. Wilkes, here," I said pointing at my client. "What do you guess he weighs? One-forty, one-fifty? You didn't have any trouble bringing him down or controlling him did you?"

"I was just using standard police procedures designed to minimize injury to myself."

"I hope you didn't hurt yourself tackling him," I said sarcastically.

I asked the clerk for the screwdriver which had been introduced into evidence and showed it to the witness.

"You found this on the floor in the dining room near where you tackled Mr. Wilkes, didn't you?"

"Yes."

"Prior to finding it on the floor, you did not see it in Mr. Wilkes' hand, did you?"

"It was dark in the house and he had his back to me."

"So your answer, for whatever reason, is that you didn't see it in his hand, did you?"

"No, but that doesn't mean he didn't have it."

"It also doesn't mean that he *did*, does it, *Officer?*"

"I suppose you could say that," he gave in reluctantly.

"And I suppose *you* could also say that you never saw the screwdriver in Mr. Wilkes' hand; let us hear you say it, *Officer.* Repeat after me. *I never saw the screwdriver in Mr. Wilkes' hand.*"

"No. I never saw it in his hand, not personally no!"

"Thank you, Officer. Now, After you tackled him and cuffed his hands behind his back, he wasn't struggling or trying to escape was he?"

"I was just using standard police procedures," he repeated defensively.

"After you tackled him and cuffed his hands behind his back, he wasn't struggling or trying to escape was he?" I demanded.

"No."

"Then you pulled him up by grabbing the back of his pants and his belt, because that's standard police procedure, right?"

"I was just helping him up," he responded.

"By the back of his pants, yes?"

"Well, sometimes we do it that way. I might have."

Jefferson was pulling on my sleeve. I turned toward him.

"What?" I asked, annoyed at the interruption.

"Ax um 'bout da guy wha' run outta da house."

"He's going to say he didn't see anybody," I replied.

"Ha you know dat?" he asked.

"Trust me," I said. "I've asked that question once before."

"Mr. West," admonished the Judge. "Are you finished with this witness."

"I need one moment to confer with my client, Your Honor," I responded.

I turned back to Jefferson. "Let *me* try this case," I reprimanded. "I don't want to ask him that."

"Ah wants ya ta ax em," he insisted.

"Okay, boss. I don't have to serve your time, and you're not paying me anyway," I said.

"Upon your arrival on the scene did you observe the man running from the direction of Miss Krenshaw's house?"

"There was no one outside except Doctor Warner and Miss Tanner."

"I told you," I said to Wilkes.

"He be lyin'," Wilkes pronounced.

"Let's get back to this screwdriver for a second. You only found the one screwdriver at the scene didn't you?"

"Yes, just the one."

"And that was the one shown in the picture wasn't it?" I asked showing him the picture of the dining room.

"Yes."

"And it was the same screwdriver alleged to be used by the intruder as a weapon, correct?"

"As far as we were able to determine."

"This is not an ordinary screwdriver is it?" I asked.

"It's an ordinary Phillips-head screwdriver," he responded.

"As opposed to an ordinary flat head screwdriver, right?"

"No. It's not a flat head screwdriver."

"A flat head screwdriver would be better than a Phillips-head screwdriver for prying something open, or slipping into a narrow space, wouldn't it?"

"I suppose so."

"But you couldn't use a flat head screwdriver to fix . . . say . . . a camera tripod could you?"

"Not if it had Phillips-head screws," he replied.

"Look at the picture," I said as I handed him the dining room shot. "Phillips-head screws in the tripod, right?"

"Appears to be," he said reluctantly.

"What other evidence did you gather and process?"

"I found a bunch of flowers on the porch rail," he advised.

"And were you able to determine where they came from, or how they got there?"

"They had apparently been picked from the flower garden in the grass median up at Twenty-Ninth Street near Charles Street, but I don't know how they got there."

"How did you ascertain where the flowers came from?"

"You could tell from the way the stems were torn that they hadn't been cut off with scissors, or some other sharp instrument, and they are the same kind of flowers that were planted in the median just up the street on Twenty-Ninth Street near the Baltimore Museum of Art."

I was amazed that Wilkes had not been charged with illegally picking the flowers. I was having a good time with this witness, but couldn't think of anything else to ask, so reluctantly, I let him go.

The Judge asked Marvin to produce his next witness. Marvin advised that he had planned to call the crime lab technician to authenticate the photographs and establish the chain of custody for the screwdriver, but since I had so graciously allowed them into evidence, he didn't think he needed to call them, and had decided to rest the State's case.

J udge Bliss called us to the bench and asked if I were prepared to proceed with any motions and defense witnesses. It was almost noon, and I really wanted some time to review my notes and prepare my motions for acquittal and the related arguments.

"Your Honor, I wasn't expecting the State to rest its case this soon, and I need a little time to research and prepare my motions. Do you think we could adjourn until sometime later this afternoon. We can argue the motions, then be ready to proceed tomorrow morning with the defense witnesses?"

"I'll see you in my chambers at three. Will that give you enough time?"

We both agreed to return at that time.

He announced to the jury that the trial would resume tomorrow morning at nine-forty-five and again admonished them not to discuss the case with anyone and not to converse with the parties, lawyers or witnesses. I was going to ask him to admonish them about checking out their screen door closers, but like I said, he's got no sense of humor.

18

I returned to the office after court and tried to catch up with the phone calls, mail and other matters that were screaming for my attention. Actually, Kelly had been handling everything quite competently and had even managed to squeeze a couple of decent settlement offers on two accident cases from one of the insurance companies, subject to my approval, of course.

She got me a corned beef and coleslaw with Russian dressing on rye and a Dr. Brown's Cream Soda from the deli around the corner. I snuggled up in the library with Article 27 and began preparing my Motion for Judgment of Acquittal.

I started with the Rogue and Vagabond Section because I really thought there was no evidence educed to this point in the trial which could fit the legal definition of the crime. It was the least serious of all of the crimes with which he had been charged, and the one Judge Bliss would be the most inclined to dismiss.

First Jefferson would have had to be apprehended with one of a number of defined burglary tools on his possession. In fact, the evidence clearly indicated that the screwdriver was already in the house and had been used the preceding day by the victim's father to repair the camera tripod. That was the only logical conclusion that could be drawn from the testimony.

The charge of Nighttime House Breaking requires evidence of an intent to steal goods found in the premises. Not one iota of evidence was presented; not even an inference could be drawn from any testimony, or other evidence which could sufficiently prove an intent on Wilkes' part to steal goods. A piece of ass maybe, but no goods. Do I have the balls, I wondered, to say that to Judge Bliss?

On the other hand, Section 31A, breaking and entering a dwelling house, does not require proof of any intent to do anything. The mere walking through an open door without an invitation into someone else's house is sufficient. Wilkes claims to have been invited in by Red Beard, but no evidence of this contention has yet been presented. This one is a loser at this point, but I decided to raise it anyway, then renew the motion at the conclusion of the case.

I felt strongly that the assault charges would be merged with the more serious sexual offenses because the assault was a necessary element of the greater offenses. There seemed to be little point in worrying about these lesser charges anyway. Once you've finished serving a life sentence, the rest of the sentences are a piece of cake.

I was reminded of the case several years earlier when I represented a gentleman who was charged with three felony murders and a host of other charges when he accosted couples at bus stops, shot the men to death, raped and then murdered the women. Unfortunately for him, one of the victims survived. When he was sentenced to three consecutive life sentences plus sixty years to be served consecutively, his comment to the judge was, "How am I supposed to serve that many sentences? I'll probably be dead!" The judge responded, "Just do the best you can."

This left me with the biggies. First Degree Rape . . . life imprisonment; Attempted First Degree Rape . . . life imprisonment; Second Degree Rape . . . twenty years; First Degree Sexual Offense . . . life imprisonment; Attempted First Degree Sexual Offense . . . life imprisonment; Second Degree Sexual Offense . . . twenty years; Third Degree Sexual Offense . . . ten years; Fourth Degree Sexual Offense . . . one thousand dollar fine and/ or one year in prison. The last is the one I would definitely pick. I made a note to ask Wilkes which one he likes best. He'll probably choose the first one so he won't have to pay a fine.

I was now down to the part that I hated the most; foraging through law books. In the first place they're very heavy; (2) they have no pictures; and (c) the people who write them seem to have no aptitude whatever for the English Language. I have to read and re-read each sentence over and over, and still not be sure what they meant. For clarification, a case would be cited which illustrated what the authors had failed so miserably to explain. This then required that another book be located, equally as heavy, also with no pictures. Then, I would have to read the case which was supposed to decode the meaning of the Statute. In order to decipher the case just read to help comprehend the Statute, reference was made to another case in a different book, which illustrated what the first case was trying to explain. If this process were pursued long enough, one ultimately would have read through twenty or thirty cases, the last of which would refer to the Statute to explain what wasn't understood in the first place. Talk about a warped sense of humor.

A good place to start was the section headed "Definitions." This section makes an effort to define some of the words found in the Statute. It defines *vaginal intercourse*, for example, as *genital copulation* and tells us that penetration, however slight, is evidence of vaginal intercourse.

The difference between the first and second degrees of the sexual offenses is that the first degree crimes involve use of a weapon, whereas the second degree offenses involve force *without use of a weapon*. However, both first and second degree rape require that there be vaginal intercourse.

Jefferson couldn't keep it up; he never got it in; there was no penetration; ergo, no rape. The judge will have to throw these rape charges out. Will it matter? Jefferson still gets full credit for trying.

Did he attempt to have vaginal intercourse? It sure sounded like he did to me. Did he use force? Plenty of evidence of that. Did he use a weapon? One could reasonably conclude that a Phillips-head screwdriver held to one's throat accompanied by the words, "If you scream, I'll kill you" is a deadly or dangerous weapon. The attempted first degree rape charge most definitely will not get dismissed.

The Statute goes on to define *sexual acts* as all of the things I did to Jennifer plus several acts I didn't think of, *other than vaginal intercourse.* The first and second degree sexual offenses both require penetration by some part of the body or some object into the genital or anal opening of the other person's body. Highly technical stuff, but the State must prove the crimes beyond a reasonable doubt and to a moral certainty within the narrowly defined, unembellished meaning of the words in the Statute.

Although there was testimony that Jefferson raised Marianne's nightgown and fondled her, there was no testimony and no other evidence presented that was sufficient to prove that the fondling involved even the slightest degree of penetration, an essential element of those two crimes. Fondling is generally defined as *affectionate and tender* or *loving touching or caressing.* It is synonymous with cuddling, snuggling, petting, patting or stroking, *not inserting, or penetrating.* So Judge Bliss would have to blow these two charges away just on technicalities.

The force of the same argument would likewise require a summary acquittal of the attempted first degree sexual offense. There was no evidence that he attempted to penetrate her with a part of his body, or some object other than his penis. The very definition of this section of the Statute, excludes an attempt to have vaginal intercourse.

Both the third and fourth degree sexual offenses contemplate an intentional touching of one's intimate parts against one's will or consent. No problem there. But both crimes also require penetration with a part of the body other than the penis, mouth or tongue. Same facts apply; no evidence of penetration with any part of his body, *only the attempt with his penis*. These charges should go down the tubes with the others.

So, I was left with the offenses of breaking and entering, punishable by a five hundred dollar fine and/or three years, assault with a deadly weapon, and attempted first degree rape, punishable by life imprisonment. If I can convince Judge Bliss to run the sentences concurrently, Jefferson shouldn't have to serve more than one life sentence. That's quite a bargain, considering we started out at four life sentences plus sixty-four years in addition to the common law penalties for the assaults.

I selected a few cases to support my arguments, and then decided to take a large stack of books to court with me. I tore a piece of yellow legal pad paper into a bunch of strips and stuck the pieces like bookmarks between the pages in several places in each of about eight different books. The books and the book marks had absolutely nothing to do with the case, but it would give the impression, not only that I did a lot of work, but that I really knew something that the opposition had failed to discover. Sometimes the guy with the most books wins.

Since I was forced into the library against my will;

forced to endure the frustration and boredom of sifting through all of these books and over-exerting my brain, I decided that I would inform Jefferson Wilkes that I was raising my fee to ten thousand dollars. Even that's not enough, but I hate to get beat out of so much money. I mean it's bad enough to be owed four thousand dollars and not get paid, and it's worse getting beat for ten thousand, but I certainly can't afford to get beat out of twenty-five grand. I'd have to consider declaring bankruptcy.

19

Promptly at three p.m., I was invited, along with my client, Marvin and the Court reporter into Judge Bliss's chambers for the hearing on my motions.

I dumped my pile of books on the table, making certain that the spines were turned toward me and could not be seen by Marvin. He noticed the books and furrowed his brow perplexed by what I may have found that was worth the effort of bringing all these books to court. The judge asked Marvin if he were certain that the State was going to rest its case. Marvin told Judge Bliss that he believed the State had proved all of the elements of the crimes and was satisfied that the charges would not be dismissed. The Judge looked to me in anticipation of my motion.

"Your Honor," I began, "I move for a verdict of acquittal and ask that all charges against the defendant be dismissed."

"I'm listening," he responded.

I narrated the arguments that I had prepared on

each of the charges and included in my demands for dismissal of the attempted rape as well. He asked if I had any cases to cite on the rape and the sexual offense charges. I not only cited the cases, but handed him and Marvin photocopies of the cases on point. The judge flipped through the cases and pulled Article 27 of the Maryland Code from his shelf. After a brief perusal of the applicable statutes, he asked why I thought the State had failed to prove a *prima facia* case on the attempted rape.

Of course I had prepared no argument on this offense, because I could think of nothing that at this point in the trial could possibly vitiate the allegation. You will recall, as if you need to be reminded, that I boasted earlier of a warped sense of humor. Since I could think of no serious response, I asserted that the State had improperly charged the defendant on this count of the indictment. When asked why, I responded with absolutely no restraint and in obvious disregard for the very real potential of being held in contempt of court, that my client would have been more properly charged with assault with a dead weapon.

Okay. I didn't expect convulsions of hysterical laughter, but I couldn't believe that the remark did not evoke even a tiny smile, not even from Marvin. Wilkes just nodded his head in agreement. I don't think he had a clue as to what was occurring at that moment. Judge Bliss sat there and just scowled.

He glowered at me and asked, "Was that supposed to be funny?"

"I thought it might elicit a smile," I said apologetically.

THE SWORD OF JUSTICE

"It seemed amusing when I was beset by the irresistible compulsion to say it."

"I would think you'd be more serious about the plight of your client," he scolded. "I'm having an irresistible compulsion to hold you in contempt!"

Like I said . . . no sense of humor.

Abruptly, he turned to Marvin and asked if he had a response to my arguments.

Marvin cited several cases from the annotations to the sections of Article 27 related to the first degree rape and sexual offenses which clarified the legislative intent with regard to the attempts to commit these crimes. He argued that the state had proven each element of each of the crimes charged and asked that my motion be denied.

"I'm inclined," Judge Bliss said, "to grant the motion as to all but the attempted rape, the assault, assault with a deadly weapon and the breaking and entering. When I view the evidence, even in a light most favorable to the prosecution, I reluctantly must agree with Mr. West as to the failure of the State to prove one or more of the essential elements of the crimes alleged in the indictment. I am not blaming the prosecutor for failing to elicit testimony from the witnesses that might have supported all of the charges. Rather, it appears from the testimony that the acts which are essential elements of the crimes simply didn't occur.

Don't misconstrue my ruling as an inclination in anyone's favor. If anything, I am extremely reluctant to dismiss the more serious offenses. However, I must say that I am of the opinion that the indictment is a perfect example of overkill. If I were to permit all of the charges to go to the jury, they would become so hopelessly confused, that a just verdict would be impossible. I will therefore grant parts of the motion and dismiss the following charges: First and Second Degree Rape; First, Second, Third and Fourth Degree Sexual Offenses; Rogue and Vagabond."

"I disagree with Mr. West on the merger of the Assault and the Deadly Weapons charges, but will reconsider the merger of these offenses at the conclusion of the Defendant's case. I therefore, require the defendant to go forward with the defense of the remaining charges: House Breaking; Attempted First Degree Rape; Assault and Assault with a Deadly Weapon. If there is nothing else, Gentlemen, court will resume tomorrow morning at nine-forty five. Will you be prepared to proceed with your defense at that time, Mr. West?"

I advised that I would and thanked the judge. I left the judge's chambers and sat down at the table in the courtroom with Jefferson to explain what had just taken place. Even though he was right there throughout the proceedings, I doubted that he had a clue as to what had occurred.

I did not hesitate to tell him what a stroke of genius it was that I was able to convince the judge to dismiss most of the serious charges.

"You da bes!" he said approvingly.

"Don't jump to conclusions. You're still looking at more than a life sentence," I warned. "I also want you to know that I decided to raise my fee to ten thousand dollars."

"Das aw right wid me," he said. "Youz worf ever penny."

Although it was after four, I decided to return to the office. I needed to decide whether or not it made sense to go forward with a defense. What had the State proved beyond a reasonable doubt?

The judge had decided that the State had produced sufficient evidence of a *prima facia* case of the remaining charges. That was when the evidence was considered in a light most favorable to the prosecution. But, if the evidence were viewed in a light most favorable to the defense; then what would we have? I tried to analyze the evidence objectively, but my dislike for Jefferson was like a wall between me and objectivity. The cops caught Jefferson inside the house. That can't be viewed favorably toward the defendant. How did he get in? They never told the jury, but then neither did we at this point. Why did he go inside? To rape! That's what they say, but we haven't said otherwise. We know he went in to get a drink *"cause it were hot out!"* All the points made on cross examination? Nah! Not enough to win; not enough to get the judge to take it a way from the jury. Then again, if I go forward and present a defense, the asshole is going to insist on testifying, and that'll be the end of it anyway. But Jefferson's story, albeit beyond belief, had to be told. There was no other way to contradict the evidence against him. I just had to go forward.

This trial was taking a hell of a lot longer than I thought. I needed to get back to my life. I was hopeful that I could get the lab technician and the FBI guy in and out before eleven o'clock the next day, put Wilkes on the stand and finish with him by noon. After the lunch break, Marvin would cross-examine him, and only God knew how long that would take.

The Judge would need about thirty minutes to review jury instructions with counsel and then another thirty, or forty minutes to instruct the jury. I was hoping we could present our closing arguments early enough in the afternoon for the judge to let the jury begin deliberations. They shouldn't be out very long; it's an open and shut case!

J udge Bliss began the session by explaining to the jury that as a result of a motions hearing yesterday afternoon, the court had dismissed certain of the charges against the defendant on purely technical grounds, but left for their determination the remaining charges which he enumerated.

"Mr. West, call your first witness," he directed.

I requested that the bailiff call Officer William Saxon to the stand and advised the court that he was being called as a hostile witness.

Marvin stood and advised the court that Officer Saxon had not been summoned to appear, since the State had rested its case. I then advised the court that I had issued a subpoena for the officer, which I knew had been served. One of the courtroom guards then emerged through the center doors of the courtroom with a man dressed in a badly fitting dark colored suit who identified himself as Officer Saxon. He came forward, took the stand and was sworn in.

I led him through his name, assignment to the Police Crime Lab, his fourteen years as a police officer, his education and training in forensic sciences, right up to the point where he arrived at the scene of the crime.

"Officer Saxon, When you arrived at the scene of the alleged crime you were met by Officer Delaney, am I correct?"

"Yes."

"He pointed out certain items of evidence for your examination didn't he?"

"Yes."

"Among them was this screwdriver?" I asked, holding up the baggie and displaying it to the audience and the jury.

"Yes."

"You very carefully examined this screwdriver for fingerprints didn't you?"

"Yes."

"And you found fingerprints on the handle didn't you?"

"Yes."

"But none of those prints belonged to Mr. Wilkes did they?"

"No."

"You also took fingerprints from the door knob of the front door, didn't you?"

"Yes."

"And from the screen door?"

"Yes."

"And from the door frame?"

"Yes."

"And from the glass panes in the door?"

"Yes."

"And from the glass panes in the windows facing the front porch?"

"Yes."

"And from the railing of the staircase inside the house from the first to the second floor?"

"Yes."

"The fact is that your very careful, very professional, very experienced fingerprint examination revealed no prints that matched Mr. Wilkes' fingerprints on the surface of any of those places, isn't that so?"

"That is correct."

"You did find some fingerprints, though, didn't you?"

"Yes."

"Whose where they?"

"I don't know," was his only response.

"You don't know? Didn't you take prints from the residents of the household?"

"Yes, of course I did."

"Certainly you were able to identify their prints weren't you?"

"Of course."

"So, are you telling us that there were prints belonging to some person other than people who live in the house?"

"Yes."

"And you have never determined to whom those prints belong, have you?"

"No, but they could be prints of just about anybody who was a guest in the house."

"Or," I asked, "they could belong to any unknown intruder, who was not an invited guest, right?"

"That's possible, but the only intruder we know about is your client, Counselor."

"But none of the prints any place in the house where my client is alleged to have been, are his are they?" This question was met with dead silence.

"Sorry I wasn't able to hear your answer; could you speak up a little so the jury can hear you?"

"My answer to what?"

"The question concerning none of the prints belonging to my client; or should I just have the court reporter read the question back to you?"

"There were no positive ID's of your client's prints in the house."

"Thank you, Officer Saxon. You also examined the front door latch and the locking mechanism didn't you?"

"Yes."

"This examination was done with a magnifying device similar to the loops used by jewelers, am I correct?"

"Yes."

"The device resembles a small pair of binoculars clipped to your glasses doesn't it?"

"Yes."

"The purpose of this examination was to determine if there had been a forced entry into the premises, right?"

"Yes."

"You likewise examined other possible points of entry didn't you?"

"Yes."

"Tell us what exactly you were looking for with that binocular type device?"

"Well, when entry is forced, any device used to slip the lock will leave microscopic scratches on the surfaces of the lock. So I was looking for those scratches."

"Give us an example of the kind of device you are referring to that could be used to slip a lock."

"Anything that would fit between the door jam and the door could be used."

"Like what?"

"Something thin. A thin piece of sheet metal, a credit card, or driver's license. A thin tool of any kind could be used."

"And your careful, and I assume, thorough microscopic examination revealed that there had been no forced entry into the premises, correct?"

"That is correct, Counselor." See? Didn't I tell you? Every cop calls every lawyer Counselor! I just knew he would do it. The urge was irresistible, and as you know, I am now an expert in the field of irresistible urges.

"So, Mr. Wilkes' fingerprints were not found on any surface outside, or inside of the house, were they?"

"No."

"If, in fact, Mr. Wilkes had been in the house at all, his entry into the premises would be consistent with his having walked through an open door without having touched anything, correct?"

"Not necessarily. He could have worn gloves, or wiped the surfaces he touched," he rejoined.

Suddenly this guy developed a vocabulary. I thought he had been doing just fine with "yes" and "no."

"Well both you and Officer Delaney searched the premises for clues and for evidence didn't you?"

225

"Yes."

"How do you know that Officer Delaney actually searched the premises?"

"We discussed the case and compared notes as a part of our investigation. That's what police officers do; it's part of how we conduct an investigation. We share information. There's nothing wrong with that is there, Counselor?"

"Is that standard operating procedure?"

"Yes it is."

"Neither of you found any gloves did you?"

"I can't speak for Officer Delaney," he responded.

"You just said that you discussed the case and shared information. Standard operating procedure you said. Did he tell you about finding any gloves?"

"If I answer, you'll say it's hearsay."

"Well I'd like you to answer, and I promise not to object. Did he find any gloves?"

"Not that I'm aware of."

"You didn't find any gloves, or anything else for that matter that could have been used to prevent fingerprints being left, did you?"

"No."

"And the officers on the scene didn't tell you about any gloves and no such evidence was given to you by any other person at the scene, was it?"

"No."

"The other responding officers turned all of the other evidence they found over to you didn't they?"

"As far as I know they did."

"And there were no gloves or the like among the items, were there?"

"No."

"Were you there when the defendant was placed under arrest?"

"He was already in the patrol car when I arrived."

"Did you see him that morning?"

"Yes. He's sitting right there next to you at the trial table."

"Good!," I proclaimed. "He's not wearing gloves now is he?"

"Obviously not, counselor," he retorted.

"And on August the sixth when you saw him in the police car, he wasn't wearing any then either, was he?"

"No, Sir."

"If, in fact, Mr, Wilkes had used gloves, or wiped prints to avoid detection, this would have smudged or destroyed any other prints on the surfaces wouldn't it?"

"Probably."

"Yet you did find identifiable prints on these surfaces didn't you."

"Yes."

"So those surfaces hadn't been wiped off, had they?"

"Doesn't seem that way."

"Now, in addition to the items we've discussed, you also removed the bed linens from Miss Krenshaw's bed and placed them into a large plastic bag, didn't you?"

"Yes."

"And the reason for this was so they could be transported to the forensic lab to be examined, correct?"

"Yes."

"And they were sent to the lab and they were examined, weren't they?"

"Yes, they were."

"The purpose of that examination was to locate and analyze any hair samples, semen, blood, skin, or any other identifiable particles found on the sheets that might yield some DNA evidence to prove that the defendant was in the bed, correct?"

"Yes."

"You have a copy of the lab report of the examination of those sheets don't you?"

"Yes."

"And did the lab find any evidence of any kind in the bed linens?"

Marvin who had been sitting with his head buried in his hands, burst from his chair and objected. "Your Honor," he protested. "This officer can't testify to the results of someone else's examination. That violates the hearsay rule, and fails to establish the chain of custody of the evidence."

"He's your Police Officer. It's your evidence, and I allowed you to introduce all of the other evidence in this case without establishing chain of custody," I demurred.

"Never the less, Mr. West," interposed Judge Bliss, "he's entitled to insist on the direct testimony of the lab technician. Have you subpoenaed him?"

"Yes, of course I did, but I thought I might save the court some time," I responded.

"Do you have anything further of this witness Mr. West?"

"Yes Your Honor, I do."

"Officer Saxon, did you take these photographs, or were they taken at your direction?" I asked showing him the State's photographic exhibits.

"The Crime Lab photographer took them at my request," he replied.

"Why did you instruct the photographer to take this picture?" I asked as I handed him the one of the stair case.

"It showed the route the attacker had to take to reach the bedroom were the attack took place."

"Were you present when the photograph was taken?"

"Yes."

"Study it for a moment. Does the photograph accurately portray the scene as it was upon your arrival."

"Yes."

I asked the same question about each picture. Officer Saxon explained why he had directed each of the photographs to be taken. I then showed him Mike's photograph of the 2600 block of Calvert Street. Before I could ask him any questions about it he announced defiantly that he had not instructed anyone to take this picture and that it was not even a Police Department photograph.

"Excellent!" I exclaimed as if I were genuinely impressed. "How were you able to tell this was not an official Police Department Photograph?"

He went on to explain at length how he determined this was not an official photograph, as though it really mattered. When he was finished, I got him to agree that this unofficial photo was a shot of the street where Miss Krenshaw resided. I offered it into evidence as

Defendant's Exhibit #1 over no objections from Marvin, as agreed, and then turned him over to Marvin for cross examination.

M arvin began, "Officer Saxon, during your examination of the front door did you also examine the lock?"

"Yes, It was a Yale surface-mounted lock with what I would describe as a slip bolt."

"What is a slip bolt?" he asked.

"Well, the end of the bolt is beveled at a forty-five degree angle, so that when it hits the strike plate, the bolt retracts until the door is closed and then springs back out seating itself automatically into the opening in the strike plate. If the bolt were squared at the end like a dead bolt, you would have to turn the knob to retract the bolt and then turn it again to seat the bolt into the strike plate."

What happened to "yes" and "no?" I wondered.

"What is the significance of this in terms of how entry was gained into Miss Krenshaw's house?"

"Like I said before, because the beveled end of the bolt faces outward, it can easily be slipped open with something thin like a credit card inserted between the door and the frame."

"That's all I have," said Marvin.

I was back on my feet for re-direct examination before the judge could even ask if I had any further questions. "Officer Saxon, you just testified that a lock such as the one you described could easily be slipped open with a credit card. Am I correct in assuming that you've done this before?"

"I've seen demonstrations of someone doing it."

"So you've never actually tried to do it yourself, have you?"

"No. I haven't."

"Then what you really meant to testify to was that it *looked* easy to do, right?"

"An experienced burglar can do it in a matter of seconds."

"How do you know that? You were never a burglar were you?"

"Like I said, I've seen demonstrations."

"If a credit card had been used to slip the lock, there would have been some discernible trace, like microscopic scratches, isn't that correct?"

"It would depend on a number of factors, but sometimes you can tell and sometimes you can't."

"Well, let's see! As a part of your training, you observed a demonstration by an expert of how to slip a lock with a credit card, right?"

"Right."

"After the lock was slipped, did you, as a part of your training, have an opportunity to examine the lock, to look for the microscopic marks that are sometimes left and sometimes not left?"

"Yes, that was part of the training."

"So, were you able to see the marks left by the person who gave the demonstration?"

"Yes, I was."

"Correct me if I'm wrong, Officer Saxon; the person

who gave the demonstration was an expert at slipping locks, right?"

"He was able to do it in a matter of seconds."

"Obviously then he was an experienced expert, right?"

"Obviously, yes."

"*He* left marks, didn't he? You previously testified that you used that binocular device to look for microscopic marks. Was that the same kind of device you used as a part of your training?"

"There are different brands, made by different manufacturers."

"Aren't they all very similar in quality and magnification?"

"About the same."

"So, if there were marks left, you'd have found them, wouldn't you?"

"Like I said, it depends on the circumstances."

"Okay. Then, under the circumstances of this particular investigation, if there were marks from forced entry, you'd have detected them wouldn't you?"

"Probably."

"Besides a credit card, what else could be used in the manner you described to slip the lock?"

"A plastic laminated ID Card, or a Driver's License, a thin sheet of metal, lot's of different things."

"Well, certainly if anything metal was used that would have left telltale signs wouldn't it?"

"Probably would have."

"And if anything were used to pry the lock, that would have left discernible marks, wouldn't it?"

"Yes."

"The reason you testified that there had been no sign of forced entry was because your examination revealed no such marks, correct?"

"That is correct."

I dug into my file and found the receipt for the personal affects that had been taken from Jefferson at the time of his arrest. In addition to the screwdriver, it listed everything found on his person. I walked to the witness stand and handed it to the witness.

"Officer Saxon, I have just handed you the personal property receipt given to my client at the time he was booked for this offense. You've seen one of these before haven't you?"

"Many times, Counselor."

"This is a receipt given to every person who is arrested for all of the property found on their person at the time they are arrested, correct?"

"Yes."

"This particular one is a receipt for the items found on Jefferson Wilkes when he was arrested on August sixth, isn't it?"

"It appears to be, yes."

"As best as you can determine this is an official Police Department Personal Property Receipt, isn't it?"

"Yes."

"It doesn't appear to have been altered in any way does it?"

"Nothing appears to have been changed or erased if that's what you mean."

"What is the date of that receipt?" I asked.

"August sixth, this year," he read.

"Will you please read the list of items enumerated on that receipt?"

He read the list of the items found on Jefferson at the time of his arrest. Conspicuously missing from the list was any reference to a credit card, driver's license, or any other thin, stiff object that could have been used to slip the lock as had been described.

"So Mr. Wilkes had no credit card that he could have used to slip the lock, did he?" I asked.

"None that we found."

"He has no driver's license, does he?"

"I don't know if he has one or not," he responded.

"Well, he didn't have one in his possession on the morning of August sixth, did he?"

"None that we could find."

"And none of the other objects found on his possession that morning could have been used to slip the lock as you described, could they?"

"None that we could find."

Did you search around the outside of the house to see if such an item had been dropped nearby?"

"Yes"

"And you found nothing, correct?"

"Correct."

"One couldn't slip that lock with a Phillips-Head Screw driver could he? It's too large to slide into the space between the door and the strike plate isn't it?"

"That's true."

"And if that screwdriver had been used to pry the lock or the door, you would have been able to see that, wouldn't you?"

"Yes."

"And if you had noticed such marks, then your report would have indicated that there *was* a forced entry, right?"

"That's right, Counselor"

I offered the receipt into evidence as Defendant's exhibit #2 with no objection from the prosecutor.

"I have nothing further of this witness, at this time, Your Honor."

I requested that the bailiff call Agent Lester V. Little as my next witness. It was already ten-thirty, and I was pushing it.

21

Agent Lester V. Little of the Federal Bureau of Investigation Forensic Laboratory was sworn and took the stand. He was one of the State's witnesses, who for obvious reasons, Marvin chose not to have testify. Although I didn't really care if he was a qualified expert, he had an extensive, and quite impressive *curricula vitae*, which would, in fact, enhance his credibility. Usually my role would be to attempt to discredit such a witness. Instead, I led him through a series of questions to establish his expertise and the chain of custody of the evidence submitted to the lab for examination. He offered his report of the examination pursuant to the subpoena I had served on him.

"Agent Little, you conducted an examination of the bed linens submitted to the FBI Lab for the purpose of detecting any human hair, body fluids, or other particles that would have evidential value in the prosecution of this case, did you not?"

"Yes, I did."

"And in the course of this examination, did you discover any human hair on these bed linens?"

"I did."

"I know I would be very interested, and I'm quite sure the jury would be interested in knowing how you are able to identify a person from a single hair, or from a drop of semen, or blood, or piece of skin. Would you be kind enough to explain that to us?"

Agent Little delivered a learned dissertation on the science of the genetic signature that is unique to every human creature. Like a fingerprint, every person's DNA characteristics are singular to that individual. He further explained how every cell in a human body contains the complete DNA material of that person, and how matches of that material are compared to the known DNA print of any particular person. The questions about exclusionary percentages were of no value in our case particularly since I was not challenging the lab's findings.

"The samples are gathered with a vacuum like device that collects any loose particle onto a very fine sterile screen. We took a sample of Mr. Wilkes' hair to establish our base DNA identification and then compared samples taken from the crime scene to that known DNA print."

I continued, "And were you able to identify the person to whom this hair belonged?"

"I was. It belonged to Miss Marianne Krenshaw."

"In mock disbelief, I asked, "You mean there was not a single strand of any kind of hair that belonged to Mr. Wilkes?"

"No Negro hairs of any description were found in the linens delivered to the lab for analysis."

"Did you find samples of any bodily fluids, or particles which matched the genetic signature of Mr. Wilkes?"

"No Sir. I did not."

"So as far as your scientific analysis was concerned, there was no physical evidence of any description that could prove that Mr. Wilkes was in, on, or about that bed, correct?"

"None that my examination uncovered."

I was watching the reaction of the jurors to Agent Little's revelations. First, they were very impressed by the fact that he was an agent of the FBI. It was as if Ephram Zimbalist, Jr. himself were up there testifying. They were visibly confounded by the absence of Negro hair in the bed. They were in a quandary. It was like paddling a canoe with only one oar.

"The bed linens you examined were brought to the lab in a sealed plastic bag of some sort, is that correct?"

"Yes."

"Could there have been any particles, hair, or other identifiable human cells on the bed sheets that might have fallen loose from the bed linens into the plastic bag?"

"Sure. There could have been."

"To be certain that there weren't any, you of course vacuumed the inside of the plastic container into which the linens had been placed, didn't you?"

"Of course."

"There simply wasn't any identifiable material on those bed sheets, or in the container in which they were transported to the lab, were there?"

"None that I could detect."

"Agent Little, we've established your vast experience and your technical expertise in forensics. Let me pose a hypothetical situation, and then I'd like your opinion."

"If I told you that two people had been struggling in the bed from which those linens were removed; that undergarments of each person had been removed, or partially removed, and then put back on in that bed, that the two people had gotten in and out of the bed at least twice, and that there had been some attempt at least of a forced sexual act, would you reasonably expect to find some hair samples of *both people* in the bed?"

"Yes, that would be a reasonable expectation."

"On the other hand, wouldn't you consider it to be highly unusual to find physical evidence of only one of the participants, and *none* of the other?"

"I think that would be unusual, yes."

"Given the total lack of any physical evidence such as hair, blood, semen, or skin cells, in your opinion do you think the events I just described are likely to have taken place?"

"I would be inclined to doubt it, but then again, you know anything is possible."

"But if you were asked to believe it, you would have some serious doubt, wouldn't you?"

"Well, let's say I'd be skeptical."

"Thank you Agent Little. That's all I have of this witness, Your Honor."

There was no way that Marvin could resurrect this testimony, but he gave it a valiant effort.

M arvin began. "There could be any number of reasons for not finding hair or other evidence on the sheets, couldn't there?"

"I suppose there could be any number of explanations." He responded.

"The absence of such evidence, doesn't necessarily mean that he wasn't there, does it?"

"I'm not given to speculation, or drawing unscientific conclusions. I'm a scientist. I only report on what I find, or in this case, what I did not find."

"Well, isn't it possible that whatever evidence might have been on the sheets, could have fallen off *before* they were placed in the plastic container."

"I suppose anything is possible, yes."

"Forgive me for objecting, Your Honor, but possibilities are not admissible evidence, perhaps Mr. Lewis would like to phrase his questions in the realm of probabilities."

"Yes. Possibilities are not a proper subject of inquiry, Mr. Lewis. The jury is to ignore the question about possibilities and the answer that was given by Agent Little. Do you wish to rephrase your question, Mr. Lewis?"

"I have nothing further," said Marvin.

"If I may, Your Honor, I have another question, or two on re-direct."

"Was any other evidence from the crime scene in this case submitted to the FBI Lab for analysis?"

"None that I'm aware of, no."

The dummies probably never even attempted to

gather samples from the floor of the bedroom, but that's their problem. I think I got enough.

"Thank you Agent Little. That's all I have of this witness, Your Honor."

"Is there any reason why this witness may not be excused, Gentlemen?" asked Judge Bliss. We both agreed that we would not be recalling him to the stand. It was now a little after eleven.

"Are you prepared to call your next witness, Mr. West?"

"I am, Your Honor, but may we approach the bench?"

Marvin and I moved to the bench for a side-bar conference. "Your Honor," I said. "I need some time to talk with my client about whether or not he is going to testify. If he is, I can put him on the stand after lunch. If we re-convene a little earlier, there should be enough time this afternoon to finish the case and allow the jury to begin deliberations."

The judge asked Marvin if he objected. Since it was agreeable with him, the judge decided we would reconvene at twelve-fifteen. Judge Bliss advised the jury that we were adjourned the court for an early lunch and asked that they return at twelve-fifteen. I returned to the office to meet with my client and try to dissuade him from making a fool of himself by testifying, and destroying the impact of my brilliant examinations of Officer Saxon and Agent Little.

I begged, pleaded, cajoled, threatened and argued until I was weary from my efforts to convince Jefferson not to testify. I felt that I had created enough confusion, raised enough unanswered questions to sway my twelve Agatha Christies into a unanimous agreement that there was reasonable doubt.

Try as I might, Jefferson insisted he was innocent, insisted his story, which hadn't changed, was the truth, and insisted that Jesus was standing at his shoulder as witness to the truth of his assertions. He was adamant that he would vindicate himself with his own testimony.

I believed he would be made a fool of on cross examination, and that he could not overcome the damage that would result from a disclosure of his prior criminal record. When I attempted to explain this to him, his response was, "Wha' dat got ta do wit anythin'?"

He was the most perverse, bullheaded, obstinate, pigheaded, stubborn, rapist son-of-a-bitch I had ever encountered. I swore to myself that when the judge sentenced this asshole to life imprisonment, and I had no doubt that's exactly what he would do, I would stand up and cheer. This fucker . . . no this limp-dick was hell bent on ruining my reputation.

I called Kelly into the office and dictated a letter in Jefferson's presence which I was going to demand that he sign.

Dear Mr. West:

You have thoroughly discussed with me my Constitutional right to remain silent and not testify in my own behalf at my trial for crimes, which if I am found guilty of, may result in a sentence of life imprisonment.

> *I understand that if I testify, the State's Attorney and the judge will be allowed to ask me questions about my criminal record. You have advised me not to testify, in part, because of the damage to my case and my credibility that will be caused by disclosure of my extensive past criminal history. Contrary to your advice, I insist upon testifying at my trial.*

I treated Jefferson to a hot dog, potato chips and a coke. Fitting last meal I thought as we headed back to the Temple of Justice.

Before embarking upon the afternoon session, I advised Judge Bliss that my client had decided to testify and that I wanted to advise my client on the record, but out of the presence of the jury, of his constitutional right to remain silent.

Judge Bliss asked the bailiff to delay seating the jurors until I advised Jefferson of his rights for the record.

"Mr. Wilkes, please stand," I instructed, and proceeded to advise him of his constitutional right to remain silent.

"Mr. Wilkes, you have an absolute right guaranteed to you by the Fifth Amendment to the Constitution of the United States, to remain silent and not be required to testify or give evidence against yourself in these proceedings. I've explained this to you before. Do you understand what I've just told you."

"Uh huh."

"If you choose not to testify, Judge Bliss will instruct the jury that you had an absolute right not to testify, and that they can draw no inference of guilt from your refusal. Do you understand that?"

"Uh huh."

"If you choose to testify, you will be required to take an oath and swear to tell the truth. If you lie under oath you can be charged with perjury. Do you understand?"

"Uh huh."

"If you decide that you wish to testify in these proceedings, The State's Attorney and the Judge will be allowed to ask you questions about anything you testify to from the witness stand. Do you understand that?"

"Uh huh."

"They will also be permitted to question you in detail about your prior convictions, if any, for past crimes you may have committed. Do you understand?"

"Uh huh."

"And if you have been previously convicted of any crimes, that fact may be considered by the jury when weighing your credibility. That means that they can use that information as the basis for disbelieving anything you may say, even if it is the absolute truth. Do you understand that?"

"Uh huh."

"Having been explained your right to remain silent, and understanding the consequences of your testifying in this case, is it your decision to testify, or not to testify?"

"Uh huh."

"Uh huh, what? You're going to testify?"

"Uh huh."

"I'd like the record to reflect that I have advised Mr. Wilkes not to testify, but that he has chosen to shun that advice."

"Mr. Wilkes will testify, Your Honor."

22

The jurors began emerging from the Jury Room. Everyone remained standing until they were seated. Judge Bliss took his seat behind the bench and instructed me to proceed.

I called Jefferson Wilkes to the stand. The jury was impassive. Marvin's eyes lit up like a child on Christmas morning peering through the spindles of the staircase at the gifts Santa had placed beneath the lit Christmas tree.

The bailiff instructed Jefferson to raise his right hand and administered the oath. "Do you swear, under the penalties of perjury, to tell the truth, the whole truth and nothing but the truth?"

"As Jesus be ma widness," Jefferson responded.

"Does that mean you swear to tell the truth?" the bailiff repeated.

"Uh huh," was Jefferson's reply, of course. He always says that!

"Please state your full name and address for the record."

And here in the center ring, folks, we have the show of shows . . . the event you've been so anxiously awaiting . . . let's all put our hands together and welcome the star of our show.

"Ma name be Jefferson Wilkes. At da presen' tam Ah be stayin' at 4115 Prentiss Street," he began.

Here we go! I took a deep breath and began. "Mr. Wilkes, you know you are not required to tell your side of the story don't you?"

"Uh huh."

"And if you chose not to testify, the judge would tell these folks in the jury that they couldn't hold that against you. You're aware of that too, aren't you?"

"Uh huh."

"You also know that if you tell these folks what really happened, both Mr. Lewis, here *(I turned and pointed to Marvin)* and Judge Bliss are going to have the right to ask you questions. You know that right?"

"Uh huh."

"And you know that Mr. Lewis is going to take great delight in asking you all about any prior crimes you may have committed, don't you?"

"Uh huh."

"And despite this, you insist on getting up here on the witness stand and testifying in your own behalf, don't you?"

"Uh huh."

"Why? Jefferson, *why* do you want to subject yourself to this?"

"Cause Ah wonts deez folk here to know da truf, is why."

"Then why don't you tell them what happened on the morning of August sixth?"

Jefferson began relating his version of the events of the early morning hours of August sixth. The story was the unabridged version of the fable he told me that fateful day at the Baltimore City Jail. The only difference was in the telling. Nobody had to draw every word out of him. He had top billing; he was the star and he was there to perform.

He wove his spellbinding myth from the bus ride with Zippo and Lukshin to "da white guy wid a red beard, on his face," and the "polices standin' on ma face, wid his shoe on ma face."

He told them about the *reefer*. He told them about the *flaers*. He told them about LaDelle and their anniversary, about the night shift and the day shift. He told them about the screen door being propped open wid da "li'l thing on the thing what make da doh closes." He told them about the *drink*.

During most of his testimony, I sat as inconspicuously as possible, sort of staring at my legal pad. I didn't want it to be too obvious that my eyes were rolling in their sockets with each word he uttered. Every now and again I sneaked a glance at the jury to see how they were reacting. I thought that a couple of the jurors seemed to be captivated, and were enjoying his version of the story. I thought a couple of them were going to burst out into spasms of uncontrollable laughter.

On the other hand, Marvin was having a blast. He had this big, shit-eating grin dripping from his face. He even chuckled to himself a few times. I could tell because his shoulders were kind of shaking. To his credit, he managed to contain himself so as not to laugh out loud. Judge Bliss was even having a hard time remaining impassive. Jefferson was getting a much better reaction from the crowd than I got with the "assault with a dead weapon" routine. At the end of his narration, I asked him a few closing questions.

"Had you ever seen Miss Krenshaw before?" I asked.

"Who dat?" he responded.

"The lady that says you tried to rape her," I answered.

"Ah ain neva seed her befo in ma whole life!" he said. "I ain even seed her in ma life til dis here tral."

"Not even on the morning of August sixth?" I asked.

"Un unh, not even den," he replied.

"How could you not have seen her that morning?" I asked.

"It's lak Ah been tellin ya all 'long. It were dark in 'at house. I was tackled on da flo wid ma face lookin' da uva way. Da cop he were standin' on ma face. I couldn' see her 'n she couldn' see me."

"Had you ever seen Dr. Warner before?" I asked.

"Who dat?" he responded.

"The man that was Miss Krenshaw's neighbor. The man who testified and who has a reddish colored beard (on his face)," I answered.

"Ah ain neva seed him befo in ma whole life!" he said. "I ain' seed him in ma life til dis here tral."

"Not even on the morning of August sixth?" I asked.

"Un unh, not even den," he replied.

"Is there anything else you would like these ladies on the jury to know about what happened that morning?" I asked.

"Ah jus' wants em ta know Ah din' do it," he said.

"Why do you think that lady is saying that you threatened to kill her and tried to rape her?" I asked.

"Das wha Ah cain' figure out; I sposes she jus' be makin a very wrong mistake is all."

He ended with, "As Jesus be ma widness I be tellin' da truf, wha' really happen."

"You've been in some trouble before, haven't you?" I asked hoping I might take some of the sting out of the blow when Marvin began to bludgeon him.

"Yeah, Ah were ina cupla beefs, you know some alterations, and stuff."

"You want to tell us about them?" I asked.

"Well, dis one tam I be dafenden' ma se'f wid a knife, an' anuva tam dis guy hitted his teef inta ma fist, and Ah's da one en' up goin' ta da hos'pal fo' a technical shot."

"You mean a *tetanus* shot?" I asked.

"Uh huh, one a doze too."

"Anything else?" I asked.

"Uh huh. Once Ah like borrowed dis telvision from outa frens house, an he sayed Ah done stole it."

I searched desperately for a way to avoid the next event in this fiasco. It was like a slow motion nightmare of two freight trains rumbling down the same track toward each other; you know they're going to crash; you scream out to warn them, but no one pays any attention to you; there's an earth shattering explosion and a cloud of dust. The dust settles. We see an operating room. Jefferson is lying on the table face down. Marvin is dressed in surgical greens. I'm in the observatory behind the glass window, screaming, banging on the window, but nobody hears, or sees me. It's like Dustin Hoffman in *The Graduate*, face pressed to the door trying desperately to stop the wedding ceremony. There's Marvin, with the precision of a surgeon wielding a scalpel, slowly, and without the benefit of anesthesia, manufacturing a new asshole for Mr. Jefferson Wilkes. And I am helpless to do anything about it.

"Your witness, Mr. Lewis."

Marvin wheeled a large blackboard into position where it could be seen by both the witness and the Jury. He drew an inverted pyramid, point at the bottom.

"So that we can all get a better idea of what you have told us, I have taken the liberty of roughly mapping out the route you claim to have traveled on the morning of August sixth," he began.

"Now, Mr. Wilkes, you told us that you began this little odyssey somewhere in the Hampden area, correct?" he asked at the same time writing the word *"Hampden"* next to the bottom point of the triangle on the blackboard.

"Ah don know nuffin' bout no odysseys," Wilkes replied.

"Okay, you started out here, in Hampden, right?" Marvin said tapping the spot on the blackboard.

"Un unh. No way, man. Ah done started out at my 'potment."

"Okay. After you left your apartment, you went to Hampden, right?"

"Ain't zackly sure da name a da place."

"Well, anyway, you took a bus to somewhere near Twenty-Ninth Street and Calvert, right?" he asked, this time drawing an *"X"* about a quarter of the way up the length of the line running from the bottom point of the triangle up to the point on the left.

"Uh huh."

"Then you intended to continue on foot to Fayette Street to catch a bus, a number eight bus wasn't it?" he asked, now writing the word *"Bus #8"* next to the left hand point of the triangle.

"Uh huh."

"How long has it been since you rode the number eight bus across Fayette Street?"

"Ah cain' zackly be sho'."

"What would you say if I told you the number eight bus doesn't run on Fayette Street?"

"Den, Ah guesses maybe dey change it," he responded.

"The number twelve bus has been the only bus running on Fayette Street for the past sixteen years Mr. Wilkes. You had no intention whatever of taking a bus anywhere, did you?"

"Uh huh. Ah maybe dunno da raght numma a da bus, but I were fixin' to ketch one," he insisted.

"And you were fixin' to go all the way over to the west side of town to take flowers to your ex-girlfriend, what was her name, *LaDelle*, who you haven't seen for five years, because it was your anniversary; is that what you are asking us to believe?" Marvin was practically screaming in disbelief. He drew a circle around the right hand point of the inverted pyramid and wrote, *LaDelle*.

"Uh huh. Das raght," Wilkes said in full agreement.

"So, here you are strolling down the street at four forty-something in the morning, and some mystery man whom you've never seen before in your life, and who has never seen you in his life, invites you into this house for a drink. Is that what you think we are going to believe?"

"Uh huh. Dat be wha' happen."

"Isn't it a fact, Mr. Wilkes, that the person you claim to have seen was really Dr. Warner?"

"Who dat?" Jefferson asked.

"And isn't it true that the only time you ever saw him was when you were being led out of Miss Krenshaw's house in handcuffs, and he was standing on his own porch?"

"Un unh," said Jefferson emphatically. "Onyist tam Ah seen him were yestaday."

"Isn't it a fact that there was nobody on that porch, and that you slipped the lock with some kind of plastic card?"

"Ain' no way. Ah din have no kinda plastic card, and dey was dis white guy and da doh were prop op'n, jes lak ah sayed, *period*!"

"And I think you're lying to us," Marvin accused.

"Ah ont raghtly care wha' you think, cause Jesus know ah be tellin' da truf."

"Well, it's too bad he isn't here to tell us about it," Marvin retorted.

"Oh, he be here, awraght, lookin' ova ma shoulda. You jes ain' been saved, so you cain't see um, das all."

"Why did you lock the door after you got into the house?" Marvin questioned, obviously trying to trick Jefferson into giving some kind of reason.

"Ah neva touch dat doh."

"How do you suppose it got locked?" Marvin probed.

"If you ax me, ah thinks da white guy close it when he run out. Course ah ain' no 'tective, er nuffin'."

"Are you sitting in that witness box suggesting to us that Miss Krenshaw sat there under oath and lied? That she made this whole thing up?"

"Ah ain' suhgestin' nuffin', but das wha Ah dunno, why she be sayin' all dis stuff."

"So you think she lied, is that it?"

"Ah dunno if she lahed, er had a bad dream, er what, but Ah thinks she done made a very wrong mistake."

"Now, according to your story, you were invited in for a drink by the mystery man, right?"

"Ah dunno wha he do."

"What do you mean you don't know what he does?" Marvin asked befuddled.

"Ah dunno if he be a mystery man, er a milkman, er he cou' be a mailman for all Ah knows."

"Well, Okay. Do you always undo your pants to get a drink?"

"Watchu mean?"

"Your pants were undone; your fly was open; the button was unbuttoned; your belt was unbuckled. That's what I mean. You're not going to deny that are you?" Marvin badgered.

"Un unh. Dat happen when da polices he pull me

up by ma belt. He grab da back uma pants and pull me up off da flo, an das when dey come undone."

"Just to make sure we didn't overlook part of this minor criminal record of yours, let me review your past convictions. If I get any of them wrong, you'll correct me won't you?"

"Un huh."

"Since you were eighteen years old, you have been convicted of daytime housebreaking and felony theft, correct, Mr. Wilkes?"

"Dat be da one when a borrowed ma frien's TV."

"Then you were convicted of assault with a deadly weapon, a knife, right?"

"It were a mistake. Ah be jus' defendin' mahself dat tam."

"Let's see . . . then there was another assault. Was that a mistake too?" "Dat were jus a small beef 'tween me 'nis uva guy."

"How about the drug charge. Did that just slip your mind?"

"Un unh. Dat were jus fo a pill Ah had an Ah got probation on dat. Ah din think dat counted."

"So you're no stranger to our courts, are you?"

"Wachu mean?"

"I mean you've had a lot of experience standing trial, haven't you?"

"You got it right dere in fron' a ya. You jes' readn' it to make me look bad."

"Did you testify in each of the other trials?"

"Ah ont raghtly memba."

"Did you take an oath in each of those cases and lie like you did here."

"Ah didn' lie den an Ah didn' lie now."

"Do you think that these folks in the jury are stupid and are going to believe this fairy tale you just told in this courtroom?"

"Ah ont know nuffin' bout dese ladies, an Ah ont know nuffin' bout no fairy tales. Ah jus know wha happen, an das what Ah told."

"I see no point to asking this . . . this . . . person anything further," Marvin said with disgust.

I felt that Jefferson had done as well as possible under the circumstances. I didn't think any of the jurors could possibly understand anyone having that many run-ins with the law in so short a period of time. None of them had ever been exposed to someone like Jefferson Wilkes.

J udge Bliss asked if the Defendant had any further witnesses or evidence he wished to produce. I advised him that the defense was resting its case. In a surprise move Marvin advised the court that he wished to re-call Miss Krenshaw and Miss Howell to the stand for some brief rebuttal testimony.

Miss Krenshaw took the witness stand and was reminded by the Court Clerk that she was still under oath.

"Miss Krenshaw, you heard the defendant testify that some man with a red beard was sitting on your porch at four forty-five in the morning on August sixth and that this man invited Mr. Wilkes into your house. My first question is, do you know a man with a red beard who might have been sitting on your porch at that time?"

"Well, the only person I know who has a reddish colored beard is Doctor Warner, my next door neighbor. I can think of no reason why he might be sitting on my porch at all, much less at a quarter to five in the morning."

"Was there *any person* other than yourself or Miss Howell authorized to invite anyone into your home?"

"Absolutely not."

"Thank you Miss Krenshaw," Marvin said.

"Anything further, Mr. West?"

"Yes, thank you, Your Honor."

"Miss Krenshaw, I'm looking at the photograph of the front of your house. Your front porch and Doctor Warner's front porch are divided by a brick wall which appears to be about three feet high and about twelve or fifteen inches wide. Am I correct?"

"I've never measured it, but I would estimate that your description is approximately accurate," she replied.

"The top of that little wall is smooth and flat, isn't it?"

"Yes, it is."

"A person could sit on that wall without any difficulty couldn't he?"

"Yes."

"If Doctor Warner were sitting on that wall that divides the two porches, someone, say walking down the street would have no way of knowing if he were sitting on his own porch, or on your porch, isn't that so?"

"Well, I can see where they might be confused," she responded.

"Wouldn't it be something more than confused? Isn't it true that one would have no way of knowing on whose porch he was sitting?"

"I suppose they wouldn't be able to tell," she conceded.

"Thank you, I have nothing further."

Marvin recalled Marlene Howell and asked her the identical questions. Her answers were identical to Miss Krenshaw's. I asked her the same questions, and likewise received the same responses.

I t was already three-thirty, and it was apparent that the judge was not going to attempt to conclude the trial today.

"If that's all, Gentlemen," said Judge Bliss, "I'd like to dismiss the jury for the day and get any motions out of the way this afternoon and discuss jury instructions, so we can get a fresh start in the morning. The jury left the courtroom, and we retired to the judge's chambers.

"Do you wish to renew your motions for acquital, Mr. West?"

I renewed my motion for a verdict of acquittal on the remaining charges. This time I argued that the only evidence of how the Defendant entered the premises, was his assertion that he was invited in. There had been not one scrap of evidence to contradict Wilkes. If he were invited in, then there was no breaking and entering within even the broadest interpretation of the Statute. At this stage of the proceedings, the evidence is to be viewed in the light most favorable to the defendant. His explanation of how he entered the house is uncontradicted by any evidence. In fact, the evidence fully supports his explanation.

I argued again for a merger of the Assault charges, but was left with no forceful argument on the attempted rape charge. I sure as hell wasn't going to mention the *dead weapon* again.

The judge decided to deny my motions and let the case go to the jury on all of the remaining charges.

Judge Bliss advised us that he intended to use the applicable pattern jury instructions. These are standard boiler-plate instructions taken directly from a book, called, of all things, Pattern Jury Instructions. "Do either of you have any additional instructions you wish me to read to the jury?"

Marvin advised that he would accept the standard instructions. I asked for a copy of the instructions the judge intended to deliver to the jury, and asked if he'd give me until the next day to prepare any additional instructions that I'd want given to the jury. The judge agreed.

So, it seemed that the case would drag out for yet another day.

J udgment day had arrived. The jury was seated. Judge Bliss advised them that they would hear the closing arguments, first from the Prosecutor, then from the Defense Attorney. He explained that the Prosecutor would be given an opportunity to offer a rebuttal argument, after which he would read them instructions concerning their deliberations.

Marvin approached the jury box and began with a chuckle. "Ladies, It's been a long, long time since any of us have been treated to a fairy tale like the one that was presented to us by the Defendant in this courtroom over the past few days. The defense was a pure flight of fantasy; one that would make Walt Disney green with envy.

It's as I told you it would be in my opening statement. This is an open and shut case. On the morning of August sixth, at four forty-five in the morning, the defendant, Jefferson Wilkes, illegally broke into and entered the home of Miss Marianne

Krenshaw. Armed with a pointed screwdriver, he crept up the steps of her home and into her bedroom. There, he threatened to kill her, and with the use of a dangerous and deadly weapon did violently and with force, against her will and without her consent, violate her by fondling her sexually and attempting to rape her.

The victim was in fear of serious physical injury or death. She testified that she honestly believed she was going to be killed. You will recall that Mr. Wilkes told her if she screamed again he would kill her. The pointed screwdriver would have required very little effort to thrust into her throat. Later, Judge Bliss will instruct you that a dangerous or deadly weapon can be any article which the victim reasonably concludes is dangerous or deadly enough to cause physical harm or death. There is absolutely no doubt that Mr. Wilkes is guilty of assaulting Miss Krenshaw with a dangerous and deadly weapon.

Had it not been for her concerned neighbors and the Baltimore City Police Officers who responded so promptly to her scream of terror, you would be deciding whether Mr. Wilkes would be guilty of rape instead of attempted rape. But for the rapid response of the police, Marianne Krenshaw would have been raped, and possibly killed.

Mr. Wilkes announced his intentions. *'I want to make love to you.'* He then set about trying desperately to engage in vaginal intercourse with his victim who begged, and resisted within the limits of what her fear of imminent injury or death would permit. Making love is quite the opposite of rape. Rape is a violent act of hatred, not love. Miss Krenshaw expressed it best when she testified that Mr. Wilkes was intent upon rape, not making love. There is absolutely no doubt that Mr. Wilkes is guilty of an attempt to forcibly, and violently rape the victim in this case.

He was interrupted in the act of committing a rape. He was caught *inside* Miss Krenshaw's house, literally with his pants down." Marvin emphasized. "We heard from the two neighbors who called the police. They watched as the police arrived and moments later brought the defendant out of victim's home in handcuffs. Officer Delaney told you about his capture of the defendant inside the house. Everyone involved in this incident was able to identify the defendant without hesitation. There is absolutely not one shred of doubt that Jefferson Wilkes was the perpetrator of this heinous crime.

All you have to do to conclude that Jefferson Wilkes is guilty of each and every remaining count of the indictment, is to think about the evidence presented to you by the State and the character and veracity of the witnesses against Mr. Wilkes.

The victim, Marianne Krenshaw, has a master's degree in social work. She is a professional Social Worker who works with delinquent children. You observed her as she testified during this trial. Is this lady the kind of person given to flights of fantasy? I don't think so. Is she likely to fabricate some outrageous story? Hardly her style. Can you think of any reason, any motive, why she might climb onto that witness stand, take an oath to tell the truth, and then lie to get poor Mr. Wilkes, whom she had never seen before in her life, and whom she now wishes she still had never seen, in trouble? I don't think so.

Miss Howell, a registered nurse confirmed that the doors were locked when she got home and when she went to bed. Officer Delaney testified that the door was locked when he arrived on the scene. Dr. and Mrs. Warner testified that they heard the scream and verified that someone inside the house unlocked the door for the police.

Ms. Tanner is an accountant; her husband, Doctor Warner has a doctorate in psychology. Are these the kinds of people who would concoct a story, swear under oath to tell the truth, and then get up on the stand and lie, just to get the defendant in trouble. I don't think so.

On the other hand, we can't talk of flights of fantasy and fabrications without mentioning the award winning performance of the Defendant. *Never*, have I met another human being with the audacity, the unmitigated gall, the insolence, the crust, the chutzpah to take that witness stand," Marvin raged, pointing to the witness box, "and under the penalties of perjury to spin that ridiculous, incredible, inconceivable, outlandish, outrageous, preposterous, ludicrous, unbelievable, yarn."

I was writing furiously so as not to miss any of the multitude of wonderful adjectives Marvin was using to characterize the inspired saga and credibility of poor Jefferson.

He ranted on, "If I were a member of your jury, I would be absolutely outraged, incensed and infuriated, offended, insulted and enraged by Mr. Jefferson Wilkes who had the temerity to think even for a fleeting moment that I would believe this fairy tale he fabricated under oath. His arrogance is an infuriating disparagement of my intelligence."

Marvin turned the blackboard toward the jurors and began tracing Wilkes' journey on August sixth. "This man has the nerve to tell us that he was going from here," he said pointing to the word *'Hampden'*, "to there," pointing to the circle he drew where LaDelle allegedly lived, "by going all the way over here," pointing to the word *'Bus'* on his map. "That's like going from Baltimore to New York by way of Los Angeles.

Why wouldn't he have saved himself about ten or fifteen miles by just taking a direct route," he postulated. "I'll tell you why," he intoned. "Because he had no intention of going there in the first place. Which brings us to one of the best parts of this ridiculous story, my favorite part. The part about going to take flowers to Ladelle, his fiancée from five years ago," he narrated, his voice rising in pitch to a crescendo. "Whose address he didn't know, and who didn't know he was coming to celebrate their anniversary."

His face was turning red and he was becoming breathless as he continued. "He then had the audacity to have us believe that some red bearded, half naked, invisible man invited him into some stranger's house to have a drink, or perhaps smoke a little pot."

He ranted on unabated, "He has the guts to ask us to believe that the police were responsible for unbuttoning his pants, unzipping his fly and unbuckling his belt.

Not only does his ridiculous story stretch and twist the imagination beyond any reasonable limits, but we are expected to give credence to a man with a felonious history whose credibility, on a scale of one to ten is *zero*. He's already been convicted of so many crimes, even he can't remember them all."

I wondered if he were referring to the Budweiser Scale?

Marvin launched into a recitation of Jefferson's past criminal history, that read like a compendium of choices from a Chinese Menu. He concluded his closing argument with an impassioned plea to segregate Jefferson Wilkes from the world at large by finding him guilty as charged.

And what about the ozone layer, I thought, he never mentioned the ozone layer! Certainly Wilkes must be responsible for the hole!

25

J udge Bliss nodded to me and simply said, "Mr. West." I arose from the counsel table looked toward the judge as I moved slowly toward the jury. "If it please the court, Your Honor, Ladies of the jury," I began.

"If applause were allowed for wonderful speeches in the courtroom, I would ask everyone to stand and give a rousing round of applause to Mr. Lewis. Don't you think he did a splendid job? He was eloquent, captivating and succinct. He reduced all of the facts and nuances of the testimony to their basic elements and really simplified everything for us. An open and shut case. I suppose, we should just take that sword of justice I spoke of in my opening statement, and put it back into its sheath; raise our hands in surrender and go down to defeat. But, *the sword of justice has no scabbard.* We have an open case which is *faaaaar* from being shut. I know it's highly unusual for a defense lawyer to stand before a jury and agree with the prosecutor, but in this case, I'm afraid I have to agree with some of the things Mr. Lewis said. He told you that Mr. Wilkes' story was . . . let me get my notes," I said. "I want to get this right." I turned away from the rail of the jury box, walked to the trial table and picked up my note pad. Then I turned back to face the jurors and continued as I walked back toward them.

"He said that Mr. Wilkes' story was a ridiculous, incredible, inconceivable, outlandish, outrageous, preposterous, ludicrous, unbelievable, yarn. I wrote down all those illustrative adjectives as he said them," I said and held up my legal pad to make my point. "I knew that I could not have said it better.

Well I'm afraid that is exactly what his story is. All of those things," I read from my notes, "ridiculous, incredible, ludicrous, inconceivable, outlandish, outrageous, preposterous, and unbelievable.

There is one other thing it is, too," I continued. "It's also *true*! It has to be and I'll tell you why.

Mr. Lewis would like us all to believe that Jefferson Wilkes is a liar. If he were, do you think he would have lied and made up a story like the one he sat up there and told you from that witness stand?" I asked, pointing to the empty witness chair.

"Think about how truly preposterous that story was. It virtually defies belief. How could it be anything but true? Nobody, not Jefferson Wilkes, *nobody* would make up a story like that. If you were a liar and were trying to cover up your misdeeds, you'd concoct a story that was believable, wouldn't you?"

I couldn't help but notice my number four juror. Every time a rhetorical question was posed, her head

THE SWORD OF JUSTICE

bobbed up and down like one of those toy German Shepherds with the spring loaded heads that ride around inside of the rear window of some cars, heads bobbing up and down with each movement of the vehicle.

"Well, so would Jefferson Wilkes, if he were a liar." I continued. "But, you see his biggest problem is that he's stupid. Yes, I'm calling my own client stupid! You heard him testify. He is not exactly the sharpest knife in the drawer. He's not smart, or cunning enough to make up a story like the one he told you and think he could con you into believing he was too stupid to make up a better lie. He's too stupid to recognize the absurdity of it."

Now the number seven juror's head started to bob. "His second biggest problem is the combination of his honesty with his eternal religiosity. He trusts in the Lord that everyone will believe him if he just tells the truth, no matter how ridiculous it may sound. So that's exactly what he insisted on doing. He got up and told the truth even if it was too incredible and all of those other things that Mr. Lewis said about his side of the story."

Speaking of believing things, I glanced over at Jefferson, he was sitting there, intent upon what I was saying, and nodding his head in agreement. It fits. Even he agrees that he's stupid. I sensed that the illogic of my argument was catching on, so I continued, "I have to be frank and admit to you that in the beginning, I didn't believe him either. I even suggested that if he were going to lie anyway, he ought to think up a more believable story. He has been consistent in his adamant refusal to alter his story in any way, even knowing that it is somewhat difficult to fathom.

Mr. Wilkes did not have to get up there on that witness stand and tell you his version of the events of August sixth. He had an absolute constitutional right to remain silent. He did not have to get up there and subject himself to ridicule from Mr. Lewis. He was not required to disclose his prior criminal conduct, and expose it to your scrutiny. But as he told me privately, more than once, he didn't have to hide behind technicalities, because he would just get up there and tell the truth. And, whatever happens, will just have to happen he said. He would tell the truth, and you would believe him. And that's exactly what he did . . . got up there and told the truth without regard to how much it defies reason.

A great deal of emphasis seems to have been placed on the fact that Mr. Wilkes has been involved in prior legal entanglements. *A nice way to call him a criminal, I thought*. We need to put all that in its proper perspective.

Keep in mind that he is not guilty of the charges for which he is now standing trial simply by virtue of the fact that he may have been guilty in the past of other wrongdoings. No inferences can be drawn of his guilt, or innocence because of past misdeeds. The convictions for prior misadventures can only be considered when you judge his truthfulness and veracity, but he's not automatically a liar just because he has a prior record.

Neither is he guilty of these charges because he's stupid and doesn't know the best way to get from

Hampden to Warwick Avenue, nor because he doesn't know the correct number of the bus that would take him there. He's not guilty because he was going to take flowers . . . you remember . . . the flowers he picked from the median strip up on Twenty-Ninth Street that were found by the police on the porch . . . Because he was going to take those flowers to his old girlfriend. Maybe that doesn't make sense to us, but it made sense to him at the time, and taking flowers to somebody at five in the morning might be further evidence of his stupidity, but it is certainly not evidence of some criminal intent.

"We discussed the question of reasonable doubt during my opening statement. Let me remind you that Judge Bliss will instruct you before you enter into your deliberations about what your verdict must be if there remain unanswered questions about material evidence, or indeed even if you're just not sure. Remember, I asked that you pay very close attention to the evidence presented, but focus even more closely on the evidence that is *not* presented.

Let's examine what you have seen and heard. Let's examine what you did not see or hear. Then let's ask if there are any questions that have not been answered by the State to our complete satisfaction. Are there any lingering doubts about any issue? Is there a reasonable doubt about whether or not Mr. Wilkes committed this crime?

Well, it seems to me that there are questions raised by the State which have not been answered to our satisfaction. There are questions raised by the evidence that have not been answered to our satisfaction, and there are questions raised by what we have not seen or heard that also have no satisfactory explanations."

I selected our unofficial photograph of the twenty-six hundred block of North Calvert Street and held it up for the jury. I explained that they would have a better opportunity to view the picture more closely when they retired for their deliberations.

"Examine this picture. Every house is identical. Indeed, even the people who live in the house were unable to determine which was their house. Officer Delaney couldn't identify the house from the photograph. What would make anybody decide to pick this particular house? It looks exactly like every other house in the block. Why this one? Why not the one next door, or the one down the street? How could Jefferson Wilkes have known that this house wasn't occupied by, say . . . a couple of world-class wrestling giants, like The Masked Assassin, or The Mad Crusher? Suppose the owner of this house kept two pit bulls as pets.

I'll tell you what made him pick this particular house. There was a man on the porch who invited him in; just like Mr. Wilkes told us. He walked in through the propped open screen door and through the open front door.

Why should we believe him? We *have* to believe him; there is no other choice. *His* version is the *only* version we have. His version is uncontradicted by any witness . . . by any evidence. In fact, all of the evidence in the case supports his story. Officer Sutton, an experienced expert from the Baltimore City Crime Laboratory, who carefully examined the premises with a pair of high-powered lenses, and who expertly dusted all points of entry for fingerprints, testified that there was no sign of forced entry, and none of Jefferson Wilkes' fingerprints anywhere at the scene. Among the other exhibits you can examine is the receipt given to Mr. Wilkes for everything found in his possession at the time of his arrest. Note that there was nothing among those possessions which could have been used to slip the lock as Officer Sutton tried to have us believe.

Mr. Wilkes is not a magician. He didn't close his eyes and mutter some mystical words that caused him to suddenly materialize on the other side of a locked door, leaving no fingerprints and no evidence of forced entry. He walked through two open doors, in exactly the manner he described . . . *in exactly the manner supported by all of the evidence.*

Oh! And how do we know he was telling us the truth about the mystery man with no shirt and no shoes who invited him in?" I walked over to the pile of exhibits at the clerk's desk and selected the police photograph of the staircase that Wilkes allegedly *used to creep up in the darkness of the night.* I held it up for the jury to see.

"We know he was telling us the truth, because the mystery man with no shirt and no shoes isn't such a mystery after all. Look closely at the photograph which, according to Officer Sutton, accurately represents the scene at the time of the incident. There, hanging over the railing is the not so mysterious man's shirt. And there, at the foot of the steps, lay his tennis shoes, just where he left them when he ran out of the house. Look at them. Examine them closely. That sweatshirt is too large to fit the ladies who live in that house. Those tennis shoes must be size twelve. They do not belong to either of the ladies that live in that house. They surely don't belong to Miss Krenshaw's ex-boyfriend who moved out seven months ago. They belonged to the man with no shirt and no shoes who invited Jefferson Wilkes into that house, and then ran out when the police came on the scene.

We're left with what is alleged to have happened in Miss Krenshaw's bedroom. I wasn't there so I don't really know what happened. You weren't there so you really don't know what happened. The witnesses except for Miss Krenshaw weren't there so they really don't know what happened. Everyone just did a lot of assuming and speculating. Mr. Lewis wasn't there and he really doesn't know what happened. And after we put all of the evidence together, all of the testimony, all of the exhibits, all of the scientific evidence, or in particular, the lack of any scientific evidence, none of us knows what really happened. And if we don't know what really happened, what must we do? *We must find the defendant not guilty.*

Here is what we do know. We know that Mr. Wilkes was not in her bed. We know that because the FBI who thoroughly examined the linens from that bed found no evidence that Jefferson Wilkes was there. They found no trace of his hair, his bodily fluids or anything else that could have placed him in that bed. They found plenty evidence that Miss Krenshaw was there . . . none that Mr. Wilkes was.

Think about what is alleged to have taken place in that bed. A man pulling his pants down, then struggling with a woman and then pulling his pants back up. Then he gets out of the bed, moments later he climbs back into it, once again tugging on his pants to get them down, again struggling with a woman in the bed, then hastily struggling to pull his pants back up and jumping out of the bed. Obviously, the experts, Officer Sutton and FBI Agent Little, a forensic scientist, reasoned that with all of this hostile activity, there would have to be hair, or other evidence in that bed. It doesn't even require any police or forensic expertise. Common sense tells us that at least one strand of the defendant's hair would be found in the bed after all of that activity. Examine the Police photograph of that bed. It depicts the scene of a struggle.

Nothing! The experts found not a trace. Conclusion, when viewed most favorably toward the defendant as you will be instructed by Judge Bliss; *he wasn't there.* The *only* conclusion; *he wasn't there!* Indeed, even Agent Little, the FBI expert, said he'd have serious doubt about whether or not Mr. Wilkes was in that bed.

Look at the testimony of the other witnesses. Miss Howell, the roommate, asleep in her bedroom just across the hall, in the very same house. She didn't hear a scream. She didn't hear the phone ring at least ten times. She didn't hear any conversations. She didn't hear the defendant go clomping down the steps with Miss Krenshaw in pursuit screaming he tried to rape me. Do you know why she didn't hear anything? Was it maybe because there wasn't anything to hear? Do we know for sure? Isn't there more than just reasonable doubt?

The deadly weapon. An ordinary Phillips-head

screwdriver. When we think of screwdrivers, we normally think of the common flat head variety. One that can be used to pry the lid from a jar, or the lid from a paint can. One that could be used to pry a door, or window open. If one were intent upon prying something open, like a window or a door and forcing his way into a home, he would not come equipped with the screwdriver found on the scene in this case. That screwdriver doesn't work well for anything other than inserting or removing Phillips-head screws. Those are screws that have sort of a star shaped groove in the head. They can only be turned with a Phillips-head screwdriver which has a star shaped point that fits down into the head of the screw. These screws are used mostly to fasten machined metal parts commonly found in electronic equipment, automobiles, cameras and of course *camera tripods*."

On August fifth, Miss Krenshaw's father came to her house armed with a Phillips-head screwdriver. His intent was to fix her camera tripod with the screwdriver that is one of the State's exhibits. The very same camera tripod shown so clearly in the dining room photograph. The photograph depicts the Phillips-head screwdriver lying next to the broken camera tripod. Mr. Wilkes didn't bring that screwdriver with him. It wasn't his screwdriver. It was there all along.

Whose screwdriver was it? Well, don't forget that the fingerprints found on that screwdriver did not belong to Mr. Wilkes. I don't know whose prints were on it because the State failed to tell us that. But, if Mr. Wilkes ever used that screwdriver for anything, why were his fingerprints not on the handle of that screwdriver? He didn't wear gloves. He didn't wipe them off." I shrugged my shoulders, raised both palms toward heaven and assumed a puzzled expression to emphasize the unanswered question.

"I liked all of the people who testified here. I thought they were nice, and were trying very hard to tell what they could remember about what they saw and heard that morning. But I think that their observations were not too keen at four forty-five in the morning. And I think that their memories of the details are more the result of suggestions offered while they were being prepared to testify, than by their actual recollections of what really happened.

Not one of you at this very moment, as close as you are to me, can see whether or not my pants are buttoned, or if my belt is hooked or my fly is partially unzipped, because my suit jacket is covering the top of my pants. And if I were not wearing a jacket, but my shirt were not tucked in and was hanging over my pants, you still couldn't see. Well everybody agreed on one thing. Mr. Wilkes shirt was hanging out. Yet, they all decided that his pants were unbuttoned, his belt was not fastened and his fly was partially unzipped, even though they couldn't possibly see the top of his pants.

Do you think you could tell if my pants are fastened or not without being able to *see* if they are? Of course you could. If my pants were unbuttoned and my belt were unbuckled and my fly were partially unzipped, the moment I took one step, my pants would fall down around my ankles. Mr. Wilkes' pants didn't fall down around his ankles. If they did, you can be sure we'd have heard about it." *Now I was talking from personal experience.*

I removed a clean sheet of paper from my yellow legal pad and walked over to the jury box. "Let's just see what the State has proved *beyond a reasonable doubt and to a moral certainty,*" I said holding up the blank piece of paper.

"Let us suppose this piece of paper represents the entire picture of this case . . . all of the evidence, all of the testimony, all of the reasonable inferences that could be drawn . . . nothing missing . . . no unanswered questions. If we had such a complete picture, we would have no difficulty making a rational judgment about this case. But, let's have a closer look at this picture. If any part of it is missing, then we have reasonable doubt. And if we have reasonable doubt, we are required to find the defendant not guilty. Judge Bliss will tell you more about this in his instructions."

I tore a corner off of the paper and held it up for all to see. "This small piece of paper represents the State's failure to prove beyond a reasonable doubt how Mr. Wilkes entered the house. No forced entry."

I tore another corner off. "This represents the doubt created by the failure to find any finger prints."

"And this piece," I said, tearing off a third corner, "represents the failure to find any evidence of the defendant being in the bed as alleged."

As I tore the fourth corner from the paper, I said, "This missing piece is the apparent inability of the State to explain the man's shirt hanging over the banister."

"And this piece," as I ripped another piece from the

center of the paper, "the failure to explain the size twelve sneakers at the foot of the steps."

I folded the paper and tore another piece from the center, and continued to tear holes in the paper for each point where any question, no matter how remote, was left unanswered. I ended up with a handful of confetti in my right hand and a torn up piece of lined yellow paper full of holes in my left.

"One element of reasonable doubt would be enough to require a finding of *not guilty*," I proclaimed, letting one small piece of paper flutter from my raised hand to the floor.

"In this case, though, there's nothing but reasonable doubt. Too many unanswered questions to reach any kind of decision to a *moral certainty*." I contended, tossing the remaining torn pieces of paper into the air and watching as they drifted to the floor.

"Just look at our picture of this case," I asserted, holding up the remnants of the piece of yellow paper. "It's full of holes, the corners are missing. It's like an incomplete puzzle.

You can't, to a moral certainty, erect a case free of reasonable doubt from a puzzle with so many missing pieces. You can't convict a man of a serious crime with evidence that leaves so many unanswered questions. You can't send a man to jail, when you don't know what happened beyond a reasonable doubt and to a moral certainty. Could you live with a decision to imprison this man by looking at this picture?" I asked again holding up my piece of torn yellow paper.

"I know that you *cannot*; I know that you *will not*. I know that you will find Mr. Wilkes *not guilty*, because you have *no other choice.* Thank you for your kind attention and may God bless you during your deliberations!"

I returned to my seat at the trial table and sank exhausted into my chair. I looked at Wilkes and thought to my self, I should have raised my fee to twenty-five grand. That closing alone would have been worth the price!

26

Marvin bounded forward like the charge of the light brigade to deliver his rebuttal argument. He nearly knocked me over as I was returning to the trial table.

"I don't think a standing ovation would suffice as a reward for the oration given by Mr. West." I'd be more inclined toward a prize of some sort," he began.

"He and his client are a perfect match. One gets up and lies and the other swears to it.

Mr. West's efforts to convince you that Mr. Wilkes was telling the truth, is even more absurd than the preposterous flight of fancy concocted by his client.

This sword of justice that my colleague has been swinging around this courtroom has two edges. I think both he and his client better duck, because that sword is about to land on both of their heads.

The impudence of those two to suggest that you accept their bizarre tale as an example of *truth* and *justice* is to give new meaning to the word *chutzpah*. You have been privileged to watch an expert use one of the oldest tricks of the legal profession. He put a stick into the water and stirred up the mud so that you can't see clearly to the bottom, and then tries to convince you that there is no bottom because you can't see it.

Don't be fooled, because when the mud settles, you can see the bottom very clearly. Common sense dictates that the bottom is still there even if it cannot be seen. That same common sense must be applied to the facts of this case so that you are not blinded by the mud that Mr. West has stirred up from the bottom of the pond.

There isn't a scrap of doubt about the defendant's guilt in this case. The bare facts are that this man was inside of the victim's house at four forty-five on the morning of August sixth. That he did not belong there. That neither of the only two people who occupy that house invited him in, or gave him permission to be there. That once inside, he crept up the steps, into the victim's bedroom and threatened to kill her. He announced his intention of having vaginal intercourse with her, and then attempted by force, under the imminent threat of bodily harm and against the will of the victim to do so. Had it not been for the neighbors and the rapid response of the police, he would have succeeded.

If you do not find this man guilty of the crimes he committed against this innocent victim, he may break into your house one day, and it will be you who is awakened in the middle of the night and raped and killed."

Marvin turned to walk back to the trial table, and hadn't taken two steps when I was out of my seat approaching the bench. I did not want to voice my objection within the earshot of the jury. But before reaching the bench, I was making my objection known.

"Your honor, Mr. Lewis's last statement to the jury was outrageous and totally improper. His statement was made for the sole purpose of inflaming the jury. It could serve no other purpose. It did not bear in any way on the evidence produced during the trial. It bore no relationship to anything argued by the defense. It was a totally improper rebuttal argument, and was so prejudicial as to render this trial a nullity. As much as I would hate to have to try this case again, I am compelled to move for a mistrial. Nothing less could right the wrong that has been committed."

Judge Bliss advised that he was going to declare a recess and that we would discuss my motion in his chambers at that time. He returned the jury to the jury room, explaining that this was going to be a brief recess, and that they were not to discuss the case nor begin deliberations until he had instructed them. As the jury once again filed out of the courtroom, we adjourned to the judge's chambers. We were invited to sit in the two chairs at Judge Bliss's desk.

He said, "I don't have to give a great deal of thought to your Motion for a mistrial, Mr. West. I agree that Mr. Lewis's remark was improper, highly inflammatory, and somewhat prejudicial. But at this point, I do not believe it warrants a mistrial."

The judge then turned to Marvin and landed into him. "I can't believe you'd risk a conviction in this case by making such a stupid remark. You have as open and shut a case as there ever was. You are assured of a conviction and you take the very substantial risk of a reversal on appeal for your inflammatory, prejudicial and totally uncalled for remarks. I frankly think any conviction in this case will be reversed on appeal. Don't ever do anything like that in my court again.

Mr. West, I hope you understand my position. I am very reluctant to take a four-day case away from this jury. Your motion is noted on the record, and I will give my ruling on the record to protect Mr. Wilkes' rights in the event of an appeal. I will, if you wish, instruct the jury to ignore and give no consideration to Mr. Lewis's improper remark. When we return to the courtroom, I will charge the jury with the instructions previously agreed upon. If there are no objections, we'll break and let the jury begin deliberations after lunch."

I thanked the judge for his consideration, but decided against having the judge make any mention of the impropriety of the inflammatory statement. I believed that to do so would only focus more attention on the prejudicial comment, and it was better just left alone. It was obvious that the judge believed a mistrial should have been granted. He was unequivocal in his belief that an appeal of any conviction would result in a reversal. But it was also obvious, that if convicted,

Jefferson would serve at least two years until his appeal was heard and a decision was rendered. So as a practical matter, he wanted to be certain that Jefferson served at least some time for the offense.

After having reviewed the instructions he intended to use, I had decided that it would be better to agree to those, than to demand additional instructions. Often in an effort to obtain concessions, a can of worms is opened which could lead to the inclusion of other less favorable charges to the jury.

W e left his chambers. The jury was seated in the jury box and Judge Bliss began reading them the agreed upon jury instructions. He advised the jury of the requirement that their verdict be unanimous, and of the need to consult with fellow jurors, but still maintain independence of their own convictions as to the weight and effect of the evidence. He instructed them as to the presumption of the Defendant's innocence and the requirement of the State to prove guilt beyond a reasonable doubt and to a moral certainty. He read them the detailed definition and the necessary elements of proof required for a conviction for Attempted Rape.

Unfortunately he also advised them that the closing arguments of the lawyers are not evidence. I thought my closing argument was the most favorable evidence in the case for Jefferson.

Court was recessed for lunch, after which, Jefferson Wilkes' fate would be placed in the hands of the twelve ladies of the jury. The time of reckoning was upon us. What would they decide? I had already made my decision, and it was unanimous.

I knew what I had decided. I decided to treat myself to a very much deserved Stoli Crystal Gimlet with a twist of lime on the rocks in a snifter.

27

U pon our return from lunch, the judge sent my twelve little ladies packing to the jury room for their deliberations. He then ordered me to clean up the mess I had made with the confetti of reasonable doubts I had sprinkled all over the floor.

Judge Bliss suggested that we remain close to the courtroom, as he felt that the jury would not take very long with their deliberations. He, as did everyone else including me, believed this really was an open and shut case. It was at least consoling to know that it was not my fate in the hands of that jury. I would never want to be in a position where my life, liberty, or property were in the hands of twelve strangers. Especially these strangers.

Here were twelve ladies, the youngest of whom was a fifty-three year old housewife, married to an electrician. My favorite, number four, was seventy-one; a widow and retired librarian. Not one juror shared even a single trait in common with Jefferson Wilkes.

They were white; he was black. They were female; he was male. They came from different ethnic, religious, and cultural backgrounds. None had ever lived in the ghettos of the inner-city. None had ever had much exposure to black laborers. Absolutely nothing in common.

This was the reverse of the Rodney King trial. Jefferson Wilkes was different, he was to be feared, disliked and dismissed. But this time it was the black man who was on trial. It was his fate in the hands of this jury, not the fates of three white policemen.

On the flip side of the coin though, these jurors had little or nothing in common with the victim either. There was a great disparity in their ages. These were women who were raised and grew into adulthood in a different era, with a completely different code of moral behavior. The victim's life style was as foreign to them as was Wilkes. They were not likely to be overly sympathetic toward Miss Krenshaw, nor feel much in the way of empathy. She, after all, was immoral, or at the very least a sinner, having lived with a man, not her husband. I sensed their negative reaction to Linda Tanner, who had the audacity to continue to use her maiden name after marriage.

I felt strongly that I had created a considerable amount of doubt. There were certainly enough puzzling twists and turns to the facts as they emerged from witnesses, and no shortage of surprises as the case unfolded. The more I thought about it, the more I started to wonder what really happened. I almost had myself convinced that there was really reasonable doubt.

What plausible explanation was there for the lack of forensic evidence? In truth, there was no rational explanation for the absence of fingerprints, or Negro hair in the bed. There was no logical explanation for the lack of evidence of a forced entry. And let's not overlook the sweatshirt and tennis shoes at the foot of the steps. Whose were they? Could the victim have been mistaken about what happened, or if it happened who it was that attempted to rape her? Well, like I told the jurors, I wasn't there, so I don't know what really happened. Was there enough evidence to explain what happened without reasonable doubt and to a moral certainty?

Not so cut and dry. Not so open and shut. Or was it? How could any thinking, rational, nominally intelligent person lend any credence to the wacky tale testified to by Wilkes? Not one element of the story was believable. No part of it made any sense. Given his record of past criminal conduct, his testimony was without veracity and totally void of credibility. The fact is, thank God, that I am not the one who has to decide.

The jury had now been out for three hours. How was this possible? We all believed they would have no difficulty whatever deciding on Wilkes' guilt. Everyone, of course, except Wilkes. He was certain they would believe him and find him not guilty.

In a criminal case, it is generally considered a good sign for the defense when the jury is out for a long time. The longer they are out, the better the chance of an acquittal, or a hung jury.

One day, I would like to serve on a jury. I'd like to see first hand, the dynamics of the reasoning process which brings twelve total strangers of such diverse backgrounds, who most often have absolutely nothing in common, to agree on a unanimous verdict.

I can just picture juror number four in that room stubbornly refusing to be persuaded by the others; her hands folded across her chest, a defiant look on her face and a determination to stand on her position against all odds. She would hold out and ultimately hang the jury, which would result in a mistrial.

The wait for a jury to reach its verdict is easily the most nerve racking part of any trial. The anxiety level can only be compared to watching the Lottery drawing on television. You have a lottery ticket with five of the six winning numbers. Just as they are about to pick the final number, there is a power failure. You lose your electricity and your phone service. The jackpot is ten million dollars. You're sitting there in the dark wondering whether or not you should go to work the next morning and tell your boss to shove his lousy job.

The long awaited knock at the jury room door indicating there was a message from the jury finally came at six-forty. The Courthouse had emptied, but for those of us involved in the Wilkes trial. The judge resumed his position at the bench. Marvin and I took our seats. We were informed that the jury had reached a verdict.

As the jurors were seated in the jury box, I studied their faces seeking a clue as to what they had decided. Their faces were impassive; there was no way to tell. Wilkes was seated beside me at the defense table. Marianne Krenshaw was seated next to Marvin at the prosecutor's table. The forewoman passed the verdict sheet to the bailiff who handed it up to Judge Bliss. He unfolded it, read it and passed it to the bailiff to be read aloud. He directed Wilkes to stand. We both rose to hear the verdict.

The bailiff announced the jury's decision. "On the charge of Breaking and Entering, we find the defendant Not Guilty."

"On the charge of Assault, we find the defendant Not Guilty."

"On the charge of Assault with a deadly weapon, we find the defendant Not Guilty."

"On the charge of Attempted Rape, we find the defendant Not Guilty."

Marvin's mouth dropped open with the shock of what he had just heard. Marriane Krenshaw let out a gasp of anguish as if she had been stabbed in the heart. Her eyes welled up with tears and she began to sob.

As badly as I wanted to win, I have to confess that I was as shocked and dismayed as everyone else in that courtroom, except of course, Jefferson Wilkes, who sat there with a big smile on his face displaying his pearly whites, which at that moment I would have enjoyed shoving down his throat.

Judge Bliss glared at the jury forewoman, but avoided eye contact with me and Jefferson.

"Miss Krenshaw," he began, "I cannot begin to convey the Court's feelings to you on the travesty of justice that has occurred in this case. I can only express the Court's deepest regret for the failure of the judicial process in this matter, and my apology to you for the miscarriage of justice that has occurred in this courtroom."

He then turned back to the jury and said, "In my years as a lawyer, in my service to this community as its State's Attorney, and in my years on the bench, I have never seen twelve rational people come to a worse decision. I would normally thank you for sacrificing your time to serve the community, but I can't bring myself to give thanks to a group who so utterly abandoned reason and common sense to rob the State and the victim of the justice they deserved." Without another word, he rose and stormed from the courtroom.

I, too, was tempted to apologize to the victim and the judge. I sat there gathering my thoughts and reflecting on what had just taken place. Our judicial system sometimes fails. Like everything else in life, it is not perfect. Despite its flaws, though, it is still the best system of justice that exists on the face of this earth. Somehow, no matter how unjust a decision may seem at the time, truth and justice ultimately prevail. I truly believe that.

Should I feel guilty about the result in this case? Hell no! I did what I was supposed to do. I forced the State to prove its case with admissible evidence beyond a reasonable doubt and to a moral certainty. Did they do it? Obviously not! Not, at least, in the eyes of the jury. They apparently were over-confident of their case. When the evidence failed to prove vital elements of the crime, they gave up. They didn't cover all of the bases. Had they, I couldn't have convinced those twelve people that reasonable doubt existed.

Was Jefferson Wilkes really guilty? Did he really commit the crimes? Did he just get off on a technicality?

Well, the answer is that it really does not matter. The people of the State of Maryland had their day in court, and they weren't up to the task.

Wilkes turned to me and said, "Ah tol ya dey'd b'leave me."

At that moment, if I had a gun, I could have killed him, and probably gotten away with it. Everybody but the jurors would have applauded. Boy, was I pissed. Because Wilkes got off? Nah! Why? You got it! Because that miserable, lying, rapist, piece of shit didn't pay me. That's why!

EPILOGUE

It had been nearly five months since the Jefferson Wilkes trial.

Jennifer left her job at the Western Run Apartments, moved in with an architect who was fixing up an old house somewhere. Sharon moved to Los Angeles. I was still hanging out at the Bear's Den, but only on Wednesday nights.

I finally settled Kim Steiner's case and found out where the drunk that creamed her had been drinking the night of the accident. So, now I go to McSweeny's Lounge on Friday nights, where a whole new cast of characters with a different collection of legal problems drown their troubles.

On Thursday nights I've been climbing the social ladder to hob nob with the Zone 8 folks at the Pimlico Hotel Lounge. I figured I'd have a better chance there of either meeting that younger version of my mother, or finding someone who has a sister whose foot fits the slipper.

Anyway, spring was about to be sprung. I was rushing to get out of the office for my Wednesday afternoon golf game. The phone rang. It was Kelly on the intercom. By this time, I had practically mastered that device.

"You won't believe who's on the phone," she said.

"Who?"

"The rapist," she replied. "Line one."

Kelly had mastered *"rapist"* and I had mastered the intercom.

I pressed the blinking button for the first line. "Hi Jennifer! How have you been?"

"Dis be Slats," came the unmistakable voice of Jefferson Wilkes.

"Oh, Jefferson! I thought my secretary said Jennifer."

"No, it be me," he said.

"Let me guess. You want to come pay me the rest of my fee. Right?"

"I do, but not zackly raght now."

"Well, then why else would you have called, Jefferson?"

"Ah guesses Ah be needin' yo hep."

"My help!" I cried. "You never paid me for the last case and you want me to work for nothing again?"

"Ah knowz, but ahz really gonna pay ya dis tahm."

"Now what did you do?"

"Ah ain't done nuffin' . . . zackley."

"So what do you need me for?"

"Memba dat guy in da case."

"Who the white guy with a red beard on his face, no shirt, no shoes?"

"Un unh. Not dat one; da uva one."

"What other one?" I asked, searching my memory.

"Dat Lewis guy."

"You mean the prosecutor, Marvin Lewis?"

"Yeah, dat be de one."

"What about him?"

"Dey sayin' Ah broke inta his house and robbed some stuff."

"You burglarized the prosecutor's house?" I asked utterly astonished.

"Dat's wha dey be sayin' an das why Ah needs yo hep."

"Are you in jail now?"

"Un unh. Ah already be on bail, but Ah thinks Ah be needin' yo services."

"You don't need a lawyer, Jefferson. All you got to do is stand up there and tell the jury the truth. They'll believe you; just like the last time. Listen, I got to run. I'm late for a very important meeting."

I pumped my fist in the air as I hung up. This was better than sinking a thirty foot putt for birdie to win the U.S. Open.

How about that sword of justice? Still unsheathed and poised for its next thrust at Jefferson Wilkes. The road is not always clearly marked. It often takes mysterious twists and turns. Sometimes it takes a little longer than it should. But, ultimately, justice prevails. It's true: *The sword of justice has no scabbard.*

ACKNOWLEDGMENTS

First and foremost I have to thank Beth, who read and edited each sentence, each phrase and each chapter of this book an endless number of times. By now, she can recite the story by rote.

The motivation to write books came from friends whom I entertained over the years with some of the outrageous tales from my office. They would always say, "You ought to write a book!"

Stories don't fall out of the sky. Even though they are pure fiction, and the flights of sexual fantasy, are just that, fantasy, the ideas result from an amalgam of life's experiences. So, I would be remiss if I failed to give credit to all of the people who have filtered through my life over the years. There is something of all of them in my writing.

I am grateful for the encouragement of friends who suffered through early drafts of the book. Finally, special thanks to those who asked, "So, did he do it?"

Printed in the United States
49644LVS00004B/340-387